THE
EVIDENCE

BOOKS BY K.L. SLATER

Safe with Me
Blink
Liar
The Mistake
The Visitor
The Secret
Closer
Finding Grace
The Silent Ones
Single
Little Whispers
The Girl She Wanted
The Marriage

THE EVIDENCE
K.L. SLATER

bookouture

First published as an Audible Original in February 2021 by
Audible Ltd. This edition published July 2021 by Bookouture.

An imprint of Storyfire Ltd.
Carmelite House
50 Victoria Embankment
London EC4Y 0DZ

www.bookouture.com

ISBN: 978-1-80019-727-5
eBook ISBN: 978-1-80019-724-4

CHAPTER ONE

THE FISCHER FILES

EPISODE ONE: MEETING SIMONE

I'm speaking to you from outside HMP Bronzefield women's prison on the outskirts of Ashford in Middlesex. Now, this place is a bit of a groundbreaker as far as prisons go. It was built in 2004 as a women-only facility but you won't find any Victorian gloom here or Gothic towers. The building is clean-looking, modern.

But make no mistake, this is a Category A facility for adult female offenders.

I'm about to go inside and speak to Simone Fischer, one of the inmates here. You might well have heard Simone's name before. She's a fifty-two-year-old British woman who, ten years ago, was convicted at the Old Bailey of the brutal murder of her husband of twenty years, Grant Austin Fischer.

Fischer has always maintained a strict silence, refusing even to give evidence at her own trial and has completely blocked any media visits. Until now.

For the first time ever, Simone has agreed to break her silence and tell The Speaking Fox the true story… in her own words.

This week marks Simone's tenth year of an eighteen-year sentence behind bars. Today, we'll finally begin to discover the full, true story of what happened that fateful night in 2009.

We'll find out the truth behind a sham marriage built on coercive control and why she, and her supporters, believe her conviction was truly a miscarriage of justice.

This is a Speaking Fox podcast and *I*... am Esme Fox.

*

I'm standing about two hundred yards away from the actual prison now.

There are nearly six hundred women accommodated here, plus there's a mother-and-baby unit, too. It's a big place. I'm approaching the building and I can see there's a constant stream of people entering and leaving. Visitors, officials wearing lanyards and delivery couriers.

Just going in...

So, I'm inside the foyer and it's bright in here... smells a bit like my old school hall an hour after lunch.

OK, I've just been through the security and admin process, quite thorough as you'd expect and now I'm heading into the prison proper. I've got my own prison officer here to take me to the room where I'll have my scheduled thirty-minute meeting with Simone. I'll talk as we walk. It's a noisy place as you can hear, metal doors slamming, lots of footsteps around us.

I think it's about a five-minute walk... is it? Yes, the prison officer is nodding.

When I heard Simone had agreed to see me, I thought about the best way to prepare to get a complete overview of the case. To start, I read and watched everything I could get hold of online. There's an incredible volume of stuff that's been written and recorded about Simone and her conviction.

Next step was the endless hours I spent cataloguing online images, YouTube videos and audio news reports about the Fischer family. There's a plethora of stuff out there with little to separate genuine reports and fake news. Seems everyone and his dog has an opinion and feels the need to air it.

I have a theory about that – about the strength of feeling that comes across in all this. I think the detail people struggle with, is the fact the Fischers' twelve-year-old son, Andrew, was actually playing on his computer game in the next room when his father was killed.

I've read the original court transcripts and researched a variety of opinions on how Grant Fischer's blood ended up spattered all over the kitchen units. It's blunt, yes, but it's the truth. And the truth is what we're seeking in this podcast. The truth is what we have pledged not to shy away from, no matter how unpalatable.

Here we are now, outside the interview room. I can see Simone Fischer through the glass door. She's smaller in real life than I expected. She looks the exact opposite of the type of woman that might beat her husband to death.

Sorry? Right, no problem.

So, the officer's just asked me to wait here while she checks everything is in order in the room. Simone is sitting at a table, dressed casually in jeans and a lemon tunic top. The women at Bronzefield are permitted to wear their own clothes. Her brown hair is tied back in a loose ponytail and I'm struck by her ordinariness. She looks like your mum, your aunt… a random woman you might see shopping in the supermarket.

Yet the majority of the British public detests her. This woman who faced her abusive husband and said, 'No more'.

The officer is on her way back to me again. Looks like I'm going in.

*

Esme: Hi, Simone!

Simone: Hello, Esme.

Esme: This is your chance to reach our listeners with your truth, speaking from your heart. Do you feel ready to make a start?

Simone: I've been waiting for the right time for a very long time. I'm ready.

Esme: Forgive me, but I'm going in strong with my questions. I want to tackle a comment I've seen repeatedly during my online research of your case.

Simone: Go for it.

Esme: Did you ever fantasize about murdering your husband, Simone? Go through the ways you could kill him… plan exactly how you might do it?

Simone: If only it had been that simple but no. I'd… I'd forgotten what life should be like. Does that make sense? To me, it was just the way things were now and I never questioned why I was settling for it. I only tried to get through it.

Esme: You were just trying to get through life.

Simone: That's it, yes. You asked about death? Well, not once did I consider he might go before me, I thought… I honestly thought he would eventually kill me. Or that I would kill myself because of him. I was so far gone it never occurred to me I had a choice in the matter.

Esme: Can you remember a time you didn't feel that way? Maybe when you first met or in your early marriage. I'm assuming things were fine to begin with… But when you first noticed the signs, when he first started treating you badly… can you remember thinking 'I'm not standing for this' or 'I need to get out'?

Simone: You've got to understand that this wasn't a case of one day things are fine, the next day he starts controlling me. People like to think in black and white, but it was far more subtle than that. Grant had a very special talent. When I met him, he appeared to be caring and reasonable for the first year, when in fact, underneath, he was a master at guiding my thoughts and decision-making processes. Even more impressively, he could do this while making me believe *I* was the one who was in control. He was like a magician in that respect.

Esme: Can you give me an example?

Simone: Let me think... OK, so, when we began dating, I was very young and close to my mum. She died a couple of years after we got married but when I met Grant, I lived just a few streets away from her and I'd pop round every day without fail. Do a bit of shopping for her sometimes, when she'd had a bad day – she had respiratory problems – or maybe do her laundry, ironing, that sort of thing.

Grant said from the start he thought it was wonderful, the way I took care of my mum. He used to say it showed what kind of a person I was: giving and caring. Then over time he started saying Mum was leaning on me far too often. He'd say things like, 'How come she can go to Bingo but she can't hang her own washing out?'

The clever bit was that he always seemed to come from a position of worrying about and caring for me or for Mum. For instance, at the end of a long day, he'd say, 'I'm worried you're doing too much running after your mum like this, darling. It's not good for her to become too reliant. You need to help her become a bit more independent for her own self-worth.'

It all sounded perfectly reasonable. He was the voice of common sense in my mixed-up head.

Esme: That's what you told yourself?

Simone: That's what I believed.

Esme: You said that's how it started. How did things progress?

Simone: Well, in terms of Mum, he'd organise things at times he knew I'd usually go around there. Like he'd get surprise cinema tickets for an early film showing after work when I'd normally call at Mum's. He wrapped his need to get me away from Mum in a nice thoughtful act, so that if I complained or accused him of anything, it just made me look ungrateful.

Then, just like that, Mum stopped ringing and texting. If I made plans to go around she'd say there was no need as her neighbour was helping her out, which I always found strange because they'd never got on that well over the years.

Esme: You accepted she was OK without you?

Simone: Not at first. I went round a couple of times to make sure she was OK and she was nervy and distant like she really didn't want me there. And she wouldn't hear of me doing any tasks to help her out. I still made an effort to see her, but I always felt like she was kind of trying to get rid of me. Then she asked me not to keep coming around.

Esme: That must've been upsetting for you.

Simone: I was heartbroken. I felt so… rejected. Still, I just thought she'd got more independent, like Grant said.

Esme: But you found out differently?

Simone: Mum died about six months later and when I had to clear her flat, I found a letter addressed to me. In it she said that Grant had been round there and told her to leave me alone. He'd said that I'd had enough of running around after her but didn't know how to tell her. He told Mum I'd been to the doctor's with depression caused by worrying about her… Sorry, I can't…

Esme: It's OK. Take your time. Here, I've got some tissues in my bag… there we go.

Simone: Thanks. It's just hard, you know? I went around to her neighbour to ask if she had helped Mum out, and she had the grace to look guilty and said she hadn't seen her for months before she died. She said she didn't even know Mum was struggling with her health.

Esme: I can see that was tough for you. Did you confront Grant about what he'd done?

Simone: I did. I was hysterical and he was absolutely horrified. He cried. Can you believe it? He actually cried and said Mum must have been mentally ill and hallucinating, that he'd never do anything so callous. Then he got angry and said Mum was cruel to do that to me… to leave a letter full of lies, as he called it. But he was particularly hurt that I chose to believe a sick old woman above him.

Esme: And what was your reaction to what he said?

Simone: I'm ashamed to say I believed him. It's hard to explain, but he was so genuine. I know this doesn't make any sense, but it came down to the fact that I wanted to believe him and chose to do so. It was all subconscious but I was in the grip of his control, you see. It was like I couldn't think for myself anymore, like I'd got so used to him telling me what to think and what to feel, I just blindly accepted what he said.

Years later I met one of Mum's oldest friends and she confided that Mum had told her the exact same story. That she'd been so upset. She told this friend she was afraid of Grant and afraid of what he might do to us both if I kept going round there. I can remember thinking 'let sleeping dogs lie'. Mum was gone by then and so I said nothing to him. I knew he would just make me feel like it was all in my head. He did that all the time.

Esme: Gaslighting.

Simone: I hadn't heard of that term back then.

Esme: It's shocking to think that, over a relatively short time, he was able to destroy your strong key relationship, with your mum… almost without you noticing it was happening.

Simone: That's the thing I find hardest to bear now, thinking about how Mum must have struggled alone… after us being so close for so long. I've had plenty of time to think and I've spent the last ten years blaming myself. How could I have just taken Mum's word for it when she said she was OK? Why didn't I just keep going around there to check on her, to do the things I'd always done, despite Mum insisting she was fine?

Esme: It's a kind of brainwashing, I suppose.

Simone: There have been so many examples like that, over the years. Friendships, my job as a cook in a local school, the book club I'd been attending for three years before I met him. They all bit the dust after Grant came up with solid reasons why I shouldn't be doing that sort of stuff any longer. All for my own good, apparently.

Esme: Sounds like the classic tactic of isolating you from friends and family.

Simone: Absolutely. I've had a steep learning curve since undergoing the voluntary therapy sessions here at Bronzefield. For the first two years it felt like waking up from a drugged sleep. I still can't believe how I blindly accepted everything he told me, how he played my insecurities in his own favour. In the end I had nobody but him, you know. Nobody to turn to, nobody to stop me from drowning in anxiety and depression… nobody but him.

Esme: And this treatment… it just went on and on in your marriage?

Simone: Yes, it was one of many things I now understand he was systematically subjecting me to over time. There was the stinging criticism about almost everything: how I dressed, what I cooked for dinner, the television programmes I chose to watch. He'd keep a mental tally of every single thing I'd done wrong in his eyes, however small. Everything would be brought up as 'evidence' against me at key times, especially if he was deciding something like whether I deserved a new outfit or a haircut.

I can see from your expression you're shocked. But it's true that every single thing I did or didn't do… it was all in his power and I didn't even realise it. The list just goes on. Incredible, isn't it, that I didn't understand what was happening… that I thought everything that was wrong in my life was my own doing? Incredible and pathetic.

Esme: There are thousands of people out there who will recognise everything you're talking about. There are thousands more who will hear this podcast and wake up to what's happening to them, too.

Simone: I hope so. If nothing else comes of this, then just one person realising what's happening to them… that they're not going crazy, but someone is doing this to them. Then it will be worth it.

END OF EXTRACT

CHAPTER TWO

HMP BRONZEFIELD

ESME

After my interview with Simone, an officer accompanied me back to the foyer of the prison. There was a small seating area there, tucked away behind a wall of artificial plants in white containers. There were people milling around but nobody in that particular space, so I sat down for a few minutes. I didn't quite feel ready to leave the prison and Simone's words were still replaying in my head.

I still can't believe how I blindly accepted everything he told me, how he played my insecurities in his own favour.

I'd had a feeling this podcast was going to be a good one and I wanted to savour it while it lasted. The difficult subject matter, the truth about Simone's marriage, had the potential to help a lot of people.

Prior to the first episode there had been some toing and froing between myself and Simone. A combination of a milestone of spending ten years behind bars and my work highlighting miscarriages of justice in *Women in Prison*, a popular side project I ran at my old job at Sky News, had seemed to change Simone's mind about letting the media help her at last.

I'd always been fascinated by the case and when I started The Speaking Fox, I'd decided it would make the perfect debut podcast.

The first recording had gone well. Simone had been open and candid and I really liked her as a person. Some of the things she'd talked about grabbed me on a visceral level that I hadn't been expecting.

Incredible, isn't it, that I didn't understand what was happening… that I thought everything that was wrong in my life was my own doing?

I sat for a few more minutes, just thinking about it. I felt sympathy for Simone and relief for myself that I'd never been in an abusive, controlling relationship with someone like Grant Fischer.

When I left the prison building and made my way to the car, I felt a knot of discomfort in my stomach. I couldn't seem to put my finger on precisely what felt so wrong.

I was halfway home before the feeling began to fade.

CHAPTER THREE

SUNDAY 8.35 a.m.

ESME

The frantic knocking started as part of my dream. But I was soon shaken from my slumber, eyes snapping open. I glanced at the clock and felt shocked at how long we'd overslept.

Zachary had had a bad night, the first in a while, and I'd been up with him a few times. Eventually, he'd dropped off but I couldn't get back to sleep. I'd popped in my ear pods and listened yet again to the first episode of my debut podcast series, *The Fischer Files*, which had aired globally just a few days ago. I'd also reflected on my thoughts about the interview afterwards. Finally, I'd slept, too.

But now the knocks downstairs morphed into thumps. Fists, instead of knuckles. Big whacking thuds on the front door.

I swung my legs out of bed at the same time as my phone lit up. Like always, I'd turned it to silent just before I went to sleep but now the screen was full of missed call notifications, text messages and voicemail alerts.

I staggered across the room and reached for the fleecy dressing gown I'd thrown over the chair before getting into bed last night.

The door opened and light from the landing flooded in.

'Mum?' Nine-year-old Zachary's pyjama-clad form appeared in the doorway. His voice sounded shaky, his eyes wide with alarm. My eyes were instantly drawn to his maimed leg, cruelly silhouetted against the hall light. The thin, striped cotton of his PJ bottoms flared out and my heart squeezed in on itself.

He'd cried out in pain at two o'clock and I'd made him some warm milk. I sat up with him for two hours until the painkillers kicked in and the terrible aching in his hip joint finally faded enough for him to get some rest again.

Someone shouted through the letterbox. A man's voice, muffled and urgent. I couldn't decipher what he was saying.

'Don't worry, Zachary.' I kept my voice light, even though my throat felt dry and my heart was racing. 'It'll be something and nothing, you'll see.'

But Zachary did look worried. He'd already been through so much suffering after the accident. My boy was not stupid. He could tell from the raw panic stamped all over his mother's face and the ferocity of the banging downstairs that there was definitely *something* happening.

I ran past him onto the landing. 'You stay up here while I see what's going on.' I thundered downstairs.

I glanced back up and saw my son, limping without his stick. He arrived at the top of the stairs. I wanted to tell him it was OK, but that would amount to lying. It was not OK at all.

With trembling hands I unbolted the locks, top and bottom, and turned the catch. I opened the door with the chain on.

Two suited men stood on the step.

'Esme Fox?' the tall one asked, making an effort to soften his tone.

'Yes?' My voice came out as a whisper.

He held up ID. 'I'm Detective Inspector Peter Sharpe and this is my colleague, Detective Sergeant Jon Lewis. You reported your sister, Michelle Fox, as a missing person, two days ago?'

I nodded and they glanced at each other. I knew then that they'd found her.

CHAPTER FOUR

THREE DAYS EARLIER

It wasn't much of a party, just a few drinks in the office to celebrate the unexpected success of the first episode of the podcast a couple of days ago. Yes, we'd hoped for a decent number of downloads and it didn't take much to make an impact. It wouldn't take that many to get us in the top fifty percent of podcasts but what we didn't expect was 10,000 global downloads in a matter of days after the first episode had aired.

We pushed the desks and chairs back against the wall and created a bit of space.

Michelle splashed cheap fizz into a glass and missed, stepping back and squealing with laughter. I'd seen her earlier, drinking with our researcher, Justine, at about three o'clock that afternoon. Now, it was nearly six.

I took the glass from her and carefully filled it as a new track started on the clubbing playlist Mo had put together, a booming bass beat vibrating through my body.

'You did it,' Michelle said, slightly too loud, too obvious. 'It's official, you're a genius.'

'*We* did it. The whole team.' I smiled, then added for devilment, 'But I suppose you're right about the genius bit.'

We both laughed but I had this uncomfortable feeling that we were perhaps celebrating slightly prematurely. Only one episode of *The Fischer Files* had been produced and released. At the cutting edge of podcasting, anything could happen. Granted, the streaming numbers were beyond our wildest dreams and had created a buzz in the podcast world, but still… there was a way to go before *The Fischer Files* could be counted a runaway success.

I looked over and saw Toby, our new production assistant, standing alone by the drinks table. He looked so downcast, lost in his thoughts.

'Are you actually listening to me?' Michelle said loudly in my ear, making me jump.

'Sorry, I was just…' I leaned closer so I didn't have to shout above the music. 'Is Toby OK, do you know? He looks a bit subdued.'

Michelle rolled her eyes. 'You just can't help it, can you? Do you enjoy being in a state of angst, even when things are going brilliantly?'

My sister could get argumentative when she drank. I gave her one of my looks.

'Relax, Esme. That's all I'm saying. It's not always up to you to fix other people's problems. This is supposed to be your big celebration!' She raised her glass up in the air too quickly and cava slopped over the rim.

The music dipped then disappeared completely and my production manager, Mohammed Khaleed, clapped his hands. 'OK, people, listen up!' The chatter died down. 'We just had a tip-off the announcement is going live on Entertainment Radio in the next sixty seconds.' He pressed a button and the presenter's voice rang out.

Mo turned up the volume and Michelle squeezed my upper arm. Over by the drinks table, I noticed Toby glance at me and then help himself to another bottle of beer.

Now, here's something you don't hear every day. A former Sky News journalist is celebrating the global hit of her controversial investigative podcast that throws new light on the Simone Fischer case. Fischer, who stabbed her husband of twenty years to death in their kitchen while their young son played computer games in the room next door, has always steadfastly refused to give a single interview... until now.

Esme Fox, director of her own eponymous small media company, The Speaking Fox, announced plans for The Fischer Files *earlier this year. Fischer has never denied killing her husband and has maintained a stoic silence since the day of his death. Even in court she refused to give details of the marriage she says drove her to act with diminished responsibility. Fischer was sentenced to life imprisonment after the trial jury came to a unanimous guilty verdict. The judge ruled she should serve a minimum of twelve years without chance of parole.*

Fox spoke to Entertainment Radio and told us that The Fischer Files *was produced and released only a year after leaving her job as an investigative journalist for Sky News.*

Podcast listeners have unanimously described the first instalment as 'addictive' and 'compulsive' after word quickly spread via social media channels. Its mainstream appeal sent listening figures soaring into the tens of thousands, and downloads are expected to double when the second episode is released next week. Industry insiders are predicting that The Fischer Files *is set to smash both podcast-streaming and downloading records.*

Fox said, 'I'm naturally beyond thrilled at the response to the first episode. I'm also truly delighted that Simone Fischer's voice will finally be heard. Women in our society are treated particularly harshly in cases like this, and often the story of abuse and vilification that lies behind a case such as this one remains ignored. That's happily not the case for Simone. After years of silence, The Fischer Files *is finally giving her the chance to tell her story to the world.'*

Well done, Esme! Tune in next week for an update on episode two of The Fischer Files.

Now, moving on to the eventful social life of popular soap actress...

Mo turned off the broadcast and the room erupted.

'Congratulations, Esme.' Mo appeared at my side and clinked his glass against mine. 'Is everything prepared for tomorrow's big meeting? Need me to do anything?'

'I've got everything under control,' Michelle remarked. 'We're ready.'

It *had* to be ready. TrueLife Media was a successful television production company who had approached me the day after episode one of *The Fischer Files* aired. Based on that single episode, their CEO Damon Yorke called with a proposal to make a TV docuseries following the podcast. 'I've just got a tremendous feeling about this, Esme. Our legal guys think there's a real chance the Supreme Court may review Fischer's case but even if they don't, the public have an appetite for this story. With you at the helm, we can bring Simone's case to a whole new audience.'

What he really meant was that I probably had the power to influence Simone to take part in the series after years of her cold-shouldering the media.

But the right deal with TrueLife could send the figure at the bottom of the business balance sheet soaring beyond our ambitions, securing the future of the company and everyone's jobs. Yorke was right in that it could help Simone's case, too. It was an excellent opportunity and we couldn't afford to waste it, and yet I knew it would be a tremendous amount of work on top of pulling myself in a thousand different directions as it was.

A deal with TrueLife would cement The Speaking Fox into the industry. Although podcasts were relatively new in the world of media, since the release of the mega-successful *Serial* podcast in

2014, hundreds, maybe even thousands of companies, had jumped on the bandwagon. Missing out on the fabulous opportunity TrueLife were offering would be utter madness – this opportunity would guarantee I could give Zachary the future he deserved, helping to compensate for the injuries he'd be forced to take with him into adulthood.

'It's the best reason for us to get an early night, I think.' I looked at Michelle. 'Drink up, girlfriend.'

I waved goodbye to everyone and they all cheered. Even Toby appeared from a side door and raised his hand. It was a great atmosphere and we left the party in Mo's capable hands.

At least, I thought that's what I was doing.

CHAPTER FIVE

In the cab, I felt relieved when Michelle quietened down a bit. She was merry, but far from wasted – which was a good thing, because she needed to be on the ball first thing tomorrow morning.

I checked my emails. Another two unsolicited hate messages judging by the subject lines, and both from email addresses I didn't recognise. I opened the first one.

Simone Fischer is a cold-blooded murderer. Have you no conscience at all? What about her poor victim?

The subject line of the second one read: *How do you sleep at night?* I didn't bother opening it.

'Trolls,' I said by way of explanation when Michelle looked over. 'Direct to the spam box they shall go.'

I'd been getting them since announcing the new podcast months ago but they'd really ramped up now the first episode had aired.

'What's your impression of Simone Fischer, really?' Michelle said, the edges of her words slightly blunted. 'As a person, I mean?'

I thought for a moment. 'I feel sympathy with her.'

'Right. God only knows what she had to put up with in that marriage.' Michelle stared out of the window. 'We'll soon find out, I suppose.'

'Mostly, I wonder how an intelligent, independent woman, like Simone was when she met Grant Fischer, could not realise she was being played and controlled. She could have got out while it was still fairly easy but she seemed completely oblivious to what he was up to.'

'Fascinating. I think a lot of people are probably in that same situation.' She paused. 'Guess that's why TrueLife are sniffing for a piece of the action. Sometimes I think we should do more with it. I mean, rather than bring TrueLife in, look at expanding the story ourselves.'

I pushed my phone into my coat pocket. 'First things first,' I told her, not for the first time. 'We need to walk before we can run.'

I applauded her ambition but sometimes, her ideas bordered on unrealistic.

Michelle and I both lurched suddenly forward, our seatbelts straining as the cab driver slammed on his brakes.

'Idiot!' He cursed as a silver sports car swerved dangerously close in front of us and then immediately took off again to skirt around the next vehicle.

I gasped, grabbing the seat in front, seeing a scene unfold again in front of my eyes… the police cars, the ambulance… my son's broken body in the road, the sound of my own screams. I felt the same wave of dread rising up in me and I swallowed hard in an effort to battle the nausea.

'You OK?' Michelle touched my arm and I blinked, clearing the awful pictures from my head.

I sat bolt upright, my hands clenched, staring straight ahead. I took a breath to ease the tightness in my chest.

'I'm fine,' I said, pulling at my seatbelt to loosen it again.

'You're still so nervous in cars after what happened to Zach,' she said. 'Maybe you should see someone. Just a thought.'

Eighteen months before, when he was seven, my son had been the victim of a hit and run. Some crazed idiot had sped by a side road near the school and mowed Zachary down. Despite a local appeal and a cash reward put up by my ex-husband's wealthy parents, Brooke and Eric, no witnesses came forward and the driver had never been found.

Zachary's injuries were comprehensive. His left leg was shattered and, for the first week, amputation was a real possibility. He also suffered a head injury when he hit the asphalt, which brought about ongoing mood swings that he hadn't had prior to the accident. Thankfully, over time, he had made excellent recovery but after a year, doctors gave us the bad news that his leg would be permanently bowed, and certain sports would remain beyond him for the rest of his life.

Whenever I thought of what he'd been left to face for years to come by some cruel, anonymous coward who was still out there enjoying life, I found it difficult to cope with the ensuing feelings. The fury and sadness merged to create an emotion so strong and powerful, I couldn't even name it. But it always ended the same way: me blaming myself that I failed in my duty to pick him up on time. Failed in my duty to keep him safe.

My phone buzzed in my pocket. I reached for it and Michelle rolled her eyes when she saw my ex-husband's name lighting up the screen. I answered it on loudspeaker by accident and then managed to drop the phone on the floor of the cab.

'Only me, ringing to see if you're back at the house yet,' Owen's voice said brightly from somewhere near my feet.

I leaned forward to speak, feeling about with my fingertips under the seat. 'We've just left the office now, I'll be home in about fifteen minutes. How's Zach feeling?' He'd had a physio appointment at the hospital, straight after school.

'He's doing great, aren't you, champ?' I heard Zachary grunt vaguely in reply. I'd have been willing to bet my life he was playing on his Nintendo Switch, even though I'd told Owen a million times he wasn't to have it until after he'd done his homework. But was it worth the hassle of raising it with him right now, in the back of a cab? No.

'Perfect. Listen, I know I'm supposed to be keeping Zach for another hour or so but... is it OK if I pop over to the house? I've got a little something to help celebrate your news. I'm so chuffed for you, Esme.'

My heart sank a little at the thought of Owen coming over. I could really do without it tonight.

Michelle sat forward and dramatically mimed *No!*, waving her hands at me. I turned slightly away so as not to laugh.

'Thanks,' I said, ignoring a dig in the ribs from Michelle. 'I appreciate it, Owen, but you really didn't need to do that.'

'It's not much, just something to mark your success... well, anyway, you'll see when you get back.'

My heart felt heavy when Owen ended the call. I was so looking forward to kicking back and chilling out with Zachary and Michelle. We'd planned to get an Indian takeaway and download some movie Zachary was desperate to watch.

I knew Zach would love his dad being there too, but lately, Owen had been outstaying his welcome at the house and it really changed the dynamic of the evening. I found I wasn't able to fully relax with him there, and Michelle wouldn't be herself either, making it difficult for us to chat about the meeting tomorrow once Zachary went to bed.

Even though everything was what I'd call 'amicable' between me and Owen – we'd agreed to stay on friendly terms for Zachary's sake and we hadn't started divorce proceedings yet – it just felt wrong to be carrying on as though we still lived together. It could be confusing for Zach. Although we were still legally married, I considered Owen to be my ex-husband in every other sense but he didn't seem to have the same vision.

I scanned the road in front of the cab, on the lookout for any more crazy drivers.

Michelle looked at me. 'Esme, it's got to stop, you know. Owen is taking more and more liberties. Jeez, he'll be moving back in soon!'

'He won't. I wouldn't allow that to happen.'

'You talk as if you're in charge and yet he seems to make all the decisions. Have you never noticed that?'

There wasn't any love lost between Michelle and Owen. She thought he was a bit of a waster and he considered her to be too interfering. Both descriptions were off in my opinion, and it was no fun being stuck in the middle of it.

But Michelle hadn't finished yet, she was on a post-drinking roll.

'Let's think about the last few days… he came over to pick Zach up for a sleepover and ended up staying an hour before taking him. He found some reason to scout around your garden shed for some mystery tool he desperately needed when he brought Zach home after school yesterday. Now, he's bought you a gift that involves him coming round yet again and finding an excuse to gatecrash the evening.'

'I know, I know.' I sighed. 'I've been hoping the situation will get better but—'

'It just keeps getting worse,' she finished for me, throwing herself back in the seat. 'I've noticed. He fobs you off with excuses all the time. Always has done. Maybe it's time you stopped being so gullible.'

I was beginning to wish I'd just left her at the party and got a cab back on my own. I steered the conversation away from mudslinging.

'Thing is, Zachary finally seems more settled at school and his teacher says he's doing well again. I really don't want to rock the boat with Owen when he's such a big part of Zach's everyday life. He needs that stability.'

'I do get that, but his father being around so much could just be plain confusing for him, too. Owen is reading you all wrong, Esme. He treats the house as if he still lives there, and when you don't challenge him, he thinks that means you're happy with things as they are.'

I shifted in my seat and gripped the inside handle as the cab swung into a side street. I didn't want to hear it, but I couldn't think of a suitable retort, largely because what she said was… well, the truth. The house was still full of Owen's belongings. Through necessity – him picking Zach up from school sometimes and bringing him home – Owen still had a set of keys. But in addition to this, he'd often walk in unannounced, pour himself a glass of juice from the fridge or make a cup of tea without asking. He had a temperamental boiler at the bedsit and he sometimes announced he needed to grab a shower at the house if he had no hot water.

'He was in favour of you two separating, wasn't he?' Michelle remarked, ignoring my silence. 'It wasn't as if someone forced his hand?'

She was right again. When Owen and I separated, it had been a very civilised affair and an entirely mutual decision… on the surface, at least. Over time we'd managed to turn into completely different people and there had started to be blazing rows: resentment and fury flaring up over the most inconsequential things, like who had forgotten to put the immersion heater on for hot water or who had failed to take out the correct refuse bin for collection.

I glanced over at Michelle. She'd clamped up and was staring out of the window now. It was so easy for her to see where Owen and I were going wrong and what we should do to put it right.

She didn't have complicated emotions getting in the way or a vulnerable son to worry about. Sometimes I envied the simplicity of my sister's life, the way she managed to excel at the different strands.

I craved more time with Zachary and yet constantly piled more and more on myself to make the business a success. All so I could somehow try and offset the negativity of the accident and give my son the future he deserved.

Some days, that felt more impossible than others.

CHAPTER SIX

SUNDAY 8.39 a.m.

I stared at the two detectives on the doorstep. My heart felt like it was ready to leap out of my mouth.

'What's happened? Have you found my sister?'

The shorter detective, Lewis, said, 'Is it OK if we come inside to talk, Ms Fox?'

I looked past them, out on to the street. Fortunately there was nobody around to witness their visit, and I wanted to keep it that way. If the press got wind of this they would revel in the scent of a story. Some of them had been scathing about my announcement for the launch of *The Fischer Files*. I stood aside and gestured for the detectives to come inside.

'My son's upstairs. I'll just need to check if he's OK before we talk,' I said, closing the front door behind them.

'Of course. Take your time.'

I asked them to take a seat in the living room and ran upstairs.

Zachary stood on the landing. His face looked so pale in the early light. 'What is it, Mum? Who are those men?'

'They're just here to talk to me, sweetie. Can you do me a really big favour and stay in your bedroom for a while?'

'I want to come downstairs and hear what they're saying. Do they know where Aunt Miche is yet?' His chest heaved as his breathing became more irregular. I stepped closer to him so I could check if he was actually taking in air. After the accident he suffered from the most awful panic attacks, that would often strike out of the blue. 'When is she coming home?'

I reached for his hand and his eyes filled up. 'Hey, we're going to sort this out, OK?' He squeezed my fingers and nodded but he didn't look very convinced. 'Come on, watch a bit of TV in your room and I promise, the moment they've gone, I'll tell you all about what they said.'

Zachary sniffed and walked back to his bedroom with me, his head hanging. He climbed back in bed – I could see the panic on his face and I felt helpless. He shouldn't have this kind of worry at his age. At the same time, I couldn't focus properly because I was desperate to see what the police had to say. I tucked him in and kissed his forehead. 'I'll be as quick as I can, sweetie. Watch something happy.' I handed him the remote control and he took it silently. I closed his door and headed back downstairs, swallowing down a rising feeling of nausea.

My scheduled visit to Simone Fischer tomorrow flitted into my mind. Nobody else could help me out by taking my place; I had to be the one to go. Everything I'd planned and organised could suddenly flip, with a domino effect.

'Do you know where my sister is?' I said, as soon as I walked into the living room.

The detectives glanced at each other again. Sharpe sat forward and laced his fingers in front of him.

'Please, Ms Fox, sit down.' He waited until I'd done so before continuing. 'I'm very sorry to tell you that Michelle has been admitted to the Queen's Medical Centre. She was found by a member of the public and I'm afraid she has suffered some very serious injuries.'

My hand flew up to my mouth.

'What kind of injuries?' I whispered. 'Is she going to be OK?'

'I'm afraid it's too early to say,' he said gravely. 'She's been badly beaten and has been slipping in and out of consciousness.'

'Oh no. No…' My skull felt as though it was squeezing in on itself. 'Where has she been for the last two days? Lying in a ditch somewhere? Where was she found?'

Panic pushed at my words, making them come out fast and jumbled.

'An early-morning dog walker found her, just off a trail, in a wooded area of Wollaton Park. Her car was found at the entrance to the park and that's being combed for evidence as we speak.'

I dashed away the tears with the back of my hand. Like most Nottinghamians, I knew Wollaton Park well. It surrounded the Wollaton Hall, an Elizabethan country house that stood in the centre of the 500-acre warren of walking and cycling trails that included a deer park. You could easily get lost in there if you didn't know your way around.

'What would she be doing in the woods?' Michelle didn't walk for exercise, she was a gym bunny, often calling there after dropping Zachary at school. There was no reason I could think of why she'd be out there.

DC Lewis cleared his throat. 'She wasn't doing anything as such.' He looked at his colleague. 'She was… left there.'

'You mean someone attacked her and then just… just *dumped* her there?'

Lewis lowered his eyes. 'I'm afraid that's exactly how it looks, yes.'

CHAPTER SEVEN

When the cab arrived outside our house I noticed, with a twist of irritation, that Owen's violet Smart car was parked in my spot on the driveway. He'd agreed to park on the road whenever he came over so I could park my car for the night without having to go out again to move it. I'd left my car at work but still. That's hardly the point.

I paid the cab driver as Michelle climbed out. 'I'll speak to Owen if you like, Esme. If it makes it easier, I can tell him it's time to back off a bit.'

I shook my head. 'I'll sort it.'

Inside the house, I heard Zachary let out a hoot of excitement. He limped quickly into the hallway to give me a hug, his face bright.

'Dad has brought something over for you,' he said, leading me into the kitchen. 'It's a present.'

'That's nice.' I plonked my bag down on the side as Owen appeared in the doorway. 'You didn't have to do that.'

'It's not much but… I just wanted to mark your special moment.'

He walked across the room, opened the longest cupboard and pulled out a large package wrapped in brown paper and string.

'Ooh, wonder what *that* is,' Michelle said for Zach's benefit. He pressed his lips tighter as if he was trying to contain the surprise.

'Hope you like it,' Owen said coyly, winking at Zachary.

It was quite obviously a picture of some sort. I cut the string and unwrapped the paper to reveal a framed version of our official *The Fischer Files* advertisement poster we'd used online.

'It's for your office,' he said.

'Oh, that's… *different*,' Michelle remarked. I heard the ridicule threaded through it, so I'm sure Owen did, too. Yes, it was a bit naff and cheesy but I appreciated the gesture all the same.

'Thank you, Owen. It's lovely.' I propped the frame up on the hob so it rested on the stainless-steel splashback. 'It's really thoughtful of you.'

The way he was looking at me, like he used to in our early years together… I squirmed a little inside. I'd agreed to him coming over and now I felt worried I was sending out the wrong messages again.

Michelle went upstairs to get changed and Zachary grabbed his game off the worktop and sauntered out.

Owen headed for the garden, apparently to get more of his tools out of the shed. 'There's a leaking water pipe under the sink at the flat,' he grumbled before closing the back door. 'The place is falling to pieces. To tell you the truth, Esme, I'm really starting to hate living there.'

I took a glass of water into the living room where Zachary was playing Super Mario. A few moments passed before he realised I'd sat down.

'Mum, do you think Dad might move back in with us?' He put down his controls and looked at me, his eyes bright. 'I know he moved to be closer to work but I think he likes being here best.'

So Zachary had noticed, too.

'Your dad will always like coming here to see you, Zach,' I said lightly. 'But he doesn't live here anymore, you know that.'

His expression dulled and he picked up his controller again without replying.

His face brightened again when the back door slammed as Owen returned from the garden.

'Dad, wanna help me get this last star?' he yelled without looking at me.

Owen appeared at the living room door. I noticed he'd slipped off his trainers and he must have left his toolbox by the back door.

'I need to get around that trap, see, Dad.' Owen nodded to the screen. 'This is my third try to get the star and I can't move to the next level without it.'

'OK, make way for the expert then.' Owen walked over to Zachary and gave me a wink. 'I'll help in an advisory capacity and then it's not cheating. Right, son?'

'Right.' Zachary grinned.

'Actually, Owen, I think it might be best if Zachary stops playing now,' I said. 'I'm about to order our pizzas.'

'Mmm, Dominos, I bet.' Owen rolled his eyes approvingly and Zachary laughed. 'My favourite.'

'You can stay and have some too, if you like, Dad.' Zachary beamed, looking at me. 'That's OK, isn't it, Mum?'

'Well… we were going to watch a movie too, Zachary. Remember?'

'Dad can watch it with us, can't he?'

They both looked at me expectantly.

'I've got a really important meeting in the morning,' I said. 'I'll need some quiet time and an early night.'

Finally, Owen seemed to get it. He blinked, startled by the realisation that I didn't want him here.

'Actually, champ, I just remembered I can't stay this time because I have to fix that bust pipe I told you about.' He ruffled Zach's hair as our boy let out a disappointed howl. 'Next time, eh?'

'I'll help you get your stuff together,' I said. Owen followed me back through to the kitchen.

'Thanks again for the gift,' I said, pushing the door to behind him. 'It was a lovely thought.'

'No worries.' His voice was flat now. 'I didn't realise you had a problem with me being here, Esme.'

'I don't! I mean, I don't have a problem with you coming in the house at all, it's just that… well, you stay too long sometimes.'

'Sounds like something Michelle might say.' He gave me a sardonic smile. 'I suppose it's not in her interests that we stay cordial.'

'It's difficult for Zachary to tell the difference between being cordial and us getting back together, Owen,' I sighed, rubbing my forehead with the heel of my hand. 'When you were down the garden just now, he asked if you were going to move back in with us.'

'Would it be so disastrous, really?' He stepped forward, sensing his moment. 'It's not too late for us, you know. I think we've both learned where we went wrong and—'

'Owen, please.' A dull thud started up in my temples.

'Just hear me out.' I winced as his voice broke. 'I miss you both… I miss you so much. I sit in that shitty bedsit every night drinking too much red wine and—'

'I'm sorry if you don't like your new place but that's hardly a good enough reason for getting back together!' Sometimes he could rile me in seconds and frankly, I didn't miss it. He had this way, over the years, of pretending to agree to everything we talked about when in reality he was out to get something altogether different. In fact, at that very second, I realised that I didn't miss *anything* about being married to Owen at all. I braced myself. 'Maybe it's time we did this thing properly. Splitting up, I mean.'

His face paled. 'What? You mean… you want a *divorce*?'

I felt suddenly lightheaded but also exhilarated at the thought of it, the chance to draw a line at last. I turned around and ran a cloth over the worktop.

'It would be cleaner, Owen. Gets rid of all this ambiguity. I know we said—'

'But we agreed: no divorce yet. We both agreed Zachary came first, above our own squabbles.'

'And he always will do. But the lines are too blurred between us; we need some clarity. It's healthier for everyone.'

A few moments of awkward silence. I felt lighter inside, just finding the courage to voice my feelings.

'The answer is no. I'd bet my bottom dollar Michelle is behind this idea.' His amicable approach suddenly gone, he folded his arms and leaned back on the cupboard doors behind him.

'She's not! I'm quite capable of making my own—'

'I don't want a divorce and I don't think you do, deep down,' he interjected, eyes blazing. 'It's not up for discussion. Not at this point in time.'

My throat squeezed as I turned to glare at him. 'Well, it's not just your decision, it's—'

We both whipped round as the door opened. Michelle appeared in a dressing gown with a towel wrapped around her head. 'Have you ordered the pizzas yet, Esme? Oh! You still here, Owen?'

Pointedly, Owen held out his arms and looked down at his body. 'Yep, looks that way, Michelle. Sorry to disappoint you.'

'I haven't ordered the food yet,' I said in a certain tone, willing Michelle to get the hint this wasn't a good time. 'There's no rush is there?'

'Pizza, pizza, pizza!' I heard Zachary chant from the living room.

My chest tightened. The last thing I wanted was Zachary witnessing the three people he loved the most at loggerheads. Since the accident, he easily became overwhelmed and anxious.

Silently, Owen turned and walked out of the room. I rushed after him, passing Michelle without comment when her hands flew up in a baffled 'what did I say?' gesture.

I hovered outside the living room door as Owen kissed Zach on the top of his head. I hated tension in the air like this. 'See you tomorrow, son. Be a good lad for Mum and enjoy your pizza and movie night.'

'Wish you could stay, Dad.' Forlornly, Zachary paused his game. 'Maybe next time, eh?'

I saw the sadness in Owen's eyes but what could I do? I walked to the front door with him.

'You forgot your tools,' I remembered.

'I'll pick them up next time,' he said curtly. 'It won't be more than a couple of days before I'm back over here.'

Referring to his next visit felt like a dig designed to cancel out what I'd just tried to flag up. Drawing a line. The divorce.

'Just let me know what nights you want Zach this week,' I said. We usually agreed the weekly split of time on a Sunday evening. 'We can arrange a day to continue our conversation, too.'

Owen stepped outside. 'There won't be a good time for that,' he said. 'I'll decide when I'm ready and I'll let you know.'

'It's not just your decision though, is it?' I responded tersely.

'See you soon, champ,' he called over my shoulder before flashing a sarcastic smile my way.

'Oh, and can you make sure you park your car on the road next time?' Michelle called loudly from the kitchen door.

I saw a bolt of fury darken Owen's face.

'If she knows what's good for her, she'll learn to keep her big mouth shut,' he muttered before he turned to walk away.

Michelle had always known exactly how to press his buttons.

CHAPTER EIGHT

TWO DAYS EARLIER

The next morning, I dressed smarter than I usually did for the office, in a navy shift dress and court shoes. It was cloudy out, but according to my weather app it was going to be a warm day. I slipped on a smart cream jacket anyway. The right impression was going to be important, and I could always take it off after the initial introductions.

I was the first one into the office, but that wasn't unusual. We had a relaxed attitude to timekeeping at The Speaking Fox. There were five permanent staff, not counting the freelancers we worked with. All staff worked over and above their contracted hours without complaint, particularly when we had an important project on the go. They'd all broken their backs to ensure the first episode of *The Fischer Files* was as good as it could be and we'd also had the celebrations the night before, so I wasn't surprised that it was nearly nine when Mo walked in.

'My head hurts,' he groaned, taking a deep draft from the Costa Coffee reusable cup in his hand. 'I should never have gone on to the opening of that new bar in town with the others.'

He looked a bit dishevelled, as if he hadn't changed since last night. But I couldn't remember what he was wearing and he was hardly my responsibility. I was disappointed that he hadn't taken better control when we left the party last night though.

'All set for today?' I said, shuffling my papers.

'Yeah, but… I'm at the recording studio this morning to get things ready for episode two, remember? Is that still OK? I could change the—'

'No, no, that's fine,' I said quickly, suddenly remembering our conversation about getting one of our preferred narrators in to do some voiceover work for the next episode's trailer. We'd pre-recorded the first few episodes to give us a head start and I would continue to interview Simone for the later ones to be aired in a few weeks' time. 'You're not involved in the actual meeting and Michelle will be in soon to go through the notes with me.'

'I should be back about midday. My phone will be off while I'm at the studio but Justine and Toby will be around if you need anything.'

'Cheers, we're all organised though,' I said, feeling anything but.

Mo glanced at his watch, the stubble on his chin seeming darker than ever. 'I might get off now, if you don't mind. Get a head start on the scripts. Good luck with TrueLife, Esme. I know you're going to kill this.'

'Thanks.' I grinned, sounding way more confident than I felt.

When Mo left, I pulled the meeting notes from Michelle's desk to look through before she got in the office. But just as I started, my phone began chirping – courtesy of the *Angry Birds* theme tune Zachary had insisted on loading onto it. I was intending to ignore the call until I glanced at the screen and saw Michelle's name on there.

'Everything OK?' My stomach churned, already anticipating problems.

'Everything is fine. I've just dropped Zachary off at school and I'm in Sainsbury's now, getting stuff for our barbie later. I just need to know if you'd prefer sweet potato or regular wedges?'

Michelle's voice was bright and animated. I resisted scolding her for calling me with daft decisions when I was trying to keep focused this morning.

'Either is fine by me,' I said, holding back the panic instead of telling her to get to the office on the double. 'Thanks for sorting the barbecue food out for later, Zach's going to love it.'

'No worries,' she said. 'I've got the stuff in my trolley now so as soon as I get out of here, I'll head straight over to the office so we can go through the paperwork before the meeting.'

'You're a star,' I said, feeling instantly calmer. I pushed away the meeting notes. They could wait until she arrived.

I took a few deep breaths, relieved my chest didn't feel quite as tight. I used to say, as a throwaway comment, 'I'm so stressed.' But the truth is, I didn't really know what stress was until after Zachary's accident, when I'd lie awake in the early hours, wracking my brains over how they could possibly catch a hit-and-run driver who was gone in seconds – so fast even the lollipop lady didn't see him coming – until I woke up in a sweat, worrying Zachary's head injury might cause a stroke in his sleep… the torture went on.

I looked around the small office, trying to see it with the eyes of the TrueLife executives who would be in here in a couple of hours. They were keen to see our offices in Nottingham, they said, and Mo thought the fact they didn't just summon us to London was a good sign. We looked on Google Earth and saw that their office building was sandwiched between the Gherkin and the Shard. I'd never met Damon Yorke, the CEO, in person before. We'd spoken on the phone, of course, and had a Zoom meeting with the whole team, but there was something about being face to face that just felt more urgent. More concrete.

Our office accommodation was certainly compact here – we had the top floor in a small two-storey office block. But Michelle, who had an eye for interiors, had worked her magic on a shoestring. She'd furnished it economically but stylishly with ex-demo blonde wood furniture and leafy plants in blue glazed ceramic pots that softened the empty corners of the white rooms. Sheer silver blinds from a local closing-down sale blurred an unimpressive view of parked cars and refuse bins out back, and the mock Peytil line art, that she'd bought online and hung in cheap IKEA clip frames, broke up the bare walls and added a certain Scandinavian charm.

When we'd viewed the premises, I'd envisaged the separate room as my own office but soon discovered I much preferred to sit out in the open-plan area with everyone else, enjoying the camaraderie that flourished there between the five of us. So we ended up grandly labelling this room 'the meeting room'.

There was a tentative tap on the door and when I looked up, Justine popped her head in. 'Got a minute, Esme?'

I nodded and beckoned her in.

Justine was the researcher at The Speaking Fox – I'd known her since my Sheffield University days, when we both studied for degrees in journalism. She glided into the room, her slender frame clad in the trademark floaty layers she wore in all seasons, rain or shine.

She styled her long, shiny brown hair the same every day, too. Loose with a centre parting and narrow plaited braids either side of her heart-shaped face.

Her bohemian style had remained completely unchanged since university. I'd been a bit of a rock chick back then, but in the world of work I'd felt I had to curtail my image to 'get on' when I'd landed my first job as a trainee journalist with the *Nottingham Post*.

Justine and I had kept in touch throughout our careers and our jobs had intersected on more than one occasion, when we'd both attended big local stories. There had been the major local drugs ring that was busted by Nottinghamshire Police four years ago, and also the time a convict was sprung free from a prisoner transport vehicle by an armed gang close to Junction 26 of the M1 two years earlier.

Justine was an excellent journalist and had won several awards for her news coverage. But I happened to know she was an even better researcher. That was also where her passion lay, and it was the reason her news stories stood up against the work of far more experienced journalists. She'd always been able to unearth some juicy background details her colleagues missed, or hadn't researched deep and long enough to find.

So, when I set up The Speaking Fox, the name Justine Campbell was at the top of my recruitment list, together with Mo's.

Now, Justine sat down in a cloud of patchouli fragrance and slid an A4 sheet over the desk to me. 'I thought you might like to cast your eye over this. It's my research plan outline for the *Fischer Files* docuseries. Maybe you could present it to TrueLife this morning as a tempting taster for the project.'

She'd jumped the gun a bit doing this. Managing my own team had proved a problematic climb in leadership for me. I wanted everything super-friendly and relaxed in the office – I'd known Mo and Justine a long time – but then it was sometimes tricky to pull things back if someone skipped ahead with stuff. I reached for the paper anyway. If today's meeting went well, Mo and I would have to meet with the executives a couple of times to thrash out the finer details of their planned television programme. Only then could I approach Simone with the idea.

Still, I was impressed with Justine's initiative and I picked up the sheet.

'This looks super, Justine.' I began, trying to strike the right note. 'You've lots of detail about the original police team and the early processes that we now suspect they skimmed over.'

'But?'

I paused before replying. 'It's great you've managed to get some ideas down at such an early stage, but I should flag up that the content could – and probably will – change after the meeting today.'

'Oh.' Justine looked deflated.

'Before the research outline can be approved, we'll need to iron out exactly what format TrueLife's television programme will take, specifically what areas of the Fischer case they want to focus on. I suspect they'll want the initial outline to come from their end.'

Justine moved her hands across the conference table as if she were smoothing out the wood. 'I didn't realise you were going to let a third party dictate the details of what we do. You've always said you wouldn't tolerate that after Sky.'

I'd shared with Justine just how I'd become disillusioned with my job at Sky News. The shift to online, instant news had robbed journalists like me of the sense of the pursuit of a story. We were told exactly what to report on and when to move on to the next lead.

I lay the paperwork down. 'Nobody is going to be dictating our content but obviously, if we accept this collaboration, TrueLife will have a say in what we finally produce. I wouldn't expect anything else.'

Justine raised an eyebrow and pulled a loose thread from her flouncy embroidered cuff. 'It's just... it doesn't matter.'

'Please... say what you were thinking. It does matter.'

'It's just that I hate the thought we're just going for the big payday and giving up artistic control in the process, that's all. It's really important you keep in touch with the company ethos on a number of fronts.'

A flare of impatience caught my breath and I waited for it to pass. Justine was my friend. She was also employed as a researcher of The Speaking Fox. But she wasn't a director and she was getting herself involved in decisions that weren't hers to make. I couldn't help wondering if I was to blame for her attitude. The way I'd encouraged an open-plan office environment that was so informal... it made it difficult to maintain professional boundaries with people you'd known a long time.

'I didn't mean to offend you,' Justine offered, registering the implication of my silence. 'I'm just flagging up what you've always said. The Speaking Fox is different to other companies. We make our own rules.'

I managed a smile. 'And that still stands, but at the end of the day there has to be a happy medium in being open to beneficial collaborations while retaining our autonomy.' I softened my tone. 'It's a bit early to worry about research ideas for the docuseries, that's all I'm saying. I haven't even broached the idea with Simone yet; she might hate it.'

'It's not just up to Simone though, is it?'

'No, but we'd need her input. Otherwise the programme would just be another third-party take on the case. It has to have Simone in it because that's what will set it apart. Like the podcast.'

Justine stood up and reached over the desk to take back her outline. 'Sounds like you've got everything under control, Esme. It's your story after all. I'm sure you know exactly what you want.'

That much was true. The stories that interested me were the ones about people. Their lives, their families, the emotional toll various events and incidents took on them. My hope was that the TrueLife proposal would take that one step further into the medium of television.

I answered Justine as warmly as I could manage. 'I'm sorry I can't give you more time right now, Justine, but Michelle is on her way in. As you can imagine, my mind's full of nothing else but this meeting at the moment.'

'Sure. I'll leave you to it, then.'

When Justine had left the room, I rubbed the taut muscles in the back of my neck and glanced at the clock. The executives from TrueLife would be arriving very soon... where the heck was Michelle?

CHAPTER NINE

JUSTINE

Justine took her bag, packed it with research notes and popped out of the office. It was early, but Esme would be holed up in the meeting for a while. Why did she have to be so controlling? Esme didn't seem to realise it, but she could destroy your enthusiasm within minutes.

She never remembered Esme being like that at college, or in the years that followed, when their work coincided on various stories. She'd always been optimistic and open to new ideas – that was why Justine had jumped at the chance of working with her when Esme offered her the position of researcher at The Speaking Fox.

But it soon became apparent Esme had changed somewhat from her early days in the industry. The optimism had been replaced by a new, more suspicious nature. Not exactly expecting the worst, but watching out for it just in case. It had made Esme cautious, which was not necessarily a good trait to have as a journalist, when you had to rely on your instincts and often go out on a limb.

Esme was adept at trying to cover up her newfound personality flaws, Justine would give her that. On the surface, she seemed pretty much the perfect boss, appearing to encourage her staff to listen to their gut feelings and to use creative thinking. But her secret drive to control every last detail – thus narrowing down the chances of something going wrong – lurked like a predator's shadow.

It was certainly not what Justine had expected when she'd joined the new business. Esme had wooed her with promises of full creative license in the workplace. It hadn't quite turned out that way. According to Michelle, Esme had been slowly getting worse since her son's accident. She was so much more on edge than she used to be, like now when Justine had put forth an idea that she'd hoped might help secure the TrueLife deal.

The gradual disintegration of their close relationship meant that Justine felt she couldn't air her concerns with Esme. She felt vindicated in taking her current course of action. She would keep quiet about it all, and when reality hit Esme between the eyes… well, then she'd only have herself to blame.

She walked across the small car park at the back of the offices and drove home, stopping only to pick up milk at a small Tesco Express down the road. Inside her flat, she made a cup of tea and, as she didn't want to arrive too early, waited for another twenty minutes before driving to the nature reserve.

She parked over the far side, behind the big sweeping willow at the side of the lake where two cars could wedge in and be invisible from the main parking area.

It was a bright but cooler day than earlier in the week. She watched two regal swans glide by, their feathers ruffling with the breeze. The surface of the water was blue, tipped with white ruffles as the current whipped it along. It was so peaceful here, she could almost fool herself that everything was fine.

Justine closed her eyes and took a few measured breaths. Her shoulders dropped slightly but her stomach still felt too unsettled to relax properly. The fear that she'd be caught out was strong. Sometimes getting found out felt almost like a premonition, a certainty that would come to pass… but she was in too far to stop this now.

The silver car turned into the main parking area, its chrome wheels glinting in the sun. Justine already knew the last three letters of the registration number were BKD. So this was definitely the one.

She swallowed the lump in her throat and checked her face in the rear-view mirror.

This was it. There could be no going back now.

CHAPTER TEN

ESME

As the clock ticked relentlessly towards the time of the meeting and there was still no sign of Michelle, I decided to immerse myself in the notes I'd made on *The Fischer Files*.

Before my first prison visit to interview Simone for episode one, I met with Janice Poulter, the founder of FSF, the Free Simone Fischer action group. She had links with a national group, Justice for Women, and access to a pool of legal advice and other experienced professionals who gave their time for free.

Simone was lucky to have them behind her, supporting her. The group members included legal and PR experts. They had secured a number of early releases or retrials for several convicted women over the last decade, but had yet to make progress with Simone's case – because of her unpopularity with the British public, some felt.

When Simone first agreed to take part in the podcast, I emailed Janice and asked for a meeting. I wanted to get their support. I knew it would be invaluable to understand everything the group had tried to do for Simone and what the major obstacles had been.

'Janice has the contacts to smooth the way with prison authorities to allow us a private weekly meeting,' Simone told me at our initial meeting. 'Any press communications from the prison have to be authorised by the board.'

I got the distinct impression that Janice would be a powerful ally if I could strike up a rapport with her and gain her trust.

We met in a coffee shop halfway between Ashford and Nottingham. She was middle-aged with short, mousy hair and wore slightly zany cerise-pink glasses. She gave off a relaxed vibe but I soon realised she was a focused woman who passionately believed in Simone's innocence.

'We've been trying a long time to get her justice,' Janice said as she sipped her latte. 'She seems to think you're different, that you've got a more honest agenda than the press who've tried to get her to talk before. It's probably because of your *Women in Prison* work at Sky News.'

The *Women in Prison* project had skimmed the surface of the UK prison system and it had whetted my appetite to delve deeper.

'I want to tell her story,' I said, tearing open a sugar sachet. 'I mean her *real* story. Like lots of women who commit crimes, Simone was immediately vilified by the public. Demonised, even before her trial took place.'

Janice nodded. 'I see it all the time. People will readily accept violence from men if they're pushed to their limits, but a woman? She's just expected to keep taking it and never complain. It's an attitude rooted in our society.'

Janice and I were on the same page, it seemed.

'What have been the group's main initiatives over the years to free Simone?' I asked her.

Janice puffed out air. 'We've had major rallies and fundraising events, all the usual tools we use to raise awareness. We've done everything that's worked for other individuals, but we've never been able to drum up the same support for Simone. I think what she did was just too... too violent, and the fact she did it while her son was close by. People can't accept that anyone could be pressed so hard they'd snap like that. Apart from the ones who've been through a similar ordeal, of course.'

'"What kind of mother would do that?" That's probably the most common comment on the forums,' I said. 'The sort of remark that garners the most likes.'

I hated that phrase. Owen had used it on me, after Zachary's accident. *What kind of a mother* would prioritise work above her son? *What kind of a mother* wouldn't want to spend every free moment with him?

'Don't forget there are plenty of people around who don't agree with what *we're* doing,' she told me. 'Just be aware they're out there. Not everyone believes Simone Fischer deserves to be a free woman and, given a chance, they'll show in no uncertain terms how they feel.'

We talked a bit about my future visits to the prison.

'I'll use my contact at the prison to try and smooth the way ahead for you a bit, securing the same private room you initially met Simone in as your regular meeting space.'

It would make a huge difference. I could hardly expect Simone to relax and open up in the highly visible main visiting hall.

'One more thing you need to know,' Janice adds before I leave. 'You'll probably have to put up with quite a bit of input from Simone's brother, Peter. Her son, Andrew, is the opposite of that; I've only met him once.'

'This is the son who was there that day?'

'Yes. He's a staunch supporter of his mother but has always preferred to keep out of the spotlight so he can live a normal life. He claims he can't remember a thing about that day and... well, suffice to say that he and his Uncle Peter don't get on.'

I waited, feeling she wanted to say more. Over the years as a reporter, I'd developed a kind of knowing. Not exactly a *sixth sense*, nothing as mystical as that. More of an instant reading of language, behaviour, the body language of others. And Janice was holding something back, I could feel it.

'Why is it they don't get on, do you think?

'Andrew thinks Peter enjoys the limelight of his mother's notoriety too much. Peter is… let's just say sometimes he likes to try and speak for Simone. When you do get to meet him, which I doubt will be long now, you'll need to make your boundaries clear and that's all I'll say on the matter. I don't want to get involved. I'm sure you'll reach your own conclusions.'

It sounded a touch ominous, but I didn't want to press too hard at this stage and scare Janice off.

I slid my card across the table. 'Can I ask you to pass my contact details on to both Andrew and Peter? I'd love to chat to both of them. I appreciate they might decline but I want to extend the invitation.'

She nodded and took the card and I thanked her, feeling grateful for her honesty even though we'd just met.

'I appreciate you being candid with me, Janice,' I said. 'I need all the friends I can get on this case. If we're to try and change opinion about Simone, we have to try and get to the truth.'

She smiled. 'I'd say you're going to do just fine. I like to think I'm a good judge of character and I believe you genuinely want to help her.'

'I'm going to do my level best to do so,' I agreed. 'I believe I can produce something that finally makes the public and the authorities sit up and listen. See Simone for the woman she is and not some fictionalised evil harridan.'

'I wish you luck,' Janice said. 'I hope you can get further than we've managed to so far. Anything else I can do, just let me know.'

When I made my way back to the car, I felt confident and fired up for the project. Even though the very person Janice had tried to warn me about would soon try his best to scupper everything.

To calm my nerves while I waited for Michelle to arrive, I decided to listen to the second episode of *The Fischer Files*, which would be aired in just a few days' time.

CHAPTER ELEVEN

THE FISCHER FILES

EPISODE TWO: THE MARRIAGE

I'm speaking to you again from outside HMP Bronzefield women's prison in Ashford, Middlesex.

In this week's episode I'll be asking Simone Fischer about her childhood and asking her what life was like living with a man she felt she had no option but to kill in order to escape from.

Grant Austin Fischer, the man Simone was married to for twenty years.

To quote some of the newspaper reports, Grant was 'brutally murdered on a sunny afternoon in broad daylight'. But the attack didn't happen in the street; he wasn't slaughtered by a stranger. Grant was killed by his own wife, in his own kitchen while their twelve-year-old son, Andrew, played on his games console in the next room.

Simone Fischer has always maintained she was never guilty of cold-blooded murder, that she never planned what happened that day in 2009. Instead, she says she was driven to kill after suffering years of abuse, withstanding cruel and debasing treatment on a daily basis.

Maybe you're wondering how someone finds themselves in a situation where, before they even realise it, another person is controlling their every move? Maybe you wonder how that same person comes to make a last-ditch attempt for freedom the only way they can.

Simone is the only person alive who really knows what happened that day. This is her story.

You're listening to a Speaking Fox podcast and *I*... am Esme Fox.

*

So I've just arrived in the prison car park and checked my phone and I've had a text message from Simone's brother, Peter Harvey. He says he's waiting for me outside the prison right now. That's quite interesting, I wasn't expecting that!

Just getting together my paperwork and... my handbag. Got that. Lock the car, ready to go.

There are plenty of people around the prison entrance. It's a busy place, as you'd expect. I'm just looking around the front of the building where I'd imagine Peter might be... oh yes, I've spotted a man who's obviously waiting for someone. He's checking his watch, eyes searching the approaching visitors. I haven't seen a recent picture of Peter Harvey but this guy is about five foot nine, stocky and going bald... he's looking around and... yep, I think he's spotted me.

Peter: Are you Esme Fox?

Esme: I am. It's Peter, isn't it? Sorry I can't shake your hand, I'm carrying all this stuff and—

Peter: Look, I've come here today to tell you I'm not happy about whatever it is you're up to. Why are you bothering my sister?

Esme: I'm making a podcast about Simone's case, Peter.

Peter: You're giving her false hope, is what you're doing. She keeps talking some nonsense about her getting out when your programme's aired.

Esme: Sorry you see it like that. I explained to Simone what would be involved in making the podcast and she decided it was what she wanted. I can assure you it was all very transparent.

Peter: Yeah, well, she can be impulsive sometimes, doesn't know what's best for her. That's why she needs me to oversee things. So, in the future, you need to speak to me about—

Esme: Really? It doesn't strike me Simone needs anyone to tell her what to think. I'd better get inside, I don't want to be late for my appointment time.

Peter: Appointment? I've heard it all now! Don't know whether you've noticed but Simone is a convicted prisoner, not an office worker. It's a prison visit you're here for. Are you recording all this? I thought you were supposed to tell people they're being taped.

Esme: I'm holding my phone out in front of me, I thought it was pretty obvious. Let's be optimistic, shall we? If this episode is as successful as the last one, Simone might not be in here for much longer. Shall we go inside?

*

We're heading into the prison now. Next stop, security…

And out the other side. Collecting my bag and paperwork… got it all. I've got a prison guard, Kat, escorting me like last time and Simone's brother, Peter Harvey, is here with me, of course.

Peter: Hey, please don't talk about me into that thing.

Esme: Sorry, this is a podcast production. Everything has to be recorded, that's kind of the whole point.

We've just arrived outside the room I'm meeting Simone in. The officer's gone in first like before and I can see Simone is sitting at the same table as before. She's giving me a little wave, she looks pleased to see us.

Peter: I think you'll find it's me she's waving to.

Simone's beckoning the officer in. Guess we'll just have to wait to hear what the problem is. She doesn't look too pleased. Here we go... she's coming out again now. I need to turn the recording off a moment.

*

Right, OK, back now. Simone told the officer she didn't want her brother, Peter, sitting in on our meeting. He's already left, didn't look too happy about it. But it certainly simplifies things for me. I want Simone to feel relaxed and able to speak freely in our session.

I'm going in.

Esme: Hi, Simone. Peter just left.

Simone: Good. He means well, he tries to look out for me. But the way I look at it, I had a man who told me what to think for twenty-four years... I don't need another. Now and again I have to kick him to the kerb.

Esme: What about your son, Andrew? Do you see him regularly?

Simone: He does visit me, less often than I'd like but that's OK, he has his own life now. My brother looked after him until he was sixteen. Peter didn't want to but I begged him. It stopped them taking him into care, you see.

Esme: You must have been very grateful to him for doing that.

Simone: Yes, of course.

Esme: I'd love to speak to Andrew. Just a short chat, if possible.

Simone: Well… I'll ask him but that's all I can do. He lives a private life, a life away from the stigma of what I did. I can't blame him for that.

Esme: Is that lonely for you, though? Knowing he's keeping you at arm's length?

Simone: I don't look at it like that. What's the sense in both our lives being ruined by what happened? Andrew is making a difference out there and I'm proud of him.

Esme: What does he do?

Simone: He works with young adults with learning disabilities and complex needs. I see my compassionate side in him. I'd much rather his efforts go into making other people's lives better. Better than moping around here constantly… like Peter does.

Esme: Is Andrew in touch with Peter?

Simone: Let's just say there's no love lost on either side. Peter likes his own way and he likes to be top dog. Andrew's young with his whole life ahead of him, he's not a child anymore, has his own opinions. He isn't interested in Peter's power games and I'm glad of that. I couldn't rest, stuck in here, if I thought Peter was controlling him. I'll get a message to Andrew about speaking to you, but can I ask a favour of you first?

Esme: Course!

Simone: Don't antagonise my brother. Don't mention Andrew or ask Peter to talk about him.

Esme: But why, if he—

Simone: Peter gets annoyed and then everybody's life gets harder. Please, just keep the status quo. That's all I'm asking.

Esme: I'm understand. I've got some questions I've prepared, just let me get the paperwork. I'll be recording the session as usual and, as agreed, I'll provide you with a full transcript after each of our sessions.

Simone: Fine. But before we begin, tell me a bit about yourself, Esme.

Esme: Me? Well, I started out as a journalist for—

Simone: No, no. About you, not your career. Your background, your family. Sorry… your face… have I made you uncomfortable?

Esme: No, not at all! Let's see… I'm thirty-four and I've been married to my husband, Owen, for eleven years. We've got a son, Zachary, who's nine. I grew up in Nottinghamshire and I have a younger sister, Michelle, who works with me at The Speaking Fox.

Simone: Your parents?

Esme: Both gone. My mum died when I was in my early twenties and Dad died when I was still at school. Both had heart trouble.

Simone: That's sad, I'm sorry. Are you and your sister close?

Esme: Very close, yes. She's involved in the business, too.

Simone: And your son… you just have the one child?

Esme: Yes. He's the light of my life. He was involved in a hit-and-run accident eighteen months ago and he faces a lot of challenges because of that. He inspires me every day.

Now, I'd better not talk about him anymore or I'll start snivelling and I need to keep my mind on our interview.

Simone: OK, I see I haven't penetrated the journalist's shell yet! But that's OK, we have lots of time.

Esme: I'd like us to start, if possible, with a brief potted history of your childhood, where you grew up. Your parents, your siblings.

Simone: As brief as your own? I'm only teasing! Now, let's see…

Esme: Maybe a good place to begin is with your parents. What was your relationship with them like?

Simone: If you'd asked me that a couple of years ago, I'd have said I had a pretty regular upbringing, but now…

Esme: Now you don't feel that way?

Simone: No. I mean, I've always thought it was nothing remarkable or dramatic. I think lots of women my age would identify with my kind of upbringing. I had my brother, Peter, and he was idolised by both my mother and father. He was clever, smart, but he was also sly… but they didn't realise that. They were blind to it. I was just your average girl and I suppose what I've come to realise is that I learned how to put up and shut up growing up at home.

Esme: In what way?

Simone: You know, the usual stuff. Not answering back, doing what was expected of me, helping Mum in the house while Peter sat watching sport on television. My dad, he had a temper. My mother said and did all the right things to avoid a blow-up. Looking back, I'd say I learned from watching her.

Esme: And how old were you, when you first noticed the way your mum behaved around your dad?

Simone: I don't know. I mean, I don't remember it ever not being that way. When I got older, I asked my mother why she put up with his moods and you know what she said? 'Every time it happens I think it will get better. And when it doesn't, I think of ways I can make it better.'

Esme: She blamed herself.

Simone: Yes and no… I'd say she saw it as her responsibility to keep the peace in the family, to keep it all glued together. That's a big burden to put on yourself.

Esme: Did you recognise that trait in yourself in your own marriage?

Simone: Oh, for sure. I'd catch myself counting all the good things about Grant and then weighing that against the latest incident. Like, if he'd humiliated me in a shop or a restaurant, I'd think 'I've had enough'. And then I'd start recalling all the times we'd had romantic meals out or he'd treated me to a gift in a store. Then it would always follow that, with his encouragement and denial, I'd dissect what happened and see how I could've done things better.

Esme: You took responsibility for his behaviour.

Simone: Every single time. Except on November 13th, 2009. That day, I'd had enough.

END OF EXTRACT

CHAPTER TWELVE

HMP BRONZEFIELD

ESME

It was frustrating to have to leave, just as things were getting really interesting in there. Having to leave Simone at such a crucial point killed me but I had no choice in the matter. Rules were rules.

Before I left the building, I headed over to the screened seating area I'd discovered in the foyer. Again, nobody was in there and so I sat down for a few minutes to gather my thoughts about the interview.

Simone had a way of connecting with people. With me. I completely resonated with her descriptions of how she'd negate Grant's behaviour by recounting all the nice times they'd had. I'd been there myself… was still there in some ways even though we'd separated. Instead of just telling Owen to keep away from the house, I often thought about our happy times together as a family. How we'd once loved each other so much, we didn't need anything or anyone else.

Again, my stomach felt knotted and painful for no good reason.

I crossed the road and saw someone waiting at the entrance to the car park. When I got a little closer I saw it was Peter Harvey, Simone's brother. I thought that was interesting. He must want to say something pretty important if he'd been waiting out here the whole time after Simone told him to leave us.

'Hello, Peter!' I said as he continued his silent glare. 'Are you waiting for me?'

'I just wanted you to know I'm not giving up, you hear me?' He sniffed. 'Regardless of what Simone says, I know what you're up to, even if she doesn't.'

'You think I'm up to something?'

'You can't be trusted, any of you. The media have only ever wanted to hurt my sister. She's only got me now and I intend to do right by her. I can tell the truth of what happened for her, I don't need you to do it.'

'But she's got more than just you, there's her son too, isn't there? Andrew? I understand he's still in touch with Simone.' Too late, Simone's plea not to antagonise Peter echoed in my ears.

His face darkened. 'You leave him out of it. He's made it clear he doesn't want to get involved in Simone's business. Leaves it all to me.'

'You look really stressed, Peter. Your colour… have you had your blood pressure taken recently?'

'Think you're so clever, don't you? There are things you don't know anything about. Will never know. So just keep your nose out. I'd have thought you've got enough stuff to be worrying about in your own family.'

My breath caught in my throat. 'What?'

'Oops. Hit a nerve, have I?' He grinned and looked over at the parked cars.

'What do you know about my family?' There *was* nothing to know about my family but it was a strange thing for him to say.

'Don't underestimate me, Esme. I do my homework.' The grin slid from his face, leaving cold eyes. 'Let's just leave it at that.'

Driving home, my curiosity was up a hundredfold. Was Simone just trying to keep the peace between her son and her brother, or was the real reason she wanted me to keep the two sides separate because she was afraid of Peter?

He was a horrible man. There was nothing to know about my family apart from the fact me and Owen had separated. Still, anyone with a bit of money to throw at a private investigator can find out the basic facts about most things.

So what, if he'd done a bit of basic digging? He clearly didn't trust me one iota. My own family was straightforward in comparison to his.

How curious it was that there were three people living their separate lives whilst also irrecoverably bound to each other by the horrors of the past. I sensed, against the backdrop of visits and interviews, there was still a lot not being said. A kind of menacing pause that filled the silences between their words.

Had one of them or all of this family got something to hide? Something perhaps that forced them to recoil from each other rather than bind themselves together?

My journalist's instinct told me I had no choice but to try and find out.

CHAPTER THIRTEEN

After listening to the podcast and reading my notes on my reflections afterwards, I held my make-up mirror up to the light and dabbed a little face powder on my inflamed cheeks. The meeting was due to start in fifteen minutes and Michelle still hadn't returned to the office.

I walked into the little kitchenette and ran a jug of cool water, taking it back through on a tray with some clean drinking glasses. My mind was racing, trying to work out how the hell I was going to be able to cover both bases: the creative and the business angle.

I completely regretted agreeing to this approach with Michelle now, but I'd never had reason to doubt her commitment before. We'd built the business together in this way and it had worked really well. Up until now.

I picked up the meeting notes and read through them yet again in some vain attempt to make sense of her scrawl. All the points were written in the kind of strange shorthand Michelle preferred, and that only she could decipher. For instance, under the bullet point marked 'Possible structure,' she'd listed:

Number, revisit, location, view

I could hazard a guess what she meant, but nothing that made any real sense. All five pages of notes were written in the same manner and I wasn't feeling particularly logical today. Why had I neglected to get the overview of Michelle's prep while I had the chance? It felt so hot in here and yet the temperature gauge showed it should feel comfortable.

I berated myself yet again for leaving such an important function entirely to Michelle, and not discussing it with her the day before. My excitement had overtaken everything. The heady mood of big media interest had been felt across the whole office. Nobody had expected such a fabulous industry and public reaction to *The Fischer Files* and they'd probably all taken their foot off the gas briefly to enjoy the moment. Just like I had. It had spectacularly backfired on me. Or was about to.

My chest felt tight, like I couldn't take a deep enough breath in.

I snatched up my phone and stabbed my fingertip on Michelle's number from the redial list. This was the fifteenth time I'd called her phone in the last ten minutes. I'd even misdialled a couple of times because I'd prodded the screen too hard and slipped to the next number on the list.

I glanced at the wall clock.

My impatience suddenly gave way to a spark of panic. What if something awful had happened to her?

Think. *Think!*

What could I do to trace her? I'd left a couple of messages for Mo but he hadn't got back to me, either.

I stuck my head out of the office door and called Toby over. He skulked around the reception desk like the last person he wanted to speak to was me.

'Toby, where's Justine?'

'She popped out for some stationery. Said she wouldn't be long.' He looked at me cautiously. 'Is everything alright, Esme? You look… well, sort of worried.'

'Michelle was supposed to be in about half an hour ago for the TrueLife meeting and I've heard nothing from her.' He looked at me blankly. He'd just finished university in the summer and was still accustomed to being directed in any given situation. 'Look, can you make coffee when they get here, Toby? And stick around in case I need anything, OK? Use your judgement for what's needed. We don't want them to think they've caught us on the back foot.'

'Course. Yes, that's fine.' He scuttled back to his desk.

I closed the door again and leaned against it, my palms flat on the cool surface. My heart was hammering in my chest and despite drinking a whole glass of water, my mouth felt so dry I worried about being able to speak at all when they arrived.

I poured another glass of water and drained it. Then I called Justine. It rang then went to answerphone. I left a message.

'Justine? Esme here, I've big problems. Michelle isn't back yet for the TrueLife meeting. Can you keep calling her for me, try and get through? I'm worried something's happened. If you can get back to the office in the next ten minutes, you could sit in for her, talk to them about your research ideas? That would be great.' I winced internally at having to say all this when I'd dismissed Justine's ideas less than an hour ago.

I put down my phone and closed my eyes. If necessary – and it was looking increasingly necessary – I could do this on my own. I was quite capable, it had all just taken me by surprise.

I sat down, pressed a clean tissue to my forehead. Then I got up and cracked the window open a touch. I nearly jumped out of my skin when the office door opened.

'They're here!' Toby hissed, his face flushed. 'There are three of them, two men and a woman. I've asked them to take a seat.' His fingers worked against the fleshy palm of his hand.

Time was up and Michelle hadn't showed. I'd been gullible, refused to face the fact she'd let me down.

Now I was on my own.

CHAPTER FOURTEEN

The meeting was nothing short of disastrous. Not just because I was unprepared, but because I couldn't seem to focus on anything they said, either.

'Look, I'm sorry,' I'd blurted out in desperation about five minutes after they sat down. 'My operations manager was supposed to be in here with notes and… well, she didn't show up. I wondered if it might be possible to reschedule. We could do either this week or next, or—'

'I'm afraid that won't be possible,' the woman, Irena, said crisply. 'As you know, we've travelled up from London to meet with you today and that's taken a big chunk out of Mr Yorke's diary.'

'I'm sorry,' I said wretchedly.

'I can see you're distracted, Esme,' Damon Yorke said. 'It sounds as if you've been let down and that's a shame. But we can carry on, get the general gist of our proposals over. How about it?'

I nodded, wishing I could just run out of the office, the building and shut myself in the car or something. I should have told the truth. Time was up and Michelle hadn't showed. I'd been gullible, refused to face the fact she'd let me down. Now I was on my own.

As it was, they must've thought me a fool, babbling my way through my very rough ideas for a docuseries follow-up to *The Fischer Files* and the re-examination of the case. I was so woefully unprepared.

Irena asked me a question about my ideas on podcast discoverability and I had to ask her to repeat it three times. Towards the end, they didn't even bother trying to hide their raised eyebrows and sly glances. I just couldn't keep focused. It was painful.

I poured a glass of water from the jug on the table and drank it down. The glass Irena drank from had a perfect pale pink lip print on it. A woman like her would never have allowed this mess to happen in her life, I was sure.

I felt so hot, dehydrated almost. The back of my neck felt clammy and it wasn't a new feeling. After Zachary's accident, everything changed. The future I saw for my son seemed suddenly tainted. I witnessed two a.m., three a.m., four a.m. in red digits on my bedside clock. For a couple of months, it happened every single night without fail.

During the day, I managed to convince myself that Zachary would come to harm even though he wasn't leaving the house and garden. Our GP prescribed some pretty strong anti-depressants and suggested I undertake some therapy sessions of my own.

Within a few weeks I began to feel better and, once Zachary's medical treatment and therapies were underway and he was making good progress, I was again able to focus on everyday life.

The way I felt right now was reminiscent of that and I definitely didn't want to go back there. I drew in some long breaths and blew the air back out slowly.

I glanced up at the clock. It was one of those where you had to stick each number and the hands mechanism directly on to the wall. It took Michelle hours to finish it and when Mo told her the number twelve was slightly crooked, she tore them all off, ordered another set and started again.

Another few hours and Zachary would be expecting his Aunt Miche to pick him up from school.

Toby stepped into the room and looked at me with either pity or concern, I couldn't decide which.

'I just wondered if you needed anything else, Esme,' he said haltingly. 'I have… a doctor's appointment today about my asthma

and yesterday, Michelle said it would be OK for me to leave early.'
He looked around the room. 'If you need me to stay I can cancel,
it's just that my mum—'

'No, Toby. It's fine, you go.' I stood up and felt a prickle of
discomfort in my lower back. 'Have Justine or Mo been in touch?'

He shook his head and took a step back as though I might
swing for him. Where the hell was Justine? She must be clearing
the shelves of stationery, it was taking her so long.

The phone screen lit up with a mobile number I didn't recognise.
I waved Toby out again and answered the call.

'Hello?' My throat was tight as a drum.

'Esme? It's me.'

'Owen?' I said, confused. Why was he calling me from another
number? 'My phone didn't display your name.'

'Yeah, this is my new number.' He said it like he'd already given
it to me. But he hadn't.

'Have you heard from Michelle?'

'What? No… I called to ask if she's picking Zach up today.
She's not answering her phone.'

I felt a rush of panic.

'Owen, I'm worried. She didn't turn up for a really big meeting
here at the office. She rang earlier and said she'd be on her way in
soon and then she didn't come back and I couldn't—'

'Slow down a moment, Esme.' Owen cut in. 'Firstly, is Michelle
picking Zachary up from school?'

'I don't know… I mean, she should be but I can't get in touch
with her. It's just not like her.'

There was a beat of silence at the end of the line. Then Owen
said, 'OK, here's what we'll do. I'll go to school to make sure there's
someone there to pick up Zachary and I'll swing by the house after
school, see if Michelle is back.'

I swallowed. 'Yes. Yes, thanks, Owen. That would be a big help.'

Toby had gone home, Justine hadn't returned and I'd heard nothing from Mo. I couldn't concentrate on anything so I closed the office early. The journey home seemed endless but I still got back before Owen and Zachary.

I parked the car on the drive and ran up the driveway. Michelle's car wasn't there. I wasn't really expecting her to be at the house but you never knew. Stuff happened. Cars broke down, people had ridiculous stories of how everything just went wrong, one thing after another.

Maybe, just maybe, Michelle was already on her way to pick Zachary up.

My lower back ached and I felt hot and uncomfortable. I silently prayed that's what had happened but I think deep down, from the very beginning, I knew something terrible had happened to my sister.

CHAPTER FIFTEEN

I knew within seconds of getting through the door that there was no one home.

There was a silence about the place. An emptiness that ricocheted through the rooms, amplifying the growing ache in my belly.

I called out anyway. 'Michelle?'

Silence.

I dumped my handbag on the side and searched for visible signs she'd been back to the house since the shopping trip. When you live with someone you get to know their habits, their routine. I knew immediately that Michelle hadn't been back here since she'd left the house to take Zachary to school that morning.

His cereal bowl, spoon and juice glass were in the sink for one thing. Michelle was a stickler for loading the dishwasher at the point of taking dirty dishes to the sink. She must have been in quite a rush to get out this morning, which was no surprise if she'd planned to drop off Zachary, pick up the barbecue stuff and get to the office in time for the meeting.

I ran upstairs to Michelle's bedroom. Again, the scene looked rushed compared to what I'd come to expect of her. A damp towel draped over her dressing table stool, the hairdryer unravelled across the floor and still plugged in, her bed unmade. She wasn't a clean freak exactly but she liked to leave things tidy. I knew for certain that if Michelle had been back here before leaving for the office, she wouldn't have been able to stop herself from tidying round.

I heard the front door rattle and I hurtled downstairs. My face dropped when Owen and Zachary appeared. 'Oh, it's you.'

'That's a nice welcome, isn't it, Zach?' Owen grinned.

'Hi, Zach, have you had a good day?' My voice was strained but Zachary didn't seem to notice.

'It was OK,' he said a bit glumly. He gave me a half-hearted peck on the cheek and kicked off his shoes. I raised my eyebrows at Owen and he shook his head.

'We're gonna have a kick-about in the back garden before tea, aren't we, champ?'

Zachary shrugged. 'I don't know, Dad. I might just watch TV.'

He disappeared into the living room and a few seconds later, we heard the television blasting out, too loud.

Owen came closer and lowered his voice. 'Mr Barry, the sports coach, caught me at pick up. Seems Zach's been a bit disruptive in class this afternoon. And… he didn't make the football team selection. Just the reserves.'

'Oh.' I feel my shoulders tense. Zach loved football and I knew he'd take the rejection badly. 'Would it really have killed them to give him a place in the team? With everything he's been through, I mean?'

'It doesn't work like that, Esme. They have to select on merit, you know that.'

Still, I was fuming. I'd go down there and demand they put him in the team. That new coach wasn't a patch on Mr Martindale, who'd retired last year.

'No sign of Michelle?' Owen brought me back to earth with a bump, reminding me of my panicked call from the office.

'No, and I'm really worried now. I feel sick, thinking what might have happened.'

Owen looked at me as if he couldn't fathom why I was being so dramatic. 'She's probably gone shopping out of town or—'

'Owen! There is no way Michelle would take herself off shopping when we'd scheduled probably the most important meeting we've had since the business started!'

He shrugged. 'I don't know then, maybe her phone died or something,' he said, opening the fridge and taking out a carton of juice. 'But where's that place you and her go to sometimes?'

'The Bicester outlet but like I say, there's no way she'd go there,' I said curtly. 'Owen, don't drink straight out of the carton like that. It sets a bad example to Zachary.'

'Zachary's not here to see it though,' he said and took another swig.

'You don't even ask.' My blood was boiling now. 'You just waltz in the house and carry on as if you still live here.'

He stuck the lid back on the carton and put it back in the fridge, needlessly thumping the door closed.

'Excuse me for breathing.' He glared. 'I'm good enough to rush over to check the house and then pick up Zach when Michelle decides to bail out though, I notice. Since you started this stupid podcast Zachary barely spends any time with you. I don't know how you live with yourself after what he's been through. And that sister of yours is—'

'How dare you! And leave Michelle out of this, there's no need to—'

'There's every need, Esme.' I moved to the other side of the kitchen but his eyes were trained on me like a laser. 'It's pretty obvious Michelle hates me coming round here. I've heard you two whispering like schoolgirls behind my back, seen the eye-rolling.'

'What are you going on about?'

'I know she tries to poison you against me.' His expression grew dark. 'Turns out she's not so reliable after all though, is she? What would have happened to Zachary if I hadn't called? He'd still be waiting at school, with his class teacher asking herself what kind of mother leaves a boy with a disability alone like that.'

'I haven't got time for this bickering.' He had this way of short-cutting straight to my guilt. I grabbed my handbag off the side. 'I'm going out to check on a few places. That's if you don't mind staying here to watch Zachary for an hour?' I hated leaving Zach again after what Owen had just said but I had to do something. 'Don't say anything to him about her being missing yet, I don't want to worry him unnecessarily.'

'But are you sure it's OK for me to stay here unattended? I might need to use the bathroom or make myself a coffee without asking.'

It wasn't worth the argument that would ensue if I replied.

'Where are you going?' he called as I headed for the living room to say bye to Zachary. He was absorbed in his programme so I just kissed him on the cheek.

Back in the hallway, Owen hadn't moved. I considered ignoring him but he walked towards me, hands outstretched. 'Look, Esme, this is daft. I'm sorry, OK? Let's not be petty with each other, that's all I'm asking. Not when you're obviously worried about Michelle.'

My eyes prickled and I nodded. 'I am really worried now, Owen. She called me from Sainsbury's to say she'd be at the office for the meeting. That's the last time I spoke to her so I guess it's the logical place to go first.'

'She's hardly likely to still be there if it was hours ago.'

'I know that. But maybe someone has seen her. I'll show her photo to the checkout operators. At least I'll start building up a trail of where she was seen last.'

A look crossed his face as if he was about to say something unhelpful but thankfully he seemed to change his mind. 'Do you know which branch she was at?'

There was a superstore about two miles away and also a smaller Sainsbury's Local within half a mile.

'I think she'd have gone to the big store as she was getting stuff in for a barbecue tea. The local store wouldn't have as much choice.' I felt the enormity of the task: asking staff who might have already changed shifts from this morning on the off-chance someone remembered Michelle. 'I have to do something. It's too soon to report her missing to the police and they'll ask me if I've done this stuff, anyway.'

Owen looked incredulous. 'Report her missing? Esme, she's only been gone a few hours. I think you're overreacting a bit.'

'I was relying on her for the big meeting with TrueLife today. She knew that and would never have let me down. I'd lay my life on that.' My jaw sets as I remember how I doubted her in the run-up to the meeting. I watched as Owen clearly lost his resolve to make me see any sense.

'Fine.' He shrugged his shoulders, a look of amused incredulity on his face. 'I'll stay here with Zachary, then. That way, if she comes home loaded down with shopping bags from the outlet, I can call you at Sainsbury's to let you know. Good luck.'

He went to give me a peck on the cheek, but I was already out of the door.

I drove the long way around so I'd pass Zachary's school. I travelled slowly along the road that ran in front of the main school gates. Despite regular pleadings from the Head Teacher in the weekly newsletter asking parents and carers to refrain from double-parking on the road, they all tended to do so, Michelle included.

There were parked cars dotted here and there and I cruised by and scanned all of them. At the end of the road, I turned left and then left again. I kept going until I'd ridden around the entire perimeter of the school campus but Michelle's snazzy new lipstick-red Mini Countryman was nowhere to be seen.

CHAPTER SIXTEEN

The superstore was busy with parents and kids who'd gone shopping after the school run. I saw a couple of other mums from school and nodded and smiled while keeping my distance. The last thing I wanted now was to get in an inane conversation about next month's school trip to Eyam.

I sat in the car park when I arrived at the superstore and selected a photo of Michelle from her Facebook page. I avoided any where she'd been dressed up to the nines to go out because I wanted an image that represented how she was most days. I chose one that reflected her girl-next-door friendliness, a lovely natural-looking shot of her taken on a day trip to the coast we had last summer. She looked relaxed and happy, her dark blonde hair tousled by the sea breeze, her hazel eyes bright and sparkling. My heart squeezed in on itself as I saved it to my photos folder.

Inside the store, I felt deflated when I saw how busy the place was. All the checkouts had queues, even the self-checkouts were all taken.

When Owen and I were still together, and before I launched The Speaking Fox, I had more free time. I used to spend a lot more time with Zachary and come in here regularly to do our weekly shop. As I approached the checkouts, I recognised some of the faces from my numerous visits here. But they saw hundreds of people every week; the chances of anyone remembering me were small.

I'd never had to ask about a missing person before.

I reached the first till and joined the short queue. I was tired and rattled now – a bad combination – and doubting that this had even been a good idea in the first place. I was mad to think anyone would remember her. Eventually, it was my turn. The cashier looked at the empty conveyer belt and back up at me.

'Sorry, this might seem a bit strange but I just wanted to ask if you've served this woman today?' The woman peered at my phone screen. 'It's my sister,' I explained. 'I'm trying to track her movements today as she missed an important appointment and she's not picking up my calls.'

My heartbeat picked up in anticipation that she'd recognise Michelle. *Please, please, recognise her.*

She pressed her lips together and shook her head. 'Sorry, love. I haven't served her today.'

It was the same story at the next till. I had to queue up and, fiddling with a change of till roll, the woman barely glanced at Michelle's photograph.

'She's not been to my till today, sorry.'

'But someone must've seen her!' My voice rose two octaves as I held my phone up to her again. 'Please, take another look… she was here! Just a few hours ago. Check again!'

The cashier stood up and took a step back from her seat. 'Look, I've told you, I haven't seen her.' Her eyes scanned the section of the foyer where the security guards usually stood.

People began to stop emptying trolleys and packing shopping bags and just stood and stared. That's when it hit me that the checkout operator obviously thought I was violent or mentally ill… or both.

'Esme! How are you?'

Dread prickled at the back of my neck. I turned around to see Imogen, a parent-governor and one of the mums who was very involved with all aspects of school life. Last term, I'd successfully dodged her efforts to organise a stand at the summer fête and to sew sequins on costumes for the upcoming Christmas pantomime.

'Hi, Imogen,' I said, managing a weak smile and then turning back to the cashier to avoid speaking to her further. But she seemed oblivious to the situation.

'You'll have no doubt heard about our eco-warriors initiative from Zachary. We're looking for parents who are happy to document their carbon footprint on their way to work.'

It occurred to me that Zachary barely talked to me at all about what's happening at school these days. Worse still, I realised I hardly ever sat down to chat about his day, aside from my usual automatic greeting of, 'How was school?'

Imogen tipped her head to one side and frowned. 'You look a little… stressed, Esme. Is everything alright?'

'Sorry,' I said quickly, my chest tightening under her scrutiny. 'I'm too busy to get involved with anything going on at school at the moment.'

'Ha ha, aren't we all? It's not as involved as it sounds, actually. All we need you to do is—'

'Look, I can't talk about it now,' I snapped and her eyes widened. 'Sorry but… I've got an emergency situation on at home and I have to—'

'Oh no, I'm sorry to hear that, Esme. Is it Zachary? I know he didn't make the football team. My Matthew said how disappointed he was and I said, "Thank your lucky stars, Matty. You're one of the lucky boys who's got a place." It must be heartbreaking for Zachary to be so hampered by his leg injury and such a difficult decision for the coach to have to—'

'Just stop!' I screeched, and my hands flew up to grip the top of my head. 'I can't think straight. My sister's gone missing, I have to find out if anyone saw her here today.'

Imogen's face paled but *still* she stayed put. 'I'm so sorry, Esme, I had no idea. Michelle, isn't it? What happened?' She took my arm and steered me across the supermarket foyer. I didn't resist, didn't speak because I knew I was in danger of disintegrating if I did. 'Is this where she came last? I saw you going around the tills showing them your phone. How inconsiderate she hasn't let you know where she is. Here we go, customer services.'

We stood in front of the horseshoe-shaped desk with Imogen still rabbiting on although it was just white noise in my ear now.

An assistant approached us.

'My friend needs help. She's lost someone.'

The woman instantly looked concerned. 'Have you lost a child?'

'No, no. It's her sister,' Imogen replied. 'She's missing and this is the last place she came.'

The other woman's hand fluttered to her throat. 'Oh, how awful.' She nodded at her colleague. 'Put a call out for Nasreen, Janet.' She looked back at me. 'It must be awful for you, lovey.'

'Thank you, it is,' I said, her sympathy making me feel suddenly tearful. I turned to Imogen who, despite her nosiness, has helped me out. 'Thank you. Sorry I—'

'It's fine, darling, really it is. Are you going to be OK now? It's just I've left my husband on the bakery aisle and—'

'I'm fine. Thank you.'

A navy-suited young woman appeared at the desk a few minutes later and was helpful and efficient. She escorted me to the remaining checkout stations and, after apologising to each customer being served for the interruption, showed the cashiers Michelle's photograph.

Not one of them had seen her that day.

'There are a couple of part-time staff who were on this morning and have already left,' Nasreen explained. 'If you text me the picture of your sister, I'll contact them personally and ask if they served her.'

I thanked her, but my heart felt heavy and sore. Still, I texted her the photo and said a silent prayer.

I'd done everything I could.

I took a diversion on the way home so I could call at the smaller Sainsbury's Local. There was a chance Michelle had been here and I felt hope rise again in my chest.

Again, the shop was busy. But at least there were only two cashiers. I stood in the queue and when I got to the front, I held up my phone to show him the picture.

'Excuse me, what are you doing?' An officious-looking man in a suit appeared out of nowhere, frowning at my phone.

'I just… I just wanted to know if he's served my sister today.'

'We can't give out information about our customers.'

'My sister is missing. I just need to know if she's been in here, that's all. You see, I'm trying to pinpoint where she last—'

'Data protection laws,' he said coldly, 'cannot be compromised, I'm afraid.'

The other customers were openly staring now and I felt like running from the shop as fast as I could. Without looking at the manager, the cashier took my phone gently from my shaking hand and showed it to the woman who was serving next to him.

'Seen this woman today, Barb?'

'Harold! This is not appropriate,' the manager blustered. 'You just heard me say—'

'And you just heard her say she's lost her sister,' he retorted.

The female cashier shook her head sympathetically.

'Nah, we haven't seen her in here, love. I'm sorry. Hope you find her soon.'

I thanked them both, touched by their kindness. Then I directed the foulest glare I could muster at the manager and left the shop.

Back in the car, I slumped over the steering wheel and closed my eyes.

When my phone rang I sat upright in the car seat. I snatched it up without even looking at the screen.

'Hello?'

'Esme, it's me,' Owen's voice sounded low with urgency. 'Zachary's just told me something that happened earlier at school. You really need to hear this.'

CHAPTER SEVENTEEN

I drove home as fast as I possibly could without breaking the law. What could have happened at school that's so urgent and why didn't Zachary mention anything when he first got back?

You really need to hear this…

If Michelle had been in touch, Owen would have said so. I prayed it was nothing about the football team, or something Zachary had done wrong in class, because those usually important details meant nothing to me right now. I'd hit the roof if Owen had dragged me back for *that*.

When I got back, I burst into the house, hope fluttering in my chest. I rushed into the kitchen where Owen sat at the breakfast bar, scrolling through his phone.

'What is it? What's happened?'

'Follow me.'

He slipped off the stool and walked into the living room. I had no choice but to follow. Why couldn't he just tell me?

'Dad!' Zachary objected when Owen muted the television.

'Sorry, son, but this is important. I want you to tell your mum what you just told me.'

'What, *all* of it?' Zachary rolled his eyes.

'Yes, all of it. It's important.' Owen turned to me. 'Zachary told me something very interesting about his Aunt Miche this morning. Something he saw.'

I reached for Zachary's hand. 'You're not in trouble, sweetie, but I've been trying to contact Aunt Miche most of the day and she's not answering her phone. Can you tell me what you saw?'

Zachary looked nervously at his dad for approval – an action that sent a splinter of envy into my heart – and Owen nodded at him.

'When she dropped me off at school this morning…'

'Yes?' I encouraged.

He stared at his hands. 'I got into the playground and realised I'd left my reading folder in the car. Mr Barry is giving out gold stickers to anyone who remembers it every day for a week.'

'That's great,' I said, my heart rate picking up. 'What next?'

Zachary bit his lip.

'So you ran back out the front to catch Aunt Miche before she drove off, right, Zach?' Owen chipped in to jiffy him along.

Zachary nodded. When he started talking again, his voice emerged quiet as a whisper. 'Then I saw Aunt Miche talking to the man.'

'The man?' I repeated faintly.

'The man who was standing by the railings.'

The back of my neck prickled again. 'Have you seen this man before?'

Owen pressed his hands in the air to signal me to let Zachary tell his story.

'No, I haven't seen him before, Mum. He's one of Aunt Miche's friends, I suppose.' His attention drifted back to the television again and he scowled when Owen reached for the remote control and turned it off completely. 'I ran across the school yard to get my folder but she got into the car.'

'Her car?'

'No, the man's!' Zachary sighed as though I was being purposely obtuse.

'Did you see Aunt Miche's car?'

'Nooo!' Zachary whined.

'Let him finish, Esme. You can ask him questions after.' I felt like snapping at Owen to shut up, but didn't dare break the atmosphere.

'I shouted "Aunt Miche!"' he yelled. 'Just like that. But she didn't hear me. She got into the car and closed the door.'

'Then what did you do?'

'The car drove off and I had to go into class or I'd have been late.' His forehead wrinkled. 'I won't get a sticker now.'

'Zachary, I want you to think really, really carefully. What colour was the car? Do you know what make it was?'

'It was silver,' Zachary said confidently. 'It looked like... maybe an Audi or something like that. I'm not really sure.'

'And the man you saw talking to Aunt Miche, he was driving?'

Zachary nodded. He finally looked up at me. 'Can I have fish fingers and peas for tea?'

I slipped onto the sofa beside him, half in a daze. Why would Michelle get in a man's car and drive off somewhere? Did she come back to the school later and pick up her own car? I now knew it wasn't parked anywhere near the building.

Owen cleared his throat. 'Tell your mum the other thing too, champ. About last week.'

'What about last week?' My heart started to race.

'She drove off in the same car last week, too. But I didn't see the man that time.'

My mouth fell open. 'Are you saying you've seen her drive off in that same silver car before?'

Zachary nodded.

'So why didn't you tell us that's what happened?'

Zachary shrugged and reached for the remote control. 'Because Aunt Miche asked me not to tell you or Dad,' he said simply. 'So I didn't.'

He snapped the TV on, and I looked at Owen over the top of our son's head. What the hell was going on?

CHAPTER EIGHTEEN

Her body was dumped there.

I stared at the detective, my throat closing a little more with every second that passed. 'You're telling me someone hurt her in another location and then left her in the woods like a sack of rubbish?'

'We know very few details at the moment,' DI Sharpe said. 'That's why it's important we start at the beginning and get as much information as we can about how Michelle went missing. We'd like to ask you a few questions.'

I nodded, a wave of something heavy and cloying washing over me. Lewis swiftly produced a rough book and pencil. He took down my contact details at home and at the office.

'I just wanted to check, Michelle lives here with you and your…' He checked his notes. 'Your nine-year-old son. Is that right?'

'Yes,' I said.

'And your husband, Owen Painter. He lives here, too?'

'No. He doesn't live here anymore, we're… separated.' My throat felt tight and dry. They both watched me, clearly expecting me to elaborate on our situation.

'When Owen moved out, Michelle moved in for convenience. She works for me, you see, and helps out with the school run, stuff like that. It works well.' I swallowed and paused. 'It did work well.'

'I see,' DCI Sharpe said softly. 'Could you let us have your husband's new address?'

I gave them the details.

'When can I see Michelle?'

Lewis coughed. 'We can give you details and you can call the hospital. But first, can we just get through this information? I'm sorry to have to ask but it's vital we start with an accurate picture of the day Michelle went missing.'

They hadn't initially seemed that interested when I'd called to report her missing. Had said it was possible she'd decided to make alternative plans to the meeting. For a second or two I could explode with fury at the lost time, the lost opportunity when Michelle still might have been rescued.

'It's hard, I know,' Sharpe says, taking in my expression. 'But it won't take long and then we can move on with things.'

We went through the same stuff I gave over the phone when I rang them for advice. I started with the phone call before the important meeting that didn't seem important at all anymore. I told them how I'd rushed around the Sainsbury's cashiers showing them her photo on my phone. Sharpe nodded and Lewis scribbled it all down on his neat white notepad.

Then I told them what Zachary had witnessed outside the school. Lewis stopped writing and they both sat up a bit straighter.

'What exactly did he see?' Sharpe asked.

I shook my head. 'He just said… I'm sorry, my head's just not working right. I can't seem to think straight… he said—'

'Don't worry, it's the shock. We'd like to speak with Zachary about this though, if possible, Esme. Not now, but perhaps tomorrow. In your company, of course.'

I didn't like the idea. Zachary was already displaying signs of his old anxiety and his tremor. But I knew it had to be done and it would get them off my back for now because my head felt like it might explode any second.

'OK but I'll need to agree a time with you. I've got a meeting I can't get out of in Ashford tomorrow,' I said, already trying to imagine how I was going to pull it off and failing. How on earth was I going to be able to focus on the interview with Simone in the midst of the terrible news about Michelle?

Lewis cleared his throat. 'I understand you're visiting Simone Fischer at HMP Bronzefield for some kind of radio show?'

'I'm making a podcast about Simone's case,' I said. News travelled fast. But the success of the podcast had been well-publicised locally as well as nationally.

Lewis waited, clearly hoping for more. I pressed my lips together and said nothing.

'Right. Just one more thing before we go, Esme. Did your sister and husband get on? I mean, he might've felt like he's moving out and she's moving in… was he OK with that?'

'He was, actually, yes. He knew it worked well for Zachary. Our son was involved in an accident eighteen months ago, a hit and run. He suffered leg and head injuries and he's had some behavioural problems since then, so a stable environment is key to his wellbeing. Michelle being here provided that and Owen recognised it.' At least he did in the beginning, until their relationship turned a bit sour. But that's not the sort of thing I'd tell the police.

Sharpe nodded and they both stood up.

'You were going to give me details of where Michelle is. Can I visit this morning or will I have to wait until tomorrow now?'

I couldn't wait to get in there, let her know I was there for her. Owen could come and sit with Zachary and I could sit and hold my sister's hand. She was alive and that's what mattered. That's what I was going to try and focus on.

Lewis took out his phone. 'I'll text you the details now but you'll need to liaise directly with the hospital in terms of visiting. It's not straightforward I'm afraid.'

My phone pinged and Lewis indicated I should look at my phone. I opened up the text.

ICU, West Block, C Floor, QMC 0115 924…

I let the phone fall into my lap. My sister wasn't just in hospital. She was in the Intensive Care Unit.

A feeling shot from my chest to my head like a bolt of light. I'd been so foolish… blinkered, even. Refusing to accept the reality that my sister might possibly have secrets she hadn't shared with me.

At that moment, I made a silent promise to myself to take the blindfold off.

I would not rest until the person that did this to Michelle was brought to justice.

CHAPTER NINETEEN

TWO DAYS EARLIER

While Owen sorted out Zachary's fish finger tea, I rushed upstairs into Michelle's room. Once in, I pushed the door to and sat on the edge of her unmade bed. I suppose I was hoping just by being there I'd somehow get a hint of what might have happened to her.

My worry had dissipated with Zachary's revelation and now I just felt like an idiot. I'd been on the brink of reporting her missing to the police. Rushing around Sainsbury's stores, telling anyone who'd listen that my sister was missing when, in actual fact, she was probably spending the day with some guy she'd never even thought to mention to me. And asking Zachary to lie to us, his parents! What was she playing at?

I bit down on my back teeth to harness the fury.

Had this man suggested a day out somewhere and she simply couldn't resist the temptation? Michelle had been in long-term relationships before – she'd even been engaged to some childhood sweetheart when she was younger, but that had fallen through. She'd repeatedly said, over the last couple of years, that her life was plenty full as it was. She said she didn't need the complication of a relationship and I'd never questioned it. Now, I wondered if I'd believed her so willingly simply because it suited me to have her around more.

Despite all this, I couldn't completely erase the possibility that she'd met a man who she thought was decent and he'd turned out to be a psychopath who'd abducted her. This morning. Outside school.

It sounded ridiculously dramatic and Owen would dismiss it as nonsensical, but you read about these sorts of awful things happening all the time.

Yet she'd willingly got into his car before, Zachary said. She wasn't stupid enough to do that if she'd felt the least bit unsafe in his company. I started to calm down a bit.

Then I remembered she'd called me and said she was at Sainsbury's *after* she'd got back from wherever they'd been, so that disproved the theory. Michelle had sounded perfectly normal and not under duress at all. She said she'd be leaving the shop for the office directly.

Nobody had abducted her. If she'd gone with this guy, she must have gone willingly.

As recently as this morning, I'd have bet my salary that I knew everything about my sister. We spent so much time together at both home and work, we were hardly apart recently. Particularly since Owen had left home.

I found it almost impossible to accept that she'd been having a relationship with someone without ever mentioning him to me. Now that I was essentially single too, we talked about stuff like that all the time and we were always in agreement that Zachary's wellbeing and The Speaking Fox came first in both our lives for the foreseeable future.

Michelle had seemed as committed to building the business as I was, and that's why it was such a shock when she hadn't turned up for a meeting that could have turbo-charged our course so dramatically.

I pushed thoughts of the disastrous meeting from my mind. What was done was done. It was obviously never meant to be. But it was one thing dismissing the lost TrueLife opportunity as unimportant when I faced the possibility my sister might be missing. Another thing entirely if we'd lost out because she'd decided to spend the day with someone she'd just met.

I forced myself to unlock my clenched teeth.

I looked around her bedroom. It was the second biggest in the house and overlooked the street at the front. My own bedroom faced the back garden. I never came in here if Michelle wasn't home but now it felt right to be in here – to spend a few minutes trying to make sense of what had happened.

I spotted something silver poking out from under the wrinkled sheet on her bed. When I peeled the sheet back, I saw her MacBook laptop and her work diary on top of that.

This wasn't Michelle's personal computer; it belonged to the company. She'd definitely have had this with her if she was headed for the office and our meeting. Which meant she must have planned on calling back for it after the supermarket. If in reality she'd ever gone to the supermarket.

I reached for them – just as the bedroom door opened.

'Bit of a mess in here.' Owen wrinkled his nose. 'Thought you said she was tidy.'

'She is, most of the time,' I said, slipping the sheet back over her belongings. 'Is Zachary OK?'

'He's OK, bit worried about Michelle. He seems to think he's done something wrong not telling us before now but like I just told him, a decent adult wouldn't ask a kid to lie for them.'

'Owen! That's not really appropriate, is it?'

He pulled a face. 'Appropriate or not, that's what she did.'

I looked away from him before I said something I might regret, and I opened Michelle's diary.

'Anything interesting in there?' Owen craned his neck to try and see, and I closed it again.

'Can you make sure Zachary's alright, please? I don't think Michelle would appreciate coming home and finding you in her bedroom.'

'Yeah, well, if she hadn't done a disappearing act with her new boyfriend, we wouldn't have to be, would we?' He moved towards the door sulkily, but instead of leaving as I'd hoped he would, he sauntered around the edges of the room, touching and prodding at Michelle's belongings. He picked up a hairbrush and inspected it before putting it back down; pulled out a litter bin from under her dressing table and poked through the contents.

'Stop doing that!' I snapped, and he dropped a ball of screwed-up paper like it was on fire. 'It's disrespectful… she might come home at any time.' And if she saw I'd let Owen snoop around in her bedroom she'd never forgive me. Despite the fact I was looking through her work items, I still felt protective of my sister.

'Excuse me for breathing, only trying to help,' Owen muttered, folding his arms.

I forced myself to keep quiet and opened the diary again. There was hardly anything written and I knew she was a big fan of maintaining her online diary. I couldn't help but wonder if she'd put details of meeting her mystery man in there.

'It's not on that she let you down this morning, Esme,' Owen said. He reached for Michelle's magnifying mirror and studied his own face in it, despite what I'd said about touching her things. 'I know how important the TrueLife meeting was to you. Hasn't she mentioned this guy to you at all?

'No, but that's her prerogative, I suppose.' I wasn't about to confide in Owen about our informal 'stay single' policy.

'I suppose on the plus side you now know she's obviously just off gallivanting somewhere with her new fancy man. You must feel a bit sickened about that.'

My conversation with Simone in one of the pre-recorded podcasts came to mind. Clever ways someone can make you feel like they're on your side when they aren't at all.

'I don't know that's what happened yet, Owen.' On occasion, Michelle and Owen reminded me of two kids trying to one-up each other. He'd have been delighted if I'd told him how irritated and disappointed I was feeling with Michelle, and that was the reason I was putting a brave face on. 'I'm more worried by the fact she's been meeting him at school. Seems a strange place for a rendezvous. I wonder if I ought to mention it to the school just in case this guy is dodgy.'

'Do you want me to take a look at that?' He nodded to the MacBook. 'I know you're a bit of a technophobe.'

I snapped the lid closed again and placed the diary back on top of the computer. 'I might not be an expert but I can manage to open a laptop and have a scout around,' I said lightly. 'Thanks for the offer, though.'

'You know how to use that word then?'

'Huh?'

'*Thanks*. I thought you might have thanked me for extracting such a vital piece of information from our son. About her fancy man at school, I mean.'

I frowned. 'Funny you should mention it, because I've just been wondering how Zachary came to tell you something like that. He was immersed in the television when I left so it's not the kind of thing he'd just volunteer, particularly as Michelle had asked him not to mention it.'

'Asked him to lie to us, you mean?'

'How did it come up?' I refused to be waylaid by his pettiness.

'I just asked Zach a few searching questions, that's all.'

'Like…?'

'Like did Aunt Miche tell you she was planning on going somewhere that Mum didn't know about this morning.' He paused. 'And I asked him if he thought she was a bit sly sometimes.'

'Owen!'

'What? It did the trick, didn't it?'

'It's not right. Michelle's his auntie and he loves her. You shouldn't put him in a position like that.'

'Can't have it both ways and you were hitting a dead end.' He picked up a small, faded photograph in a frame of Michelle and me, taken when she was seven and I was ten years old. I can still recall the feeling of that hot day in August. No school and a picnic in the garden with Mum's homemade lemonade.

'You don't look like sisters here,' Owen remarked.

I knew what he was getting at. I was plump with pale red hair against Michelle's slim, athletic build and blonde curls. This was Owen's preferred method of getting me annoyed. Discreetly and by the merest suggestion, so he could simply deny it if I confronted him.

Not this time. I didn't have to put up with his peevish games anymore.

I kept my voice light. 'Owen, would you mind checking if Zachary is OK? I just need a bit of thinking time about what I should do next.'

He clamped his mouth closed. Annoyed, but not able to think of a smart reason he could stay up here. I'd become better at playing him at his own game over the years.

At least, I liked to think so.

CHAPTER TWENTY

When Owen had gone back downstairs I opened up the laptop and the screen lit up with a password field. I tried Michelle's date of birth, various permutations of Zachary's name, but nothing worked.

I picked up my phone and called Mo. To my surprise he picked up after the first ring sounded.

'I was just about to call you! What happened at the meeting, Esme? It dragged on a bit at the studio so I've only just finished. Toby told me Michelle didn't turn up.'

'She *still* hasn't turned up, Mo. I'm out of my mind.'

'It's not like her to let you down. Where do you think she is? How did the meeting go?'

'Not well, I'm afraid, I'll tell you all about it later. I have no idea where Michelle is but there are some documents I really need access to on her laptop. It's password protected so is there any chance you can swing by my house and get me in?'

'Sure, no problem. I can be there in about... say, fifteen minutes?'

'That's perfect, thanks.'

I looked around the room, imagining Michelle up here this morning, getting ready to leave the house, chivvying Zachary along. Was she excited she'd be seeing this man at school?

Despite her nephew spotting her with the man this morning, there was still a strong chance she'd had some kind of accident. I just couldn't accept she'd let me down because some bloke she fancied offered to take her out for the day.

'Where are you, Michelle?' I said out loud but her bedroom offered no clues.

Hopefully Mo's IT skills would help me to come up with some answers. For the next five minutes I sat and googled phone numbers of the local hospitals so I could call them later to check she hadn't been admitted.

Downstairs, I explained to Owen that Mo was calling in.

'There was no need to drag Mo out, Esme. I told you, I could've sorted the laptop for you. He'll think you have a useless husband.'

'We're separated, in case you hadn't noticed.' He winced at my words. 'Anyway, Mo handles all the IT issues at the office.'

Owen fancied himself as a bit of a technology whizz but he was far from that. Once, on a crazy whim and for reasons known only to himself, he'd wiped the operating system off his own MacBook Air in order to convert it to a regular Windows laptop. He'd used a YouTube video as his operating manual and… well, you can guess the rest. Not only did the expensive piece of equipment not work anymore, it was unable to be reversed, even by the Genius Bar staff at the Meadowhall Apple Store.

Twenty minutes later, Mo's car pulled up outside the house.

'Bill Gates just arrived,' Owen called out drily.

I looked into the living room as I headed past to the front door. Zachary had the television blaring out and was building a Lego model. Owen was stretched out full-length on the sofa, mug of coffee in hand.

'You're a star!' I said, relieved as Mo stepped into the hall and pulled out what we called his 'bag of tricks' in the office. A black rucksack containing an unfathomable tangle of cables and powerpacks, the proof of Mo's regular boast he never threw a wire or cable away. I tried to smile. 'Thanks for coming. How did the recording session go?'

'It was fine. What the hell happened to Michelle though?'

I lowered my voice.

'I'm really worried, Mo. She'd never have let me down like that unless… she physically couldn't get into the office.' I dropped my voice even more. 'Owen is convinced she's just gone shopping or had a better offer of how to spend her day. But it doesn't add up. It's not like her.'

Mo pinched his chin, concerned. 'Doesn't sound like Michelle. She never gave you any hint she might be delayed somewhere?'

'Nothing. In fact, she called me from the supermarket to say she was heading straight back to the office. That was the last I heard from her.'

I didn't tell Mo about the guy outside the school at this point. Mo was a friend of sorts, but first and foremost he was a member of staff and, despite them all being good at their jobs, I didn't trust them not to gossip amongst themselves. It would feel disrespectful to Michelle.

Mo had accepted my invitation to come in but turned down the offer of coffee.

'I'm meeting my old flatmate for a pint in town, so I won't stay.' He put his head into the living room. 'Hey, Zach! Hi, Owen.'

'Mohammed,' Owen drawled by way of a greeting.

'Mo! Come and see, I'm making a Lego Hedwig!'

'Wow, sounds awesome, mate. Got to run now but your mum will take a photo of it to show me when you've finished, yeah?'

Zachary seemed content with this response and his brow immediately furrowed with focus again.

I led Mo into the kitchen where he opened the laptop before rummaging in amongst his spare wires. He pressed a few buttons and sighed.

'Can't do anything here, I'm afraid. I'm going to need to take it with me.'

'Oh!' My shoulders sagged. 'I thought you'd get in easily through your administrator access.'

'That will just get me into the operating system. To access the personal files, I'll have to break through her password and that takes time.'

'Well, how long do you need?' I was tempted to ask him not to go drinking and do this instead. Michelle was missing, it might be important.

'I'll need to keep it overnight,' he said, crushing my hopes of getting it back later today. 'I'll drop it off at the office on the way to the pub now and set a programme running. When I get in first thing in the morning it should be unlocked and I'll aim to have it sorted by lunchtime at the latest.'

It seemed every which way I turned, I just hit another dead end. Despite Owen telling me it was too early to call the police, I felt a conviction it was time to ask for help.

I picked up the phone.

CHAPTER TWENTY-ONE

When I came off the call to the police, my heart leapt when I read an email from Janice of the FSF group. It was brief but I was delighted that Andrew Fischer had agreed to speak to me. Janice had included his telephone number.

The officer taking the call had sounded so disinterested, I almost ended the call. I realised she'd only been missing a few hours but they didn't seem to appreciate how out of character that was for Michelle.

A call with Simone's son was just what I needed to distract me from the burgeoning worries.

After checking Owen wasn't lurking around outside the kitchen door, I tapped the number into my phone. It was answered almost immediately.

'Andrew Fischer.' He sounded bright and young.

Briefly, I introduced myself. 'Thanks so much for agreeing to talk to me, Andrew. Your mum has explained how you feel about getting on with your life so I do appreciate it.'

'Well, Mum seems to have put all her faith in you.' His voice was relaxed and warm. 'What is it you'd like to know?'

'It was just a general chat, really. For background purposes. Would you rather meet up in person? I could drive to you, wherever you are, it's no problem.'

'I'm afraid I'm a bit pushed work-wise at the moment,' he said. 'We're short-staffed here. Someone left, someone else is ill.'

'Where is it you work?'

'I'm a live-in senior carer at a place called The Spindles. It's a care home for young adults in Nether Broughton.'

'Your mum told me you make other people's lives better. She's very proud of the work you do.'

'Is that what she said?' His voice thickened slightly, as if hearing what Simone said had touched him. 'I'd like to think I add some value to the residents' lives. In fact, I've just looked at my diary and I'm due to visit Mum next month. I'd be happy to meet up in person to chat then, if it's any help?'

I'd be finished with the podcast recording in a month's time.

'Let's just have a quick chat now on the phone, if that's OK with you?'

'Sure.'

'I've been told by various people you have no memory of what happened back in 2009.'

'It's true I can't remember anything about the actual attack. I had headphones on, playing my computer game. That's the last thing I can remember. It's so weird but the doctors told me there's a name for it. Dissociative amnesia.'

I'd happened across the term before whilst researching stories, particularly where childhood abuse had occurred. A victim might block out certain information, often associated with a particularly stressful or traumatic event in the past. Memories were then able to effectively hide away in the brain, lurking like a shadow but with no way of being consciously accessed. Put simply, it was the brain's way of protecting itself from a total meltdown and, in Andrew's case, totally understandable.

Andrew said, 'After that, the next thing I remember was the house being full of people in uniforms; scene of crime officers, policemen, paramedics… and, of course, the noise. I remember the noise, like a rising wave of panic all around me. Engulfing me.' He fell silent for a few seconds before speaking again in a quieter voice. 'I never saw Dad's body but I saw my mum. She was sitting quietly in the corner staring into space. But I was used to her doing that anyway. She used to do it whenever he shouted at her, which was quite a lot.'

'What do you remember of your father's treatment of her?'

Andrew blew out air. 'I think he probably treated her very badly but I was used to it, you know? It sounds really horrible but looking back, their behaviour was never anything but normal to me as a kid. And I never saw him hurt her. Ever.'

Grant had been clever. Careful. Simone had already told me that.

'Did you speak to your mother at all, after the attack?'

Again, he fell silent as if he were summoning the pictures in his head. 'When the house started to fill with people, I walked across the room and stood next to her. She put her arm around my middle and squeezed and then she let go and didn't touch me again. She didn't say a thing. She was calm, as if she was in a trance. The social worker came and they took me away.'

'Into care?'

'For one night and then I went to live with Uncle Peter.'

Simone's plea not to stir things up between Andrew and his uncle rang in my ears but the whole point about me making the podcast was to ask questions, to give the listeners an insight into the Fischer family as it was back then.

'It must have been a relief when your uncle took you in,' I said gently. 'Avoiding you going into care at such a young age.'

'Have you met my uncle yet, Esme?'

'Yes. Just briefly at the prison, but—'

'Then you can probably imagine what he's like to live with. He's a textbook narcissist. Now, he's obsessed with gaining attention and making money out of my mother's case.'

'In what way?'

'Hasn't he told you? He's writing a book. I'm not supposed to know but let's just say I keep an eye on his emails. He's always been sloppy with his passwords.' Andrew laughs lightly, obviously a bit embarrassed at his confession. 'It's suited him that Mum has refused to speak to anyone all this time. Now you've come on the scene and he's seeing his money spinner dissolving into thin air. I like to keep an eye on my mum from afar, even though Peter doesn't realise it.'

The pieces slotted in place like a jigsaw. Peter's insistence I should filter my contract with Simone through him, his ill-disguised fury when Simone dismissed him from our interview…

'Look, all I'm saying is be careful around him,' Andrew said. 'Watch him closely because he'll shaft you if he can. He cares about nobody but himself. Trust me on that one. Mum seems to think you might create a real chance to turn the tide with public opinion and that's why I'm speaking to you now.'

'I really appreciate your honesty, Andrew,' I said. 'I just have one last question. Do you think your mum is afraid of Peter? I can't put my finger on why she might be nervous of him but it's something that's occurred to me more than once.'

'Scared of Uncle Peter?' He repeated thoughtfully. 'Truthfully, I think we all are, a bit. Don't underestimate him, Esme, that's my advice. Stay away from him when you can.'

CHAPTER TWENTY-TWO

Once the detectives left, I had no one to call but Owen. So that's what I did.

'Esme?' His voice sounded disjointed, muffled by sleep. He's always enjoyed a lie-in at the weekend.

'Owen, they've found Michelle.' I couldn't get any more out. I felt like I was drowning.

'What? Is she… is she OK? Esme, are you there?'

The room was drifting away from me but then I heard Owen's voice, strong and dependable.

'I'm on my way over now.'

The detectives left fifteen minutes ago. I held myself together long enough to speak to Zachary. I walked into his bedroom. It was quiet and dim in there, his curtains still drawn. His television was off and my eyes adjusted to the faint light that filtered through the lined fabric. I wondered if Zach had somehow fallen asleep again after his restless night, but then his head poked out from the duvet.

'Have they found Aunt Miche, Mum?' He propped himself up on his elbow and watched me intently.

My heart felt like it had stopped momentarily, and I forced myself to breathe. What could I tell my son? I didn't want to lie to him, but neither did I want him spiralling back down to that negative place where he got stuck in the months after the accident.

I walked over to the window and pulled open the curtains. Outside, the sky was cloudy and dull. Too thick for the sun to break through.

'Aunt Miche is in a safe place now, sweetie. She's being well looked after.' I sat on the side of his bed and stroked his hair. 'But she won't be coming home just yet.'

He pushed himself up to sitting and rubbed his eyes. 'Why not?

'She's in hospital. I don't know all the details yet, Zachary. I'll find out more later today. The main thing is, we know where she is now, right? And we know she's in a safe place and the doctors and nurses are caring for her. That's got to be a good thing.'

He looked unconvinced. 'Has she had an operation?'

'I don't think so. They'll be doing some tests, I expect, before they fix her up.'

DS Lewis's text flashed into my mind. *Intensive Care Unit.* People were sent there when they couldn't easily get fixed up.

'Maybe she's had an accident… like me,' Zachary said. 'Her leg could've got crushed by a car.'

My heart squeezed. 'Maybe.' I leaned forward and kissed his forehead before pulling back the covers. 'We'll know more soon. Get dressed and I'll make you some toast and eggs. Your dad's on his way.'

'Yesss!' He hissed and eagerly began to get out of bed.

Downstairs, I filled the kettle, ready to make tea when Owen arrived. Everything looked slightly strange to me. The worktop, the sink, the room. Everything around me seemed a little off-centre.

I sat on the comfy sofa opposite the French doors and stared outside feeling dazed.

Despite the clouds, it was a dry morning, the kind of day when I might have thought about persuading Zachary to go outside for a bit of fresh air. Before I started The Speaking Fox and before his accident, we used to sometimes make the fifteen-minute walk to a nearby park after school to feed the ducks. He'd groan and say he needed the time to reach the next level on his computer game but I could tell he didn't really mean it. It was our little bit of screen-free time where we'd talk about all sorts of things, just mother and son.

For months, all I'd seemed to talk and think about now was getting the format of *The Fischer Files* right, or how we might keep our general production costs down. The first few episodes had been pre-recorded but because of the limit on prison visits, I was still travelling down to speak with Simone and record the last few episodes. This would be aired each week towards the end of the series.

We were safely in front with completed episodes but I had to keep my commitment to visit HMP Bronzefield at any cost or the series wouldn't be completed on time. It sounded like I was putting business first but it was the opposite of that. I was just trying to ensure I could build security for my son's future.

For now though, I pushed all that away and focused again on Michelle and how soon I could see her.

I could hear Zachary padding about upstairs, getting ready. He was always excited to see his dad.

Owen's flat was just a twelve-minute drive away when the traffic was good. I'd never been there but he'd shown me the interior photographs on Rightmove before he moved out. It was small and basic and located in a decent part of town.

'It's just a bit of a stop-gap for the first few months until I find something better,' Owen had said when he signed the three-month tenancy agreement. He'd let the tenancy run on and had been living there seven months now.

Our family home, purchased a couple of years before Zachary's birth, was a comfortable Victorian villa in Wollaton, a leafy suburb of Nottingham. Four bedrooms, a good-sized lounge with a deep bay window, and we'd had the kitchen extended three years before.

We had a reasonable garden at the back that Owen had loved to tend, and now he was living in a rabbit hutch with small windows and no balcony.

It didn't take a genius to work out he had to be finding it very tough. It was obvious he was missing being at home but I tried not to think about it.

My breathing felt shallow and inadequate. I couldn't shake the unnerving feeling our lives were changing by the minute; that I was losing my grasp on the security a normal routine offered. I no longer knew what was going to happen next. This whole nightmare felt like a spider's web twining thicker and stronger around me with every minute that passed. Soon, I'd have no way of escaping and everything I'd tried to do to build a future for Zachary would crumble away before my eyes.

I sat on a tall stool at the breakfast bar and tried to force myself to take deeper, slower breaths. After a few moments, I picked up my phone and tried the ICU number again but there was still no answer. If only I could see Michelle. I tried to remind myself no matter how bruised and beaten she was, she was still here. She was in the best place.

But what kind of monster would do that to her?

'Mum?'

I jumped up in my seat. 'Zachary! What's wrong?'

'I don't want to go to school tomorrow if Aunt Miche isn't back home.'

Oh no… not this again. Please.

'No worrying about school today.' I pulled him closer and slid my arm around him, thinking about the looming prison visit in the morning I couldn't get out of. He gave a long, deep sigh of pure misery. 'What's wrong, sweetie?'

He shrugged. 'I keep thinking about Aunt Miche being in hospital and Dad living at the flat. Why is everybody leaving us?'

I kissed the top of his head, a weight settling on my chest.

'People's circumstances change, Zachary. Our family – you, me, Dad and Aunt Miche – we're still all here for you, even if things are a little different to how they used to be.'

'But I liked how things used to be. I didn't want everything to change.'

I rubbed at my temple. I was getting the mother of all headaches. 'I understand. Change doesn't always go our way, but the important thing is that your family love you and we are all here for you. That's something that will never change, OK?'

He gave me a forlorn nod but didn't say anything. I gave him a squeeze.

'Come on, Dad will be here soon and you've still got your pyjama bottoms on!'

'Can I stay off tomorrow, Mum? My tummy already hurts.'

My heart sank, the memories of those dreaded words fresh in my mind again. Today it was a battle I didn't feel up to fighting.

'We'll see how you are in the morning,' I said non-commitally, busying myself getting eggs out of the fridge.

After the accident he'd suffered from night terrors, waking up exhausted night after night after night. I'd found lots of advice online back then and I tried all the recommended tips: mood lighting, letting him read in bed, talking about how he was feeling. But things got worse when Zachary began to wet the bed regularly, and then started refusing to go to school altogether.

My whole body grew rigid when I thought it all might begin again, provoked by his worrying about Michelle. When he found out someone had hurt her, it might send him back to that dark place. It would be so difficult for me to cope this time without Owen's support during the night.

I heard Owen's key in the front door and I rushed into the hall. Zachary got there first, grabbing his father in a tight bear hug.

'Hey, champ, what's happening?'

'Aunt Miche is in hospital,' he said. 'We don't know when she's coming home.'

'What?' Owen looked at me as he held our son close and I nodded to confirm it. He recovered quickly. 'I'm sure she'll be OK though, Zach, try not to worry.' He held our son close. 'You on the next level of your game yet or do you need the master's help again?'

I left the two of them bantering and walked back into the kitchen to butter the toast. Owen walked in a few minutes later.

'He seems a bit hyper,' he said, picking up half a slice of toast and taking a large bite.

'Owen, that's Zachary's breakfast.' I moved the plate away from him. 'He's had a rough night with his hip. I thought I was going to have to bring him into my bed but he dropped off eventually.'

Owen's mouth twisted into a strange shape. 'Sounds so odd, that.'

'What does?'

'You saying about Zachary in your bed.' He shook his head. 'I suppose I still think of it as *our* bed.'

I looked at him. 'I'll make us some coffee.'

Owen took Zachary his toast and scrambled eggs and when he came back in we sat on the sofa opposite the French doors with our drinks. There were a few moments of silence and I could feel the weight of what had happened settle squarely between us.

I told him the story of how Zachary and I had slept a bit later and woken to the sound of hammering on the door downstairs.

'It really unsettled him, Owen,' I said, biting my lip. 'After you moving out and now Michelle… I worry he's going to slide back into his dark place again.'

'It is a real worry,' Owen agreed. 'What's happened with Michelle?'

'She was dumped in the woods. Left for dead.' A small noise came out of my mouth and I covered it with my hand. 'I can't think about it. I can't bear it. Do you think it's something to do with that man Zachary saw her with?'

Owen closed the gap between us on the sofa and slid his arm around my shoulders. I bristled slightly at his close proximity but I hadn't the energy to complain about it.

'Don't. Don't torture yourself, Esme, not when you don't know the facts yet.' His hand balled into a fist. 'I can't believe they told you half a story and then just buggered off again.'

'They gave me the hospital number, I suppose.'

Owen shook his head. 'It's not good enough, just leaving you to it like that. It really isn't.'

'I've called a few times now but there's no answer. I know they're bound to be busy but I feel like driving over there and hammering on the ward door so they have to let me see her,' I said, even though I knew it was illogical.

'The only thing that would achieve is getting thrown out by security,' Owen said, showing me his phone screen. 'Looks like they don't open for visits until 1.30 p.m. at the weekend.'

'I'd just be grateful for an update this morning.' I chewed at the inside of my cheek too hard and tasted the metal tang of blood. 'I feel so hopeless. Thinking about Michelle lying in that place without anyone there for her. It's horrible.'

'Well, at least we know she'll be getting the best care where she is,' Owen said, sipping his coffee. 'Nothing I say can make you feel better, and I'm sorry for that. I hate to see you suffering like this.' He looked out of the window at two pigeons squabbling on the grass.

'Thanks for coming over,' I said softly. 'I feel better already talking to you about it.'

'Anytime. You know that.' He looked at me over his mug. 'How much does Zachary know about what's happened?'

'Obviously, he was unnerved by the detectives turning up but I managed to persuade him to stay in his bedroom while I spoke to them. When they'd gone I didn't want to lie, so I told him that his Aunt Miche was in hospital but that she was safe.'

'And he accepted that?'

'Sort of. He wanted to know if she'd had an operation and I said they would be doing some tests to find out more.'

'I suppose it brought back memories for him about the accident.'

I nodded. 'He wondered if her leg had been crushed by a car, bless him. And then… oh, it doesn't matter.'

'And then what?'

'He asked me why everyone always leaves us. You and Michelle, he meant.'

Owen's face sagged. 'That kills me.'

'I know. I hate that he feels like the people he loves are somehow leaving him. I don't want him to feel insecure.'

Owen straightened up a bit in his seat. 'Esme, I wondered if… look, just hear me out, OK?' I shrugged and watched as he finished his drink and put his mug on the coffee table. I couldn't be sure what was coming but suddenly my skin felt itchy. 'What if I stay here for a few days… or at least until Michelle is back home? You're going to need some help with Zach and I don't like to think of you coping alone. What do you say?'

'I… Owen, I don't know. I don't want it confusing Zachary about where we stand. It would make it so much harder for him when you have to go back to the flat again.'

'I'll make the bed up in the box room so it's clear I'm not back in our bedroom. No pressure, it's up to you. But you're going to need someone to take Zach to school and pick him up at the very least for a few days. You'll want to be at the hospital quite a bit with Michelle, I'm sure, and if she has got a lot of injuries then it could be a while until she's home.'

'Zachary's already saying he doesn't want to go to school tomorrow. I thought those days were behind us.'

'Well, there you go, then. I can persuade him to go tomorrow, I'm sure of it. And if not… well, I'll stay with him while you visit your friendly murderer.'

He just couldn't help it! Having a dig in the middle of a crisis. He'd made his feelings about Simone clear from the beginning and he definitely wasn't on the supporters' side.

But I thought about how I was going to manage Zachary's care without Michelle around. It didn't feel right Owen moving back in but as he said, it might only be for a couple of nights. I'd know more tomorrow when I could get to the hospital. I had the journey to Middlesex to worry about, too. It was really important I did everything I could to minimise the impact on our son, and that realisation decided it. I swallowed down my irritation.

'Thanks. I think it might be for the best, if you're sure you're OK with it.'

His face brightened immediately. 'Of course I'm good with it! I wouldn't have offered if not.' He stood up and clapped his hands together. 'That's sorted then. I'll just get my stuff out of the car.'

'What stuff?'

He turned back in the doorway. 'I brought an overnight bag with me. You know, just in case you wanted me to stay.'

I heard the front door open quietly and close again. I walked into the living room to see how Zachary was getting on with his breakfast.

When I glanced out of the window, Owen had parked in Michelle's spot. As he turned to open the boot, I could swear there was a faint smile playing at the corners of his mouth.

Later, I listened to episode three of *The Fischer Files* again. It was the last of the finished episodes we had produced to date and so I had zero wriggle room in getting the second half of the series recorded.

My planned interviews with Simone had to take place no matter what, or the whole project would fail and my business would collapse.

CHAPTER TWENTY-THREE

THE FISCHER FILES

EPISODE THREE: LIVING WITH THE ENEMY

I'm speaking to you from outside HMP Bronzefield women's prison.

It seems that over the years, everyone has formed an opinion on what happened behind closed doors at 331 Marigold Avenue, a smart, detached red-brick house that fits in perfectly with the rest of the street.

But what happened that night eleven years ago sets that family home apart forever from every other house on the avenue.

You can find numerous online articles about the Fischer marriage. Speculation, hearsay and fake sources are rife. If you want the truth, then keep listening, because for the very first time since her conviction, Simone Fischer has exclusively agreed to tell The Speaking Fox the truth about her marriage to Grant Austin Fischer.

This is a Speaking Fox podcast and *I…* am Esme Fox.

*

I'm walking towards the prison building and I'm thinking about how I've personally read dozens of accounts of the Fischers' marriage online from various sources, ranging from complimentary work colleagues of Grant Fischer's to an interview with the Fischers' cleaner who reported Simone to be constantly 'annoyingly nervous'.

Today, I'm hoping to speak in detail to Simone herself about the insider's take on the marriage that split the country. If Grant controlled Simone, then what exactly did he do? Why didn't she leave him? There must have been a better way than killing him, right? Then there are Simone's supporters who say that people – often women – can be unaware they're being manipulated; that coercive control is now a form of abuse and Simone must have felt she had no way out. But Simone must prove that's what happened and *The Fischer Files* podcast is a major step in that process.

I'm heading for security.

*

I'm outside the meeting room now, feeling a little tense.

I used to consider myself a fairly hardened journalist, before my son had his accident. Then something seemed to tip inside me. I speak to people about all sorts of things but somehow, today, I feel like I'm about to invade Simone's privacy by asking her about her marriage.

You see, she's never spoken about her marriage in great detail, even in court. Never commented on the numerous opinions and reports out there. I wonder, will she fall back on avoidance tactics when I begin with my questions? Will she decide enough is enough and change her mind about co-operating with the podcast? It'll be understandable if she does.

She's smiling at me through the glass door. She looks comfortable, relaxed.

I'm going in there, now. I'm going to find out what it felt like to be Simone Fischer eleven years ago.

*

Esme: Could you tell me a bit about what Grant was like as a husband, Simone? How other people regarded him, how they saw him interact with you?

Simone: That's easy. He was a model husband outside the house, the perfect gentleman. He was always one to help out if the neighbours needed a hand. In fact, he'd help anyone, at home or at work. He was even voted Colleague of the Year once by his fellow salesmen, who said about him, and I quote, 'He's completely selfless and always willing to share tips and give advice to help others.'

Esme: So, an all-round nice guy, on the face of things at least… what about closer to home, your near neighbours. What did they see of your marriage?

Simone: He'd often chat to our next-door neighbours when he got home from work. Neville was in his seventies and nearly always out in the front garden if the weather was fine. His wife, Cathy, was always pottering around in the greenhouse in all seasons. Grant would come into the house still smiling from their interactions. But as soon as he closed the front door, the smile would literally slide off his face. Like most things in his life, it was all a big act.

Esme: And when you saw that – the smile slide off his face, I mean – you must've felt pretty nervous. How did you react when that happened?

Simone: By this stage, I behaved like a kicked dog around Grant and it always seemed to anger him even more. I tried really hard to have everything ready as he liked it when he got home from work, but there was always something that didn't suit. Always some small detail that would seal my fate for the rest of the evening.

Esme: Seal your fate? That's quite a strong phrase. What would come of his bad moods?

Simone: It sounds pathetic but you get into routines when you're married. Our routines though were slightly different to most healthy relationships.

Esme: In what way?

Simone: Gosh, I can feel my face colouring up. It's… it's embarrassing.

Esme: I don't want to force you into talking about anything that makes you really uncomfortable, Simone. And we can always edit out if you change your mind about certain details airing. But bear in mind, our listeners want to understand about your case. I think you'll find most of them have a high level of empathy when they hear the truth and will respect a candid approach.

Simone: That's what I want… to get it all out in the open. I want people to know what kind of man he really was under the mask. It's just… embarrassing. With hindsight, I'm mortified I allowed this to happen to me.

Esme: I understand, although there's nothing for you to be ashamed of, Simone. It's not easy revisiting this stuff and I know our listeners will appreciate that.

Simone: OK, well, one of our routines was that when Grant got home from work, he'd sit down on the bottom stair and I'd unlace his shoes, and take his jacket and briefcase. Mostly he wouldn't speak to me at all at this stage. He'd walk into the living room and greet our son, ask him about his day, ruffle his hair or kiss the top of his head. Andrew was so addicted to his computer games anyway, he'd barely notice, always in his own little world.

I'd make Grant a cup of tea and wait in the kitchen until he was ready to come in. Each morning before he left the house he'd tell me what he wanted me to cook from scratch for dinner that evening, but Grant was fond of changing his mind. Say we'd agreed pizza and he announced he fancied lasagne, I had to be ready to rush to the supermarket to get whatever ingredients I'd need.

Esme: And this was every night?

Simone: There wasn't always a problem with dinner, often it was some other issue. But generally, there was always some kind of problem. Occasionally he'd inspect the kitchen cupboards, wipe his finger over the top edges for dust. Other times, he'd head straight upstairs to make sure I'd made our bed correctly. When he was in the mood, he'd find something – anything – that wasn't up to scratch and then I'd be punished.

Esme: He would be violent?

Simone: He was rarely physically violent. I often used to think that would be preferable, you know? Get it over with, a few minutes of pain.

The things he would do, the way he'd speak to me… it was all far wider reaching. It chilled me, terrified and hurt me on a deeper level.

Esme: Could you share those things with us?

Simone: He started to belittle me more in front of our son. Encourage Andrew to call me a stupid bitch or a lazy cow. Andrew didn't know any better, he'd been taught to do it from an early age, but Grant seemed more and more amused by it.

When I got upset, Grant would laugh and hug me in front of our son, say 'Can't you take a joke, Mumsy? We're only having a bit of fun, aren't we, Andy Pandy?' And Andrew would laugh – I was never quite sure whether he knew what was really happening – and I'd have to join in to make it seem 'normal' for him.

'It's just harmless words, a bit of fun.' Grant would shake his head as if I were a lost cause. 'Why do you have to read a deeper meaning into everything we say?'

I'd see Grant out in the back garden sometimes, talking to Neville and Cathy over the fence. I remember this one time, they were closer to the house, and I crept into the bathroom to listen through the open window. Grant was telling them all about my supposed mental health problems and how he was desperately worried about the wellbeing of our son when he left Andrew in my care.

I heard Grant say, 'You'd think he was a normal boy to look at him but that lad cries himself to sleep nearly every night, Cathy. She's so cutting, so utterly cruel to him.'

After that, whenever I went outside, Neville and Cathy would either scuttle back inside or avert their eyes and pretend they hadn't seen me. They, in turn, told other people on the avenue and pretty soon, I was an outcast. In the summer, oftentimes one or more people would have a barbecue and Grant would go alone, telling lies that I didn't want to mix with other people.

Esme: So it was another way of isolating you.

Simone: Totally. Nobody would have helped or believed me if I'd approached them or confided in them about his abusive behaviour. They all loved Grant. They thought I was the monster.

END OF EXTRACT

CHAPTER TWENTY-FOUR

ESME

There was a middle-aged woman in the seating area today. When I walked into the space she glanced up from her Kindle but didn't look up again.

I sat down in the seat furthest away from her, put my bag down on the floor and draped my arm around over the back of the seat as I twisted round towards the large square window. From here, I could see everyone who was leaving the building, the road outside, the car park beyond.

Soon, those things began to blur and the conversation with Simone filled my mind. She'd talked about Grant presenting a picture to others that wasn't truthful and, after a while, she'd started to believe in it herself.

After Zachary's accident, everything changed for me and Owen. We both suffered in different ways. For me, the fear of something else happening to my son loomed large. Until I'd been to see the GP and got help, I found I couldn't leave him alone for a second unless there was someone with him. Owen was different. He couldn't forgive himself for deciding to go to a training expo in Newcastle and therefore hadn't been around to protect Zachary or to be with him directly after the accident.

Back then, once I'd started to feel better, I began to think about getting back to work again. Owen took his foot completely off the gas and drastically cut down the number of clients he'd built up as a personal trainer. That was fine by me because he took over as the main carer of Zachary. But then he started pressuring me to work less, too.

I began to feel trapped in a cycle of arguments, so a few months later, I suggested the three of us went to the coast for a weekend break to Whitby, a quaint fishing town in North Yorkshire. The fresh air, paddles and fish and chips, eaten on benches overlooking the harbour, seemed to do Zachary the world of good and Owen and I got some much-needed time to chat while our son happily dug numerous holes on the windy beach.

On our last morning, I opened up, tried to explain exactly how I felt to Owen. 'I get you want to scale back your job, but if I'm going to start the new business I have to put the hours in for us all to reap the benefits. I want to be able to give Zachary a good life, fund private therapies to try and ease the challenges he'll have to face from his injuries. You know that.'

'I do know and I'm sorry. I want to support you,' he said. 'I want the best for Zachary like you do. I'll stop talking about your increased hours, I promise.'

But he didn't stop. He just found new ways of saying it. He seemed hell-bent on making me feel the guilt he himself suffered from.

'If only you weren't going to that meeting we could take Zach to the cinema.' Or, 'The weather's picking up so do you fancy a family day out on Friday? Can you reschedule your work diary?'

Each time I'd gently remind him of his recent promise.

The final straw came one morning when we woke up in bed and he said, 'You know, most mothers would thank their lucky stars if their kid survived an accident like Zachary has. They'd want to spend every moment with him.'

When he uttered those words, I felt something die inside me. It was probably the hope that things would improve between us but also my belief that I was a good and decent mother to Zachary.

Was it true? Was Owen right, that if I was a good mother, I'd give up everything to be with my son 24/7?

His face was puce, my teeth were locked together and it was just seven in the morning. That's when we just sort of looked at each other and the realisation dawned. Our marriage was no longer serving either of us.

Inside, I felt hollow. Years together, wiped out in what felt like an instant. If Owen had put his arms around me at that moment, I think I'd have sobbed into his chest and tried yet again to come to a truce.

But he didn't do that. He folded his arms, the tendons in his neck still visible.

'Zachary has to come first and this constant arguing can only damage his recuperation. I feel bad enough about what happened to him without causing him more hurt.'

'Agreed,' I said, steeling myself against showing any emotion. 'Perhaps it's time to call it a day, Owen.'

He looked at me then, a shadow crossing his face and settling over his narrowed eyes.

'You can't just airbrush me out of your life, Esme,' he said, his voice soft and pleasant. 'I'm here to stay. Whatever it takes, whatever happens, I'll be right here at your shoulder. Nothing you could say or do can change that.'

Harmless words, Simone said Grant had called them, and now I knew exactly what she'd meant.

What should have felt like a comfort, a security that Zachary and I would never be alone, somehow had sounded like something else entirely.

Silently, I'd swung my legs out of bed and reached for my dressing gown, an icy chill tracing down my spine and pooling at the bottom of my back.

I gathered up my things and headed out. I wasn't here to rake up events from my own troubled marriage. I hadn't got the time.

CHAPTER TWENTY-FIVE

SUNDAY

By ten a.m., Zachary and Owen were sitting in the living room watching a recorded episode of *Match of the Day*.

I closed the kitchen door and called the hospital. The Intensive Care Unit phone number was engaged. At last they must be answering the phone!

For the next fifteen minutes, it was constantly engaged. Just when I was on the brink of getting dressed and driving over there with or without Owen's approval, someone answered.

'ICU, Ward Manager speaking.'

'Hello! I'm calling to see how my sister is. Her name is Michelle Fox and she was admitted to ICU yesterday.'

'Let's see.' I heard the shuffling of paperwork. 'Michelle Fox. Here we go.' The line went quiet.

'Hello?'

'Hi, yes. What's your name, please?'

'Esme Fox, I'm her sister. The police came to my house this morning and gave me this number. Can I come over and see her? What time are your visiting hours?' I felt slightly breathless.

'You can come and see her whenever you like.'

Was it my imagination or had her voice softened? Seemed I could've gone over there after all.

'Is she… OK?' I managed as my chest burned.

'Your sister is on a ventilator and currently unconscious. She's stable at the moment, but obviously we're monitoring her hour to hour. Hopefully we'll have an update later in the day.'

'Thanks, I'll be there as soon as I can,' I said, grappling with the new horror that Michelle was unconscious. I ended the call and sat staring into space for a moment or two.

The kitchen door opened softly and Owen slipped in. 'Everything OK?'

'I wouldn't say OK exactly, but I've spoken to ICU and she's stable. I'm going to get ready and go in. They said I can visit any time.'

Owen nodded. 'Zach's happy watching TV for now. He's complained about tummy-ache again; I might have a job getting him to school after all if he's still like this in the morning.'

I sighed. 'We'll see what tomorrow brings, but it's just not worth upsetting him. A day or two at home won't do him any harm. He's obviously worried about Michelle and we have to cut him a bit of slack.'

'Agreed.'

'Tomorrow morning I have the visit at HMP Bronzefield, as you know, and then I'd like to pop into the hospital again.'

'Can't you postpone your prison visits?' He said shortly.

'I can't, Owen. I've managed to get the first three episodes in the bag but after they're used up, we've nothing to air. We booked the remaining few interviews in quick succession… it's not negotiable, I have to do them.'

He said nothing. He didn't need to. The disapproval was written all over his face.

'I'm hoping I'll be back home around mid-afternoon tomorrow, so if you've got stuff to do I can try and—'

'No, no. Nothing I'm doing is more important than looking after Zachary.' I received the subtext loud and clear but Owen continued. 'And looking after you too, actually. You look exhausted if you don't mind me saying so.'

'Yeah, well, Zachary was restless all night… me too, if truth be told.'

'Go to the hospital now, if you like.' He touched my arm lightly. 'You need to see Michelle, you must be out of your mind with worry, but I'm always here. You know that.'

'Thanks,' I said, feeling a prickle at the back of my eyes at the unexpected show of kindness. 'I really appreciate it.'

'Tell you what, I'll cook us up something nice for tea when you get back.' His face brightened. 'You'll need a decent meal after your busy day.'

'Honestly, it's fine, Owen. I can sort something out for mine and Zach's tea. I don't want you to feel—'

'I'd like nothing more than the three of us eating together like we used to do. Say no more about it.'

Something rankled in my chest and I suddenly remembered Simone Fischer talking about her husband.

… if I complained or accused him of anything, it just made me look ungrateful.

Owen wanted nothing more than to move back home but he made it sound as if he was putting my welfare first by making tea because I'd be tired later. I'd just sound ungrateful if I told him not to bother. I let it go.

But it was an interesting observation. One that had never occurred to me before.

'I'll shower and get dressed for the hospital now,' I said. 'Sooner I get there, sooner I can get back.'

'Course,' he said, his voice upbeat. 'Whatever you say. You're the boss.'

But was I, really? Sometimes it felt like Owen called the shots even though we weren't together any more.

CHAPTER TWENTY-SIX

Driving on to the huge QMC campus, I managed to find a parking space near west block and bought a ticket covering me for a couple of hours. As I walked to the hospital entrance, I wondered how people who visited a loved one every day for a period of time managed to meet the extortionate parking costs.

The lift doors opened, bringing me back to the moment and I propelled myself forward, clutching a bunch of flowers I'd picked up from the hospital shop in the foyer. I pressed the C Floor for the Intensive Care wards and, soon as I stepped out, I spotted the large ICU sign. I followed the arrow pointing ahead and then turned left at the end. A man and a woman were in front of me and I could hear footsteps behind me. But as I neared the signposted ICU double doors ahead, the couple turned off and the footsteps behind me faded away. I stood alone in front of the entrance, my heart galloping in my chest.

How had we got to this? From everyday normal life to me visiting Michelle in ICU?

I pressed the buzzer and announced my name. My voice rang out in the echoing emptiness of the corridor. 'I'm here to see my sister, Michelle Fox.'

'Come through,' a female voice said, and I heard the double doors click.

Once inside, I walked down a short holding corridor. A fluttering feeling began to spread quickly in my chest. The floor and walls were white and the overhead lights stark and bright. My small heels clicked on the tiled floor and I breathed in a strong smell of disinfectant. I reached another set of inner doors. A short nurse with a large round face and cropped black hair appeared from a side office.

'I'll take you through to Michelle,' she said and looked regretful. 'Sorry, you'll have to leave the flowers here, they're not allowed in Intensive Care. You can take them back home with you when you leave.'

I placed the flowers on a small leaflet table behind me. She held up a lanyard to scan over the inner door's security pad.

'How is she?' I said.

The nurse hesitated and looked at me. 'How much did they tell you about her injuries?'

'I know she's been attacked, badly beaten,' I said, trying really hard to keep my voice level. 'They found her dumped in woodland apparently.'

I thought she'd wince but there was no reaction. She simply nodded and pushed open the doors when the security pad beeped.

We walked through into the main ward and I immediately felt unnerved. I'd never been in ICU before but I imagined a hushed, dim space with pulled curtains and patient privacy. But here we were in a noisy, large open space with harsh fluorescent lighting everywhere.

The patients lay beneath a tangle of plastic tubes and breathing apparatus. These people didn't just look ill, slumped on their pillows. They were completely unrecognisable, most lying in some awful liminal state between life and death.

The smell of antiseptic remained strong and as we walked further into the room, the noise level seemed to increase, filling my ears and my head.

I looked at the nurse, feeling a rising panic.

'Are you OK?' She lay a hand on my arm. 'It can be a shock, coming into ICU for the first time. Did you want to take a moment before you see your sister?'

'No!' I say, too quickly. 'No. I'm fine. I'd like to go straight to her, please.'

We walk another few steps before she slows down. Stops.

'Here we are. As I said, she isn't conscious at the moment because of the ventilator. But you can still talk to her if you like.'

The nurse stood back as I walked tentatively towards my sister's bed.

*

I stared down at this person she'd told me was Michelle and I felt completely hollow inside.

Her features were barely visible due to a Perspex mask and various ridged tubes that spiralled around her face and throat like vipers. But the worst thing was the noise: a rasping, pneumatic sound that invaded her body by force and sent chills cascading down my spine.

Her usually smooth, even skin looked mottled, and from the glimpses I could see, her face was almost double its usual size, blistered and patched with blue and red. If the nurse hadn't pointed her out, I'd have just walked past the bed.

'What happened to you, Michelle?' I whispered, my voice thick and catching in my throat. 'What did he do to you?'

I stood for a few more moments, wondering how long my legs would keep me standing and then remembered the nurse behind me. I turned to her and she lay a hand on my arm. I wanted to pull away from her touch, my skin felt so stripped and raw.

'Your sister has sustained a serious head injury and also internal injuries, Esme. One of her lungs has collapsed and that's why she's been put on a ventilator.'

'What happened to her?'

The nurse glanced back down the ward. 'Here's Dr Collins now, he might be able to help you.'

A diminutive man with salt-and-pepper hair and an open coat strode towards us flanked by two much younger doctors.

He held out his hand. 'Dr Collins. You're the patient's sister, I understand?'

I nodded, my voice failing me. It all seemed so surreal.

He consulted his notes. 'We'll be closely monitoring her for the next forty-eight hours and if she improves, we can consider taking her off the ventilator.'

'She'll come out of ICU?' I said hopefully, although even I could see it would likely be some time before Michelle came home.

'Too early to say, I'm afraid,' Dr Collins said. 'Her injuries are severe. Depending on whether the body can recover from the trauma, we may have to look at other solutions in order to give her the best chance of survival.'

I steadied myself against the bed frame. 'She might… die?'

He pressed his lips together. 'As you can see, she's in a bad way. The next forty-eight hours are crucial.'

The junior doctors watched me with a detached curiosity. I could imagine them writing up their reports later, under the heading: *Communicating effectively with relatives of ICU patients.*

I felt the nurse's hand on my arm again. 'Someone will be monitoring your sister all the time in here. You can rest assured she's in the best place possible.'

'It's such a shock to see her so… broken,' I said, trying to keep my voice level despite a rising tide of emotion. 'She was so vibrant, always had so much energy.'

'She suffered a very violent attack,' the doctor stated.

'You said she had internal injuries… they were caused by another person? By a beating?'

'We were given few details by the police when she was brought in and they're the people to talk to, really. But our initial thoughts are that her injuries have been caused during a physical attack, yes.

She has three broken ribs, a collapsed lung, extensive bruising to her sternum and evidence of broken and fractured bones caused by blunt trauma.'

Someone really did a job on my sister. Someone with a lot of hatred in his heart.

The police told me to ask the doctors and the medics referred me back to the police. But I didn't think they were hiding anything from me. They just hadn't a clue what really happened to Michelle and they genuinely didn't know if she was going to survive.

CHAPTER TWENTY-SEVEN

Zachary was restless during the early hours again, tossing and turning, calling out unfathomable words and phrases. Unsurprisingly, we both had a night of broken sleep.

I watched the digital hours tick past on my bedside clock radio. My body felt like a lead weight as I stared up at the ceiling. I listened to the soothing rhythm of Zachary's faint but regular breathing, a world away from the sound of my sister's artificial gasping and expelling of air.

When I left the hospital yesterday, I knew I couldn't go directly home without trying to process some of what I'd seen and learned at my Michelle's bedside. I made the twenty-minute drive to Holme Pierrepont Country Park. I walked twice around the large Regatta Lake, relishing the feel of the biting wind on my face and hands.

I felt numb. Helpless. How could I possibly help Michelle now? I'd always been a fixer at heart. If someone I cared about had a problem, then I'd automatically take it on as my own, try and solve it for them or at least offer up some workable solutions. But in this instance, I felt completely powerless. There was literally nothing I could do, and I felt utterly impotent.

I slowed down as a gaggle of geese waddled across the footpath just a few yards away from me, completely unconcerned by my presence or my despair. Michelle loved it here, loved the wildlife. She used to run around this very lake when she was younger but when she started getting knee problems, she ditched the running and adopted the gym instead. Now I wondered if she'd ever be well enough to move again.

I glanced over at the digital clock. Six fifteen, and Zachary was resting peacefully at last, his warm little hand curled around mine. I lay quietly and enjoyed observing him without his usual objections of *Mu-um*, without him dodging my embrace or taking himself off to watch TV or play a computer game. He was growing up so fast that to watch him breathing next to me, to take in his perfect features, his fluttering eyelashes, his smooth skin... it was a rare treat to do so these days.

My heart clutched when I thought of the physical suffering he'd endured in the last couple of years through no fault of his own, and an overpowering sense of wanting to protect him from the horror of Michelle's attack flooded through me.

When I'd eventually got home from the hospital yesterday, I'd talked to Owen in the kitchen and told him everything.

'My God, I can't believe it,' he'd said, his face paling. 'It sounds like whoever attacked her wanted her dead.'

I'd winced at his blunt manner and glanced at the door, nervous of Zachary suddenly appearing and hearing more than he should. 'Owen, please don't say things like that.'

'Sorry. That was insensitive of me,' he'd said. 'Do they think... will she recover soon?'

'They just don't know at this stage. It's touch-and-go but if she can get off the ventilator in the next forty-eight hours, then that's a big milestone. But even if that happens, I think it could be weeks, if not months, before she's well enough to come home.'

'And she's still unconscious?' he'd said, perplexed. 'There's no way she can identify anyone or give the police any information on who might've done this to her?'

'Sadly not. For now, anyway.'

'Jeez.' Owen blew out air. 'I think our priority has got to be getting some normality back for Zachary throughout the upheaval. Agreed?'

'Definitely,' I'd said and I saw his shoulders drop an inch. 'Within reason, though, Owen. It would be unfair to let Zach think we're back together and everything's rosy again.'

'I'll be sleeping in the spare room, if that's what you're worried about,' he'd said, a little sharply. 'I thought you'd be glad of the extra support to be honest.'

'I am. Of course I am, it's just—'

'You've got to admit that me staying here solves a lot of childcare problems for you. Unless you're planning on closing down the business anytime soon.'

'I'm not! I can't do that.'

'Well then, I suggest I move back in temporarily. I'll finish the tenancy on the flat, there's no sense in paying rent when I won't use the place. I can start bringing my stuff back over tomorrow afternoon when you get back.'

'Hang on, I need to think about this.' My head was banging. Everything was moving way too fast. Big decisions being made on the hoof.

'You worry too much,' Owen had said dismissively, heading for the kitchen door. 'You can't manage Zachary on your own, you've admitted that. As his father, I need to be here as a stable influence if nothing else. You're pulling yourself in far too many different directions and you can't possibly care for Zach in the way he needs. Now, why don't I pour you a gin and you can go up and have a nice bath?'

I'd opened my mouth to counter some of the things he'd stated but Owen was already in the hallway, humming a merry little tune to himself. I'd felt so tired, so washed out, I just let him go. Now, I felt renewed irritation that Owen had plans to install himself in the house again. Just like Michelle had said he was after doing.

I left Zachary sleeping and soundlessly slid out of bed.

I wrapped my dressing gown around me and padded past the spare room, where I caught Owen's faint snores, and downstairs to the kitchen where I made myself some tea.

An hour and a half later I kiss Zachary, leaving the problem of getting him to school for Owen to sort out.

I entered the postcode for Bronzefield Prison into Google maps and with the image of Michelle covered in breathing apparatus seared into my mind's eye, I set off to record the next episode of *The Fischer Files*.

It was going to be a long day.

CHAPTER TWENTY-EIGHT

JUSTINE

It was early. Just before seven. Just as she'd anticipated, the office car park was reassuringly empty, and that suited her requirements perfectly.

She let herself into the building using her key fob – they all had 24/7 access to the office as sometimes it was necessary to work odd hours to meet publishing deadlines – and pressed the lift button.

There was a list of things she was here to do which she hoped she'd be able to complete without anyone else popping in and forcing her to pretend to work on something else.

She'd received a generic office email from Mo last night, telling everyone the police had contacted Esme yesterday morning. Michelle had been attacked and found in the woods. She was currently in hospital but Mo hadn't mentioned the extent of her injuries.

Justine had called him back right away but he hadn't answered. She'd wanted to gauge his reaction, his thoughts as to what might have happened, but it would have to wait now.

She stepped out on the second floor and the Speaking Fox door faced her. There was a large sign on it with the company name and a crass cartoon drawing of a female fox dressed as a human in a tweed suit, taking notes. Justine had suggested getting the company name designed professionally: a smart icon that could be used across emails, letters, the website and social media.

But of course, Michelle had known better and had come up with this 'friendly and accessible' graphic that she and Esme believed would appeal to listeners and business contacts across the board.

Justine locked the door behind her, flicking the Yale switch so it couldn't be opened from the outside.

She headed over to Mo's desktop computer. She knew his password, had watched him type it in on several occasions. She sat down in his chair and turned on the monitor and then she saw it. Sitting on the desk right in front of her was a bonus she'd never expected to find today.

A Post-it note stuck on the screen, Mo's scrawl marking it clearly as 'Michelle's laptop'. Even better, it looked as if the access software he'd obviously been running overnight had bypassed the security blocks and the machine was wide open for browsing.

What a stroke of luck.

CHAPTER TWENTY-NINE

THE FISCHER FILES

EPISODE FOUR: DO YOUR BEST

You're listening to Episode Four of *The Fischer Files*. I'm speaking to you from outside HMP Bronzefield women's prison. Today I'm going to be speaking to Simone Fischer and you're going to hear, in Simone's own words for the first time, what she remembers about the day she killed her husband.

For the first time in the ten years she has been imprisoned, Simone is telling the story only she knows.

This is a Speaking Fox podcast and *I…* am Esme Fox.

*

So, I've just locked the car and I'm walking up to the prison and reflecting a little. I've done this a few times now and I actually feel like I'm getting to know Simone quite well. I've covered a lot of stories over my journalistic career. Believe me, I've had a varied taste of the terrible things some people can do to others, some very close to home.

The time has come for me to talk to Simone about the day she finally snapped and killed her husband. Sure, we've talked around it plenty, but the subject of exactly how he died has felt like the elephant in the room to me since the first time I met her.

*

Good news, I'm through security and on my way to see Simone in our interview room, escorted by Officer Donna. Donna doesn't say much… but she's smiling at me now, that's a good sign! Here we are outside the room. Donna's gone in to check everything's OK for my visit. Simone is giving me a little wave.

She's got a dress on today, hair down and looking fresh. I'd like to think it's a sign she's feeling positive about today. It can't be easy for her, reliving the horror of what happened.

*

Esme: We've got a really good sense now of what it was like to be married to Grant. But November 13th, 2009… there must have been something different about that day?

Simone: Not to start with. At first, it was the same as any other day apart from the fact I felt unwell. I woke up, slipped out of bed very carefully so as not to disturb Grant. If I woke him I knew it was certain to rapidly turn into a bad day, so I learned to be very good at being silent. Silent without even thinking about it.

See, the quality of my life hinged on lots of small decisions: making the bed correctly, cleaning the house up to standard, producing a decent meal when he got home from work. His reactions were at the centre of my world and I was completely absorbed in just getting through the day on that basis.

Esme: You'd fully accepted this was your life by now?

Simone: Pretty much. When I met Grant I was an independent working woman who managed my own life perfectly well. As the years rolled by, I never thought about how and why I'd come to accept so little in life. I never thought about my childhood, about seeing my own mum controlled by my father. I just tried to get through every day. Do my best, please my husband and everything would be OK. Annoy him and I'd only have myself to blame.

Esme: I hear you. Simone, can you take us through the day it happened… from the beginning?

Simone: As I said, it started off just an ordinary day apart from the fact I had an upset stomach. Before Grant went to work, as usual, he told me what he wanted for dinner. Salmon en croûte and not shop-bought. He wanted me to make my own puff pastry, everything from scratch, he said.

Andrew had a stomach-ache too, so I said he could stay home from school. He spent the morning in his bedroom and didn't come downstairs until lunchtime.

Esme: And Grant surprised you by arriving home early?

Simone: Yes… and I panicked. I'd spent all morning preparing the meal for later, making the pastry twice because it went wrong the first time, but I hadn't had time to put the dish together yet.

I'd had to keep dashing to the bathroom, feeling more and more unwell as the day went on. But none of that mattered. If Grant did something out of the blue and I wasn't prepared, then that was my fault. I was woefully unprepared to cook and serve his meal mid-afternoon rather than evening and he was predictably furious.

He trampled the pastry underfoot and tossed the fresh salmon fillets in the bin. He told me to walk to the supermarket to buy the ingredients again.

Esme: You'd already told him you were feeling unwell?

Simone: Yes, and he was amused. The supermarket was a mile away and I didn't think I'd make it. I asked if I could take the car and he refused. By this time I had the mother of all headaches and I nearly collapsed at the thought of all that walking and then having to make the pastry again. It's so fiddly, puff pastry. I just sat down at the kitchen table and put my head in my hands.

I heard him rustling about but I felt too ill to even look up and then something was pushed into my mouth. Raw pastry from the bin. I spat it out but he pushed in more, grabbed my hair and pulled my head back and filled my mouth with it. Ramming more and more in. I was retching, I couldn't breathe... I was terrified I'd choke and he'd just watch me die. Then I vomited all over the table. He sat down opposite me and laughed. I mean, he really laughed.

Esme: What did you do?

Simone: It's very hard to remember the detail, it feels like recalling a dream now – or a nightmare – trying to grasp the slipperiest of details. I remember his head, tilted right back, his teeth on show when he laughed so heartily. I saw the glint of metal on the side and I felt myself standing up and then... then I had a newly sharpened knife in my hand.

Esme: What recollection do you have of actually attacking your husband, Simone?

Simone: Sorry, I... my mind's gone blank...

Esme: Take your time, there's no rush. There's no pressure.

Simone: I remember…

Esme: Yes?

Simone: I remember seeing his blood… so much blood. All over my hands.

END OF EXTRACT

CHAPTER THIRTY

HMP BRONZEFIELD

ESME

I sat in the seating area in the foyer, relieved I was the only person there. I stared out of the window and unscrewed the cap on the small bottle of water I brought with me.

When I'd stood up to leave Simone after our interview, she'd reached across the table to touch my hand.

'I can tell something is troubling you, Esme,' she said gently. 'Are you OK?'

The words spilled from my mouth before I could choke them back.

'It's my sister. She's been attacked.' The relief in sharing the burden of Michelle's hospitalisation with someone else made my body slump slightly. I'd sat back down again. 'She's… she's in intensive care.'

Donna, the prison officer, who was under strict instructions to monitor my visits and keep me to the agreed thirty minutes, stepped outside the door and looked the other way.

'They don't know what happened yet,' I explained. 'Michelle is unconscious, on a ventilator. I'm out of my mind with worry. You should see the state of her, what he did…' My voice faltered as Simone pushed her chair back, the legs scraping on the hard floor. She stood up and walked around the table to me, laying a hand on my arm. I felt the warmth of her fingers pressing gently into my flesh, the faint scent of vanilla as she moved a little closer.

She said, 'Who attacked her? When you say "he," who is it that attacked her? Do you know what happened?'

When she stepped back to look at me, her expression was strangely vacant. It seemed as if she was only half-focused on me, that her mind was elsewhere.

I shook my head. 'The police know nothing at the moment and of course, Michelle can't tell us anything.'

'Come and see me again soon,' she whispered, squeezing my forearm. 'I'll tell Janice to schedule in a few more visits... if you'd like, that is. I don't want to add to your burden.'

I felt a light relief roll over me.

'I would, like that, I mean.' I nodded. 'If you're sure...'

'I am sure. Certain, in fact.' She pressed her face so close to mine her cheek grazed mine. In contrast to her hand, her face felt cool and smooth like marble. 'Janice will be in touch.'

Kat opened the door and I stepped away from Simone.

'Thank you,' I whispered, and headed for the door.

CHAPTER THIRTY-ONE

The hundred-and-thirty-mile journey home went quite smoothly. No accidents or roadworks to contend with for once, and I was back in Nottingham two and a half hours after leaving the prison.

I'd already called the hospital for an update on Michelle on my way down to the prison.

'She's had a comfortable night in that she's remained stable,' was all the nurse who answered the phone could tell me. I didn't expect any great leaps of progress but it was still hard to hear there was basically no change in her condition.

The thought of days, weeks, months passing, waiting for a crumb of improvement in Michelle's condition… I couldn't bear to even think about it. Or about how I was going to explain it all to Zachary.

I had to make a real effort to push away my dark thoughts. They were serving no one.

When I'd left the prison, I listened to the recording of my conversation with Simone on the car's Bluetooth speaker during the journey back – partly to try and force myself to think about something else other than Michelle lying in hospital all alone.

The initial recording was the very first stage of the podcast process. Human speech patterns naturally dragged and lingered, and needed a little nip and tuck to keep the content moving. Simone's interview was filled with the umms and ahhs of normal conversation, short interruptions, the few times we veered off the subject of Simone's life with Grant.

I was confident Mo would work his magic. After consulting with me about what we should keep and what we might discard, he would cut and shape the session into something that was smooth, interesting and invisibly spliced. Finally he'd enhance the diction and sound quality so it was more pleasing to the listeners' ears.

Usually after listening through the recording again, I'd put some music on or perhaps play my current audio book for the remainder of the journey. But this time, I just couldn't seem get the stuff Simone had talked about out of my head. Grant's treatment of her was so disturbing, such needless cruelty.

What did people like him get out of controlling another person so callously, keeping them suspended in a constant state of fear and anticipation of punishment?

Later, my first task would be to email the latest audio file to Mo. Secondly, I'd email the FSF group the final file for Simone to review, and, if she was unhappy with any of the material we were using, then we'd obey her wishes and cut it. I felt it was important to stick to my initial promise to do so.

Peter, Simone's brother, had been on my mind during the journey back, too. Did he really want the best for Simone… was he trying to protect her? Or did he want to control exactly who spoke to her so he was the one with all the power? I'd had the chance to talk to him when he waited for me near the prison car park but we'd got off on the wrong foot.

There weren't many people who could corroborate or deny Simone's story about her marriage but he was certainly one of them.

I resolved I'd try and make contact with him on my terms. Hopefully, if I could talk to him for a short time I'd get the measure of him and his intentions. I called Janice from the FSF group. I hadn't heard from her by phone since leaving my business card with contact details. She didn't answer but I left a message asking her for Peter's number.

*

On the way back home, I called Mo at the office and brought him up to speed with my visit to the prison.

'I've emailed you the audio file over. I'm heading for the hospital again now to see Michelle.' My voice shook and I swallowed hard.

'Listen, Esme, do you want me to come over? I can go with you, I—'

'No, no. Honestly, Mo, the best thing you can do to help is to keep things going at the office. The priority for you and Justine is to get each episode of *The Fischer Files* out. There's nothing you can do at the hospital while she's unconscious. We won't know anything for another day or two, I'm sure.'

He made a small noise of frustration and I knew then that he felt as helpless as I did.

'Listen, Mo, there was one thing...'

'Anything, you only have to say.' His voice sounded hopeful.

'Michelle's laptop. Did you manage to get in?' I thought maybe I could find some clues on there as to who the man outside the school was and Mo had said he'd have the job done by lunchtime.

But Mo's voice sounded frustrated. 'I got in but there was nothing on there, Esme.'

'I'd still like to look through her files myself.'

'No, I mean there was literally nothing on there,' Mo said. 'For some reason Michelle had wiped it completely clean, taken it right back to factory settings. It's perplexing that she didn't keep any of her files on there.'

'What? Why would she do that?' I bit down hard on my back teeth. Michelle did everything for work on there, as well as having her personal email and electronic diary stored on it. It didn't make sense. 'Surely there's a backup in the cloud or something?'

'Turned off,' Mo said. 'She'd turned all the backup facilities and even the automatic save function off. I've no idea why she'd do that.'

I suddenly remembered Michelle saying she'd handwritten the notes for the TrueLife meeting. Wouldn't it have made more sense for her to have them on the computer?

Someone spoke again in the background.

'Justine's asking if we can visit Michelle in hospital,' Mo said.

'No. Not while she's in Intensive Care, Mo. She's unconscious, but tell her I'll pop in the office tomorrow and speak to you both myself, OK?'

'Sure, take care, Esme. Remember; anything you need, you only have to say the word.'

'I will. Thanks.'

On the outskirts of Nottingham, I pulled over into a lay-by, lowered the window a notch and rested my forehead on the top of the steering wheel. After a few seconds, the feeling of nausea passed a little and I carried on to the hospital.

*

The same nurse I saw yesterday took me through to Michelle. She greeted me warmly then tipped her head to study my expression.

'I know it's hard when you're waiting for progress but you should count the fact she's had a stable night as a positive. Stability is what we look for at this crucial early stage.'

'Thanks,' I said, forcing a small smile. 'I just want to speak to her. She can tell us exactly what happened and then whichever monster did this can be brought to justice.'

The security pad beeped and we walked into the ICU ward.

'Can I give you a piece of advice?'

'Yes… please do,' I said, looking at her.

'Keep an open mind about Michelle's progress. When she is conscious again, she might not remember anything. Or she might have difficulty articulating things.'

I stopped walking and looked at her. 'Are you saying she might not be able to speak?'

'I'm not saying that because I don't know but anything is a possibility right now.' We started moving again. 'Just try to keep your expectations in check and protect yourself a little, that's all.'

I thanked her and she left me at Michelle's bedside. She didn't wait like before, instead she attended to another patient on the opposite side of the ward.

I sat down next to my sister and held her hand. The ventilator pulled air in, then forced it out… in, out, in, out… with horrible regularity. And Michelle just lay there, motionless, swollen and bruised.

'I love you,' I said, choking back tears. 'Zachary sends his love. We want you back home. We miss you. Please fight, Michelle. Fight to come back to us.'

I squeezed her hand and stood up. Then I walked away before I broke down completely.

CHAPTER THIRTY-TWO

On the short journey home from the hospital, I opened the window fully and let the wind blow away the smell of the place from my skin together with the dread that had settled on my face.

When I pulled on to the drive, I breathed a sigh of relief. Finally, I could decompress.

But as soon as I opened the front door, the noise hit me.

Owen was yelling, not in an angry way but in an attempt to make himself heard above Zachary's wailing. I rushed through to the kitchen, my heart in my mouth. It didn't seem that long ago that Zachary had one of these meltdowns most days.

I stood in the doorway and, for a few moments, they were both unaware of my presence. Zachary was still wailing and had cunningly wedged himself under the kitchen table, right into the corner where Owen couldn't reach him. Empty pans and cutlery were strewn across the kitchen floor, the detritus of Zach's earlier fury. He'd kept hold of a plastic reusable Costa cup and was currently hammering it on the underside of the kitchen table in time with his strident yelling.

'Zachary, for God's sake, stop this!' Owen shouted. 'It's not helping you and it sure as hell isn't helping me.'

'Hello?' I called out.

Owen turned to me, raking his hands through his hair. 'Thank goodness you're back.'

Zachary scooted out from under the table, dropped the plastic cup and rushed across the room, hurling himself at me.

'Mum!' He grabbed me around the middle and looked past me out into the hall. 'Is Aunt Miche with you?'

'Hey, what's all the drama about?' I said softly. 'Aunt Miche isn't home yet, but I've seen her in the hospital.'

'What did she say?' He looked up at me, his face red and swollen, his eyes bloodshot but hopeful. 'Did she have an accident?'

'She was still sleeping when I got there.' I looked at Owen, who I could see was trying to read me. 'She's had an accident but we're not sure exactly what happened yet. We're just waiting for her to wake up and tell us, Zachary.'

'Do they think that might be soon?' Owen said, biting his lip. 'She was asleep last time you went, too.'

'Reading between the lines, no,' I said quietly. 'It might be a while until she wakes up.'

'What a nightmare,' Owen shook his head.

'Maybe I should have stopped her getting in that car,' Zachary said in a small voice, before tightening his arms around me and burying his head into my stomach.

'It wasn't your job to do that, sweetie.' I squeezed him and kissed the top of his head. 'Aunt Miche is a grown-up and she did what she did.'

I raised an eyebrow at Owen.

'Zachary's been a bit upset,' Owen said, his words loaded with innuendo. 'He wanted to go with you to the hospital and see if Aunt Michelle is OK.'

'Remember all our chats about this, Zachary?' I hugged him closer to me. 'We decided there are so many better ways of talking about stuff, telling us when you're upset. Acting up like this just makes you feel ten times worse. You know that, right?'

No response. I was trying to gently encourage him to move away from me slightly, but his head remained buried in my stomach and his grip felt pincer-like around my middle.

'Come on, champ. Give Mum a break, eh?' Owen moved towards us as if to prise Zachary off me and I shook my head. A few more minutes stood immobile like this wouldn't kill me, especially if it helped calm Zachary.

After the accident, he used to get like this all the time on school mornings. After loving school in the years before the hit and run, he'd start to get dressed and then suddenly stop, sit on his bed and announce calmly, 'I've decided I don't want to go to school now.' If we tried to press him, he'd throw himself on the floor and scream the place down. His injured leg would often get bashed about – he seemed oblivious to this in the throes of his meltdown, but he'd pay for it later when it throbbed even through the prescription painkillers.

The stropping, as Owen labelled it, became his preferred method of protest in many places: at the supermarket if he got told 'no' to stuff he wanted to put in the trolley, at the park when it was time to come home. Although to all intents and purposes he looked like a regular spoiled brat to passers-by, the doctors explained that the head injury he'd sustained in the accident had affected his reasoning. The way he now coped and behaved was no longer in a socially acceptable manner, but there was little anyone could do about it. Least of all us.

During the months immediately following the accident – the toughest time – I learned just how inflexible and judgemental some strangers could be, and how others could show kindness and understanding.

Seeing him like this again chilled me to the bone. The thought that Zachary's old behaviour might have returned, brought on by the worry of his missing aunt, made my chest ache.

I looked at Owen and he gave me a discreet nod and mouthed, 'He's fine,' over Zach's head. Typical! Glossing over the facts because he didn't want to think about it. Owen was totally out of control when I'd first got back. Shouting over Zachary was never going to calm him down and he should know better by now. He'd seemed so stressed himself when he didn't know I was watching from the doorway.

'Can I go and see Aunt Miche in the hospital later, Mum? We can take a chocolate orange, her favourite.'

I took Zachary's hand and led him into the living room. We sat on the sofa together and Owen followed us and perched on the arm of the chair.

'I'm going to level with you, Zachary, because I think you're old enough and you have a right to know. Aunt Miche is really poorly at the moment and she's sleeping lots.'

His expression didn't change. 'Why is she sleeping lots? What's wrong with her?'

'Well, she's been hurt quite badly but she can't tell anyone how it happened at the moment. The doctors are helping her breathe and to do that properly, they've had to put her to sleep for a while.'

'Why? Why can't she breathe?' Zachary's eyebrows drew together.

'Because she's hurt herself somehow. They found her in a wood and she was in a pretty bad way.' I squeezed his hand, hoping I hadn't overstepped the mark and gone too far. The last thing I wanted was to risk an influx of traumatic memories for him. 'I know it's very upsetting but I think you're sensible enough to know the truth about what's happened.'

'I bet she tripped over a tree trunk,' Zachary remarked. 'Jack Hart at school fell over one in a wood and broke his arm.'

I nodded. 'Well, we should know more in a few days. I think it's a bit more than a broken arm with Aunt Miche but the doctors are watching her very carefully and she's in the best possible place.'

Seeing him struggle to make sense of it all pulled on my heartstrings. Andrew Fischer hadn't been that much older when his father was killed. It must have been so terrifying and confusing for a young boy. His whole life changing beyond recognition in an instant as it did.

Owen came over and ruffled Zachary's hair. 'Sounds like the hospital are doing their very best to get Aunt Miche back home soon, right, buddy?'

Zachary nodded. 'That man I saw with her outside school… he didn't hurt her, did he, Dad?'

There was a sudden, loud knock at the door.

'Who's that?' Zachary looked alarmed.

'I'll go,' Owen said, shooting me a look. He closed the living room door behind him.

Zachary ran over to the window, craning to see. 'It's those detectives again, Mum. The same two that came to talk to you yesterday.'

CHAPTER THIRTY-THREE

I held my breath and my chest tightened with every second that passed.

I heard Owen speak out confidently in the hall. 'Sure, no problem,' he said. 'Come through.'

I walked out into the hallway, Zachary pinned to my side.

'Hello again, Ms Fox,' DI Sharpe said. 'It's just your husband – ex-husband – we need a word with for now.'

My instinct was to ask them to come back later. After all, we'd only just got Zachary calmed down again. It was interesting that they'd guessed Owen might be here – I supposed his violet Smart car parked outside gave the game away.

'They're just here to ask me a few questions, Esme.' Owen swallowed, glancing at our son.

'I see.' I took Zachary's hand. 'Come on, let's go upstairs a little while.' My head felt so full of awful possibilities, it was fit to burst.

'No, I don't want to go!' Zachary stood rigid, his nostrils flaring. The detectives glanced at each other.

'Zachary, we need to give Dad some space to talk to the detectives, OK? It won't be for long,' I said gently.

'I want to hear what they're saying,' he cried out as I half guided, half pushed him gently toward the bottom of the stairs. If he threw himself on the floor I knew I'd never get him up there. The detectives looked slightly alarmed but Owen quickly led them into the living room. From behind the closed door, I strained to hear him explaining about Zachary's accident and the effect it often had on his mood and behaviour.

Upstairs in his bedroom, Zachary stalked from the window and back again to his bed half a dozen times, his breathing erratic.

'Come on, sweetie, sit down and we can watch something together.' I kept my voice as calm as I could but inside, I felt like screaming.

'It's not fair,' he raged, his voice growing louder. 'Nobody ever tells kids anything!'

He had a point but what choice did we have? What was happening was way beyond what a boy of nine years old could handle.

'It's best we give Dad a little privacy to talk to the detectives, that's all. Come and sit here next to me.' I patted the bed.

Suddenly, Zachary stopped striding and cocked his head to one side, listening. Then I heard it, too. Owen was raising his voice. 'Why do I have to come down to the station? Surely you don't think *I've* got anything to do with it!'

Zachary turned to face me, horror-struck.

'They don't think *Dad* hurt Aunt Michelle in the woods, do they? Mum?'

'Wait in here, Zachary.'

'Where are you going?' He watched me walk to the door.

'I'm just going to check everything's OK down there. Stay here with the door closed, I'll be back in a minute.'

Zachary growled in frustration but when I looked back he'd sat down on the bed, his eyes wide and troubled.

Downstairs, the two detectives stood facing Owen. His eyes darted around the living room, his fingers chafing on his jeans.

'Is everything alright down here?'

'Everything's fine,' Sharpe told me smoothly. 'We were just asking Mr Painter about one or two things.'

'They want me to go to the station with them, Esme.' Owen's voice sounded thin and peculiar.

'It's a request, not an order at this stage, sir,' Lewis said calmly. 'Just to answer a few questions.'

'Can't you speak to Owen here?' I said. Surely the questions were only routine?

'We could, but some people prefer to go to the station than to go through the process at home.' Lewis looked at Owen. 'Sometimes the family home isn't the best place to do it, especially when there's a child around.'

Owen was petulant. 'I'll go then,' he said. 'It's no big deal, right?'

The detectives didn't answer but both moved swiftly towards the door.

'Let me know if you need me to pick you up afterwards,' I told Owen, following them into the hallway.

'We can arrange a lift back for him, Ms Fox,' Lewis offered. 'No need to inconvenience you and your son.'

Owen looked tetchy. I lay my hand on his arm, our previous tensions forgotten.

'Call me when you're finished. It'll only be routine questioning, I'm sure.' I looked to the detectives for confirmation.

'Shouldn't take too long, hopefully.' Lewis said, non-committal. They all trooped outside.

While Lewis led Owen towards the unmarked police car, Sharpe doubled back suddenly.

'One thing before we go, Ms Fox. May I step inside again for a moment?'

I stepped back into the hallway to let him in. He glanced up the stairs as if he was mindful of Zachary and then indicated we should move to the living room.

'What is it?' I said tersely.

'Can you tell me anything about your ex-husband's whereabouts the day your sister went missing?'

I thought for a moment. 'I suppose the first sign I had she was missing was when she didn't turn up for the work meeting. Owen actually called me at work a couple of hours later.'

'That was unusual?'

'Not *unusual* exactly, he often calls me about arrangements for Zachary. But Owen wasn't due to see him until the following day.'

'Can you tell me what you talked about during that call?'

'He was calling to see if Michelle was definitely picking Zachary up from school.'

'And that was because…'

I hitched my shoulders up. 'He didn't say but I told him Michelle had gone AWOL and wasn't answering her phone. He offered to pick Zach up and then drop by the house to see if Michelle had returned.'

'Did he say where he'd been, up until calling you that day?'

I shook my head. 'He doesn't have to be accountable to me for how he spends his time. We're separated.'

'So I understand. Just to confirm then, Owen picked Zachary up from school and where did he take him?'

'He brought him back here, to the house. I left work soon after Owen's phone call and I came home to see if there were any clues as to Michelle's whereabouts. I got back before Owen and Zachary did. I told you when we last spoke, I went to ask the staff at the supermarkets if they'd seen her and Owen stayed here with Zachary.'

'Yes, you did and that was very helpful, thank you.' He looked down at the floor and frowned. 'One more thing. Did you see anything of Owen yesterday?'

'Yes. When you'd left here, I was upset and I called him. I told him Michelle had been found and he offered to watch Zachary while I went to the hospital.'

'What was his reaction… when you told him what had happened?'

'He was shocked, as you might imagine! Why are you asking stuff like this? You'd be far better spending your time looking for the mystery man she was seen with outside school.'

'Of course, and we have that in hand. We have to cover all bases as early as possible in the investigation. It gives us the best chance of hitting the ground running in a case like this, where there are very few leads.'

'But you do have some? Leads, I mean?' A channel of heat ran through my chest.

'We have one or two lines of enquiry we're pursuing, yes. You'll be the first to know of any developments.'

I nodded, my hope thinning fast again.

At the front door, Sharpe turned to me. 'Would you say Owen and your sister have an amicable relationship?'

It was an odd question to ask.

'They get on OK, if that's what you mean.'

'Yes, that is what I mean. It's just that with Mr Painter moving out and your sister moving into the house, it seems reasonable to wonder if there was a little friction between them.'

I thought about Michelle's increasing irritation that Owen regularly overstayed his welcome and spent too much time here. The niggling little exchanges they often had, as if they were sniping at each other but managing to keep from me just how deep the resentment lay.

'There's no problem between them,' I said. 'They get along fine.'

CHAPTER THIRTY-FOUR

It took a tremendous effort to play events down with Zachary. When the detectives and Owen had driven away, I called him downstairs and – terrible mother that I am – suggested he played his computer game to relax.

An hour later, Zachary still wanted answers. 'Why has Dad had to go to the police station?'

My head was thumping and my legs felt as though they were about to give way. I sat down on the sofa and patted the seat next to me, but Zachary sat aloof in Owen's armchair instead.

'They just want to ask him a few questions,' I said carefully. 'They're talking to lots of people because they're trying to piece together what happened to Aunt Michelle, sweetie.'

He thought for a moment and frowned. 'But Dad sounded upset. Like he didn't want to go.'

'Well, I don't suppose anyone wants to go to a police station, do they? I expect he would have rather—'

'Dad said *surely you don't think I've got anything to do with it.* Do they think he's the one who's hurt Aunt Miche in the woods?'

'No! I don't think so, Zach. We know Dad wouldn't hurt anyone, but the detectives don't know us, do they? They don't know Dad, or me… they have to talk to everyone so they can tick them off their list.'

'But if Aunt Michelle tripped in the woods and hurt herself, how is that anyone's fault?'

I covered my face with my hands. I was trying, really trying, but I was starting to doubt I could do this all on my own. I felt like I might keel over. My mind's eye was still full of Michelle's swollen face, buried under a heap of medical equipment.

I felt a small arm slide around my shoulders.

'It'll be alright, Mum,' my son said warmly, resting his head on my arm. 'Dad will be home soon and then we can all watch a movie together.'

'What a great idea.' I pasted a smile on my face and hoped he wouldn't notice my brimming eyes. 'Tell you what, I'll make you a sandwich and a glass of milk and you find a good film for us all to watch later.'

Zachary seemed happy at last so I left him to it and went back into the kitchen. I closed the door and collapsed onto the sofa, just staring out of the glass doors and trying to make sense of what had happened.

After about fifteen minutes, my phone rang. I jumped up and snatched it from the breakfast bar.

'Ms Fox? This is Nottinghamshire Police. Owen Painter has asked us to let you know we'll be keeping him in overnight for further questioning tomorrow.'

'*Tomorrow?*' I cursed myself as I realised I'd screeched out and lowered my voice, praying Zachary hadn't heard. 'You're keeping him in for what sort of questions? This is ridiculous. You're wasting time while the real culprit is still out there.'

'Someone will be in touch.'

'But… it's been so quick! He's only been gone about an hour. What has he said that makes you think he knows something? Has he been arrested in connection with the attack on my sister?'

'I'm sorry, I'm not at liberty to discuss it further with you.'

And that was it, I couldn't get another thing out of her. My insides turned to liquid. This was really serious. They were keeping him in overnight and that spoke volumes about what they thought he could tell them. Whatever he'd said during the initial questioning must've led them to believe he was hiding something.

Had Owen even got a lawyer? I'd never thought to ask the officer who rang because he was innocent. I would bet my life on that. I couldn't deny things had moved on a step, though. This was clearly not just *a few questions* he was being subjected to.

At that moment, it occurred to me then that I should let Owen's parents know, but I couldn't stand the thought of dealing with Brooke, his overbearing mother, on top of everything else that was happening. Yet the alternative was to manage all this alone, as well as feeling sick with worry about Michelle and trying to protect Zachary from any fallout.

It was starting to feel an impossible mountain to climb.

The only thing I could do was to pray this all got resolved, and soon. That the police would completely exonerate Owen and focus their efforts on whoever was really to blame for attacking Michelle.

Like the mystery man Zachary saw her with at school.

CHAPTER THIRTY-FIVE

I don't know how, but the next morning I managed to get Zachary to school.

He looked so tired and pale and I felt rotten sending him, but I knew it was for the best. Routine stabilised him, stopped him overthinking and, although 'normal' was out of the question right now, I knew school would give a bit of structure to his day and enable me to focus on getting some kind of a plan together.

My efforts to be truthful with Zachary had fallen through yesterday following the phone call from Nottinghamshire Police informing me they were keeping Owen in for further questioning. I couldn't possibly tell him what was really happening to his dad, it would have been impossible for him to sleep a wink.

A few minutes after I'd put the phone down and sat staring hopelessly at the kitchen worktop, Zachary came in.

'Mum? I found a film I think Dad will like, too. It's about this soldier who's trying to find his brother and—'

'That's great, Zachary,' I'd said lightly. 'It'll just be you and me tonight though, Dad's tired and got a headache so he's gone back to the flat to rest.'

His face fell. 'Those stupid detectives have ruined everything! Can I ring Dad? He can rest here while he's watching the film.'

'Maybe tomorrow, sweetie. As I said, he's exhausted.'

Wordlessly, he'd gone back to the living room and I felt like a failure for lying to him, even though it had seemed the right thing to do to spare him the details.

He slept in my room again and although he cried out in his sleep a couple of times, he rested better than the previous night and his leg didn't keep him awake at all. More than could be said for me. In between staring at the clock and battling the terrible low I felt when I thought about Michelle, I combed through every conversation, every interaction between Owen and Michelle that I could recall. Was there something more between them that I'd missed… more than just the odd bit of sniping and bickering? Were the detectives right to interrogate Owen about the attack? At 3 a.m. it seemed a distinct possibility. At 7 a.m., it seemed a completely ridiculous notion he had anything to do with what happened.

'I don't want to go to school,' Zachary said when I suggested it was time to get ready this morning. 'I want to see Dad. And Aunt Miche.'

'I know you do. I don't want to go to work either, but then later we can do something nice. Just you and me.'

He scowled. 'What about Dad? He missed out on the movie last night so he needs to come over to make up for it.'

Last night, I'd sat through ninety minutes of a film I couldn't recall one line of dialogue from. I'd just zoned out and thought through a thousand terrible scenarios involving Owen, Michelle and the police.

'We can call Dad later,' I said. 'If he feels well enough I'm sure he'll come over.'

'When can I visit Aunt Miche in the hospital?'

'Soon, I promise.' I chivvied him into the bathroom, feeling like my head might blow off if he asked me one more thing. 'Wash your hands and face and let's get moving. Sooner we're out, sooner we get back home, yes?'

He ran the tap and stared down into the sink. When I left the room I heard him close the door softly behind me.

*

I silently offered up thanks when Zachary went to school without further debate. I waited with him in the playground and when Miss Carling, his class teacher, came to the classroom doors to greet the children, I took the opportunity to grab a quick word with her.

'Zachary might be a little delicate in class for the next few days. His auntie is in hospital.'

Her hand flew to her mouth. 'I heard a group of parents discussing something that had happened but I didn't know if it was just gossip. Has she been... I don't want to pry but—'

'She's been attacked, yes. She's in a really bad way.'

'How awful. I'm so sorry, Esme. Please do let me know if there's anything we can do here at school to help at all.' She grasped my hand. 'Don't worry, I'll keep a really close eye on Zachary. We'll look after him.'

'Thanks so much,' I managed to say, turning away before I turned into a snivelling wreck.

After the school run, I drove to the office and found Mo and Justine sat drinking coffee, discussing some paperwork. Both their mouths fell open when they saw me.

'Esme!' Justine jumped up and rushed over to me. 'How's Michelle? I could barely sleep for worrying about you both.'

Mo walked over. He looked drawn, his brow furrowing with concern. 'Listen, Esme, anything I can do... and I mean *anything*, you only have to say.'

Justine wrapped her arms around me and for a moment I froze, terrified I'd break down. I'd wanted to keep this out of the office, to try and separate my work and personal life. But their warmth and sympathy thawed me almost instantly and I felt so alone and confused... I was fighting a losing battle.

'Thanks,' I sniffed. 'She's... in a bad way, I'm afraid. Still on the ventilator and they don't really know what happened to her yet.'

Toby appeared. 'Hi, Esme, I... I hope you're OK,' he said awkwardly from the doorway, twisting his hands together before disappearing again before I could thank him.

'What actually *has* happened?' Justine placed her hands on my shoulders and held me slightly away so she could see my face. 'Mo said she's in hospital but how did she get there?'

My breathing felt ragged, my throat raw. 'We don't know much yet,' I managed to croak. I'd promised myself I wouldn't say too much.

'Esme, you're amongst friends here,' Mo said softly. He looked terrible, like he'd lost weight. 'Anything you say to us won't go any further, you know that. You look... exhausted. Are you bearing up? Is Owen staying at the house with you?'

The mention of Owen's name made me feel sick, like a weight bearing down on me.

'Listen, I have some good news. Episode two is whipping up a storm – early signs are it's going to do even better than the first one,' Justine beamed, squeezing my upper arms. 'I wanted to give you that brilliant news even though it feels inappropriate. Sorry.'

'No, that's... that's brilliant.' How on earth could I have forgotten about today's episode? Easily, that's how. But it was amazing news all the same.

'What about Zachary... is he coping with it all?' Justine pressed me.

It was too much. Everything. I just couldn't hold the emotion back any longer. I dissolved in Justine's arms.

'Michelle's unconscious. She doesn't even know I'm there.' I heard myself babbling and when Mo handed me a clean tissue, I covered my nose and mouth with it to shut myself up.

'But what on earth happened to her?' Mo asked. 'How did she get those sorts of injuries?'

I blew my nose. 'She was viciously attacked, but beyond that…they don't seem to know anything at the moment. Except…'

I didn't know how to say it. My chest tightened so quickly it took me by surprise and I sat back on the desk, gasping for air.

'I think she's having a panic attack,' Justine cried.

Mo pushed a brown paper bag near my face then Justine said, 'Breathe into that, Esme. Slowly, not too quickly. That's it. That's better.'

'Toby?' Mo called. 'Can you bring Esme a glass of water, please?'

'All this… it's so hard for you to deal with but you're not alone. We're here for you, Esme,' Justine said softly as she helped me lower into a chair. 'Keep breathing. In, out, nice and slow. That's it.'

'They don't know who attacked her. They don't know anything,' I managed. 'And it gets worse. The police took Owen in for questioning yesterday afternoon. He's still there.'

'They've got Owen?' Mo gasped in disbelief. 'They kept him overnight?'

'Shh. You can tell us later, Esme,' Justine soothed. 'Don't go upsetting yourself even more. It must be horrendous for you, and for young Zachary, too.'

'He doesn't know much yet.' I dabbed at my damp, hot face. 'I'm trying to protect him but he's not daft, he knows things aren't right and he was there when Owen left with them for the station.'

Toby brought the water through.

'Thanks, Toby,' I said, taking the glass from him. I expected him to turn around and leave again but he just stood there, staring at me.

'Thank you, Toby,' Justine said a little curtly. But still, he didn't move.

I took a sip of water and met his eyes. 'What's wrong, Toby?'

'Sorry. I was just – I hope everything's OK, Esme,' he said, finally coming to his senses. 'I… I can see you're upset.'

'I'll be OK. Thanks, Toby.'

He turned and scuttled off again.

'He can be a strange one at times.' Mo frowned, his eyes following Toby out.

I'd planned to just pop into the office for ten minutes to show my face, reassure everyone Michelle was OK and pick up some paperwork relating to the next episode of *The Fischer Files*. But I'd managed to mess that approach up.

I didn't want to even think about the next planned visit to HMP Bronzefield but I had to go. I had no choice unless I wanted to blow the whole project. There was no way Simone would agree to seeing anyone else and so many things were scheduled in order for the podcast to go out as planned that it would be impossible to claw it back if I failed to go there.

Simone offering me more frequent visits was both a godsend and a logistical nightmare. Travelling to the prison again, so soon after yesterday, had felt like an impossible task at first. But now I was back in the office my thinking calmed enough for me to realise the return journey was only five hours out of the whole day. I could call at the hospital on the way back to see Michelle. So long as I could get Zachary safely into school, it was totally doable.

Rather than going back home as I'd initially planned, I decided to stay in the office for a while. I felt safe and supported there and I didn't want to go back to an empty house. I set up in the same small meeting room the disastrous TrueLife meeting had taken place in.

Justine brought me a coffee.

'Have TrueLife been in touch at all?' I asked her.

'Nothing yet,' she said regretfully. 'I can arrange for Toby to get them on the phone if you want to—'

'No, no. I'm not surprised, I just wondered on the off-chance. The main thing is that we keep the podcast production on track.'

It was cool and private in the meeting room as I begin to work on the *Fischer Files* notes I'd written a few days ago, when

Michelle had only just gone missing. I'd still been hopeful she'd come home, head hanging after some crazy decision to ditch any plans and go off and have some fun. Blissfully unaware then of just how completely my world was about to explode. It was a constant battle, trying to concentrate. If I wasn't wondering how Michelle was doing, I was imagining Owen, stuck in the police station after a sleepless night, answering their inane questions. I was thinking about Zachary, desperate to see his father.

The ICU nurse had given me a leaflet detailing a simple guide to visiting. One of the things that varied from a regular ward was that they'd requested no phone calls from family members until 10 a.m. if possible. Obviously I hadn't known this when I'd called on the first morning, but now I did, and I waited until ten exactly.

I must have tried half a dozen times to get through the day before but incredibly, I was answered first time.

'It's Esme Fox here, I'm calling to see if my sister, Michelle Fox, has had a restful night and if there's been any progress at all?'

'Let's see.' I heard the shuffle of notes. 'Yes, she's had a good night – and actually seems to have picked up very slightly. The ventilator readings are encouraging and, although we've a long way to go, things seem to be moving in the right direction.'

I dropped my head. 'Thank God, thank you, God,' I whispered, before thanking her and ending the call. Now I just needed the police to release Owen from questioning.

Mo came in to get one of the studio time logbooks and instantly noticed my brighter mood. 'Good news?' He smiled.

I nodded. 'The hospital say Michelle had a good night and is making some progress with her breathing. It's early days yet, I know, but... oh, Mo, if you'd seen her.'

I bit down on my tongue to stop the emotion surfacing again and felt glad when Mo didn't instantly rush over to comfort me.

'I understand, Esme, and that's great news. I don't know how you're getting through it, to be honest. But coming into work...

I'm not sure that's the best thing for you with everything that's happening. Why don't you leave it to me and Justine to sort out?'

'Thanks, but it's better than sitting at home thinking through the endless awful outcomes, Mo. I've already lost us the possibility of interest from TrueLife, it seems. We've all worked so hard on *The Fischer Files* and it's getting the success it deserves. I can't just abandon Simone. This is her life, her chance for justice. I can't turn my back on her after she trusted me. She's asked me to increase my visits and I'm going to do it.'

Mo looked aghast. 'I assumed you'd want us to cancel – or at the very least, reschedule the remaining visits to the prison, Esme. Nobody would expect you to work under this kind of pressure, even Simone. Have you explained the situation to Simone?'

'I'll be fine.' I shrugged and picked up my notes again as Mo left the room shaking his head.

Things were looking up for Michelle slightly at the hospital and, God willing, it would be the start of her full recovery. I felt a duty not to abandon Simone or our new business, and it was just a few more sessions I'd have to get through to safeguard the remaining podcast episodes.

For the first time, I allowed myself a tiny glimmer of hope.

All that was needed was for Owen to be cleared of any wrongdoing and for the police to find and lock up the monster who really hurt my sister.

Then there was a chance that life could slowly get back to normal. Normal was exactly what we all needed.

CHAPTER THIRTY-SIX

JUSTINE

Esme had looked ill when she first arrived at the office.

She'd had some sort of panic attack where she couldn't breathe but then she'd quickly calmed down. In fact, when Justine passed by the meeting room on the pretence of visiting the photocopier, she was actually smiling and talking animatedly to Mo.

He'd told Justine he was out of his mind with worry when Michelle had initially failed to turn up for the TrueLife meeting.

I bet you are, Justine had thought. Mo had even called round to Esme's house to pick up a laptop. Creeping his way into Esme's favour, no doubt. It sickened her.

When Justine had come into the office on Monday for an early-morning session, it had proven to be a lucrative plan. Not only did she get to snoop around Mo's desktop computer but there had been the added bonus of finding Michelle's laptop, its security walls disabled, too.

Neither Esme nor Mo realised that Justine was somewhat of an IT expert herself. She had a natural interest in it and, after university, had studied for an additional qualification to aid her research skills.

Mo's overnight programme run had removed all passwords from the machine, so it had been no problem to plug her portable hard drive into the laptop and download all Michelle's files on to it. On a whim, Justine had taken the machine back to its factory settings to prevent Mo downloading all the files, too. If he thought he was going to get any information off there he could think again.

Yes, Justine had a lot of little surprises up her sleeve that would shock the lot of them. They were all guilty of underestimating what she was capable of. She had bided her time for a while now but soon all would be revealed. It was crucial she picked the right moment to light a match under the stack of dynamite she'd been carefully packing.

Justine stood near an internal window that was partially screened by a tall yucca plant. Esme was looking brighter now for some reason. Justine's head jerked as she heard a shuffling noise behind her.

'What the… oh, it's you!' Justine's hand flew to her mouth. 'Jeez, you made me jump a mile there!'

'What are you doing skulking around in dark corners?' Mo said jokingly, then frowned at the window when he saw it afforded a good view of Esme sitting in there.

'Skulking?' Justine said, in an offended tone. 'I was just checking Esme was OK. I don't want her crying alone into her paperwork if she needs to offload, that's all.'

'Ahh, I see. I've just been in there and she's feeling a bit better. She's just spoken to the hospital and it seems Michelle's showing signs of recovery.'

'That is good news,' Justine said.

Mo nodded. 'We need to get things back to normal here. So we can all crack on with the business again.'

'Indeed,' Justine said. She smiled as she walked away. 'I'd like nothing more myself, Mo.'

She couldn't wait to see his face when everything blew up.

CHAPTER THIRTY-SEVEN

ESME

The door to the meeting room flew open.

Toby stood there, gripping onto the door jamb. 'I'm sorry to disturb you, Esme, but there's a woman here!' he blustered, his face red. 'She's insisting you've got to see her or she's going to force her way in. I tried to explain you're busy but…' He paused and pushed his hand through his short, dark blonde hair. 'She told me to save my breath and that she's not leaving until she speaks to you.'

I took a second to process what he was saying. My head still felt fuzzy and my whole body was aching. All I really wanted was to be left alone. Was that really too much to ask?

'What? Who is it?'

I heard raised voices outside in the main office. It appeared Mo was now getting involved with the determined visitor.

'She won't tell me her name. She's maybe in her early sixties, done up like a dog's dinner and holding her handbag like the Queen.' Toby wrinkled his nose.

My heart sank at his description. I had a feeling I knew exactly who this was. 'Ask her to wait in the foyer for five minutes, Toby. I need to work up to this one.'

He nodded and disappeared and I clamped my hand to my forehead.

That was *all* I needed on top of everything else. I took a sip of water and sat up straighter in my chair, trying to look on the bright side. Maybe she'd changed since I was last in her company. Maybe she'd somehow grown to be a nicer person, altogether more pleasant and polite… although it certainly didn't sound it from the way she'd treated Toby so far.

I heard voices approaching and the sharp clipping of stiletto heels on the laminate floor, then there she appeared in the doorway, in all her glory.

Toby bobbed around ineffectually at the shoulder of her immaculate cream bouclé jacket, its pale gold buttons glinting in the light. Owen's mother, Brooke Painter.

Toby craned past her shoulder to meet my eyes. 'Sorry, Esme, she just—'

'*She*? It's Mrs Painter to you,' Brooke snapped, in the same caustic manner I'd been at the mercy of myself a few times in the past.

'It's fine, Toby. Thank you.' I gave him a nod and he was away in a flurry of obvious relief. I stood up and walked around the desk. 'Hello, Brooke. It's nice of you to come. I just wish it was in better circumstances.'

Emotions rose up inside me and for a sudden crazy moment, given the opportunity of someone who might just understand, I almost felt like flinging my arms around her. She seemed to sense this and shifted her weight uneasily from one stiletto to the other, as if she might have to leg it if I dared to show her any affection.

'Everything OK in here, Esme?' Mo's head appeared around the door, first glaring at Brooke and then raising his eyebrows at me.

'Heavens, what's all this ridiculous fuss about?' Brooke fumed at Mo. 'Of course she's alright, she's not made of glass, you know!'

'Everything's fine, Mo, thanks.' He nodded and closed the office door without looking at my mother-in-law again. I had to try and rescue the situation or, given Brooke's volatile temper, things would get much worse. 'Please, Brooke, take a seat. How are you keeping? You look well.'

'I'm fine, thank you – but as you might expect, it's not me I'm worried about,' she said brusquely as she sat down and brushed some non-existent flecks from her tailored black trousers before looking up at me. 'I'm sorry for what's happened to your sister, Esme. You must be out of your mind with worry, but I'll be straight with you. I've not trawled a hundred and seventy miles down here on the Newcastle to Nottingham train to console you. I'm here for Owen.'

'Well, I'm glad we've established that early on,' I said. I wondered how the hell she'd found out so quickly and who had told her Owen was in police custody.

Brooke glowered. 'Someone needs to be looking out for Owen and I've come here, to you, to get the full story of exactly what happened.'

She hadn't softened any in the twelve months since I'd last seen her. A couple of times a year Owen travelled up to Newcastle for various training events to maintain his fitness qualifications and he always stayed overnight at his parents' house. It was probably for the best I saw very little of them. Brooke and I had consistently rubbed each other up the wrong way almost from the day Owen took me home to meet his parents, nearly thirteen years before.

'Is Eric with you?' I asked her. Owen's dad ran his landscaping business in Newcastle and managed the grounds for several premium hotels there. He rarely took a day off.

'No. Eric was going to drive us both down, but I told him I'd get the bones of this mess clarified and then we'd discuss our next move.'

I glanced at the clock. 'Look, it's only just turned one. Let's grab a sandwich and I'll fill you in on everything.' I couldn't have eaten a morsel myself, but I wanted Brooke away from the office and I certainly didn't want her anywhere near the house. For the sake of a couple of hours stuck in a café where I could bring her up to speed with what had been happening, she'd hopefully be on her way back to Newcastle by teatime.

'Go out, you mean? I was hoping we could go straight to the house. I have a small suitcase in reception.' She narrowed her eyes. 'I assumed I'd be able to stay with you and Zachary for a couple of nights. After all, you had four bedrooms the last time I counted.'

It was a statement, not a request, and I felt like screaming with frustration at yet another thing landing on my plate.

I swallowed down the impulse to tell her in no uncertain terms that no, she would *not* be able to stay at the house and she only had herself to blame because I'd had zero notice of her arrival. Instead, I took a breath and steeled myself.

'Yes, that's fine, Brooke. Zachary will be thrilled to see you.'

If he still recognises you that is, I added in my head. Why did I find her so hard to tackle? It was because she was so confident and firm in saying and doing what she wanted.

When Owen and I had first told them, ten years ago, that we were expecting baby Zachary, Brooke insisted that they host a big family party at their large house near the quaint village of Corbridge in Northumberland. As if that wasn't bad enough, Brooke, without asking if it would be OK, took out a quarter-page announcement in the *Northumberland Gazette*. I was barely three months pregnant and felt nervous about letting everyone know in such a manner when it was early days still.

'Don't worry, Esme, everything's going to go perfectly, you'll see.' Owen had planted a kiss on my forehead by way of allaying my fears. 'It's just Mum's way of showing us how proud she is.'

Yet despite all the early showboating, Owen's parents had made woefully inadequate grandparents.

Between Eric's corporate landscaping business and Rotary Club commitments, and Brooke's involvement in the Hexham Ladies' numerous charity luncheons, there was little time for them to devote to family… to their only grandson. We tried to encourage their involvement as much as we could. But there always seemed to be some flimsy reason they weren't able to make Zachary's important milestones: his birthdays, school plays and sports presentations prior to his accident.

After the hit and run, and during their only hospital visit, Brooke offered to have Zachary stay to convalesce at their house.

'Countryside and fresh air, that's what he needs.' Brooke declared in front of Zachary and the nurses. 'Not cooped up in a small house on the wrong side of town. I know you have to work, Esme.' She turned to Owen. 'But *you* could bring Zachary up and stay with us a while, darling. It will do you good after all the trauma and I'd love to spoil you both.'

It was an insult and meant as one. But at the time, I was more furious with Owen than with her.

'She means well,' he'd simpered when I tackled him about not defending our care of Zachary. 'Maybe we could all go up there for a couple of weeks. It might do us good, too, and—'

'You must be joking.' I cut him off. 'I'd rather pull all my teeth out one by one than spend two whole weeks listening to your mother spouting her bigotry. Plus, she's made it quite clear she doesn't want me there.'

I knew I'd gone too far by the way his mouth sagged, but I didn't care. As far as I was concerned, it was painfully clear that Brooke had no time for us as a complete family. She'd only ever wanted Owen and Zachary. Most of the time, I was just an inconvenience that got in the way of her plans.

Owen periodically visited them through work, but Zachary and I had only seen them once more since he'd been in hospital. About a year ago, Eric had to collect an expensive piece of landscaping equipment and they drove down to Leicester, stopping off at ours for a two-hour visit on the way.

So when Toby announced her impromptu arrival here at the office, I was gobsmacked to say the least.

'Are you feeling alright, Esme?' Brooke's nasal tones cut through my musings. 'You seem somewhat distracted.'

You don't say.

There was no hint of warmth or empathy in her voice and, suddenly, I didn't know if I could do it. Whether I could actually put up with her around me for a minute longer – never mind for a few days with everything else that was currently happening. Brooke might not have realised it, but her son and I were no longer together. Our marriage was on the rocks. Therefore I owed her precisely nothing.

'Brooke, I'd hate for you to take this the wrong way but I'm sure you can understand this is a really testing time for us as a family.' I was cringing inside but there was no escaping the bluntness of what I had to say. 'Come back and see Zachary today, of course. But it's not a good time to stay over.'

'Why ever not?'

I stared at her. Was she seriously asking that question? Owen was at the police station and my sister was at that moment lying unconscious on a ventilator in the ICU unit of the Queen's Medical Centre.

Brooke broke the silence. 'I know there's a lot happening at the moment, but surely you could do with an extra pair of hands?'

'I'm managing OK,' I said weakly.

'Nonsense! I've only to look at you to see how pale you are. You're clearly not eating properly. If you're not taking care of yourself, then how can you possibly care properly for Zachary… and Owen, for that matter?'

She was a bully. Maybe a world away from Grant Fischer but made of the same core stuff. But I was no Simone.

'Excuse me?' Blood roared in my ears.

'I don't mean you're neglecting them… as such. I mean your mind must be racing. In that situation, anyone could be forgiven for letting things slip through the net.'

'I care for Zachary perfectly well and as for Owen... he's a grown man, not a child.'

I was pretty sure Owen hadn't said a word about our separation. He'd have been dreading his mother's reaction. She might not have been keen on me, but she'd hate the thought that her friends, all ladies who lunch, would raise their eyebrows snootily at the unexpected development. She'd always loved to brag and exaggerate about her son and his family even though there was no substance to it. Still, I did feel it was up to Owen to break the news to his parents. It wasn't something I wanted to use as a weapon in a moment of annoyance, tempted as I might be.

'And on top of everything else, I understand you've got yourself involved in defending that odious woman who murdered her husband? The whole country despises her. Please tell me it's not true.' Brooke pressed her lips together so tightly they disappeared for a moment.

'I'm sorry, Brooke, but I'm not going to discuss my work decisions with you at this point in time. It's just not going to be possible for you to stay at the house on this visit.' I wanted her toxic presence gone.

'I see. Well then, I shall make enquiries at the little bed and breakfast on the High Street, how's that?'

The Old Post Office, run by a man in his seventies whose son, Colin Wade, worked as a reporter at the national newspaper that had printed the most sensationalist articles about Simone Fischer over the years. It would be disastrous for Brooke to be in contact with him. He was the kind of man who would revel in any insider information she could give him. Give Brooke a pink gin and an audience and there would be nothing they *didn't* know by the end of her stay.

'I'm here now and I'm determined to spend some time with my grandson. He needs his family around him at a time like this.'

'He's managed perfectly well so far seeing you once a year,' I said tartly.

Brooke stood up to her full height and looked at me coldly. 'There's no point in trading insults. Frankly, I'd have thought you'd have better things to do. What time does Zachary get home from school?'

'Look. Let's not start off on the wrong foot,' I sighed, the journalist's vicious articles flashing into my mind. 'You can stay at the house but please don't expect too much, Brooke. I'm in a bit of a mess there as you can imagine and—'

She held up her hands.

'Say no more, it's really not necessary. I can help you out while I'm here.' She gave me a thin smile. 'There's nothing I like better than a good cleaning challenge.'

CHAPTER THIRTY-EIGHT

Back in the car and on the drive home, I filled Brooke in on events so far, starting with Michelle's no-show for the TrueLife meeting. It quickly became clear that Brooke had no interest at all in exploring the possibilities of how Michelle might have ended up in hospital. I suppose at least she was consistent from the moment she'd stepped into the office: she was here for Owen's welfare and nothing but.

'Eric's got a fantastic lawyer lined up, Bruce Condor. If they keep Owen, he's agreed to travel down from Newcastle tomorrow.'

'Is it someone Eric knows?'

'They play golf together.' No surprise there, then. The Old Boys' Club at work again, no doubt. 'At five hundred an hour, Bruce is giving Eric a hefty discount,' Brooke added smugly.

Five hundred was Bruce's discount rate? I was in the wrong job.

I stopped off at a small supermarket, grabbing a few basic items and something for tea while Brooke waited in the car. When I came back out again, she was spoiling for a fight before I even started the engine.

'Now, dear. Eric has been doing some research on what's available publicly about your little business and I know we've already touched on it, but it seems you've got yourself involved with a very unsavoury character, this Fischer woman.'

Smarting from the 'little business' comment, I allowed a lengthy pause before replying.

'As you say, that's part of my business, it's nothing at all to do with Owen or the fact the police are questioning him.'

'I understand your thinking. On the surface, it seems to have little to do with Owen's predicament. But actually, the fact that woman brutally murdered her husband in cold blood has rather a lot to do with sparking other people's opinions. As Eric says, it's a case that tarnishes anyone who's foolish enough to go near it.'

Her words prodded at my throat, goading me. 'I've no intention of choosing my cases in line with other people's opinions and expectations, Brooke,' I said testily. 'I think it's best if we leave my work out of any discussions about Owen. It's nobody's business but mine.'

She gave the sort of laugh that infers disbelief. 'It would be very convenient indeed if your affiliation with a convicted murderer could be so easily ignored, Esme. But as Bruce astutely observed this morning, the reality of your involvement is that people – perhaps even the police – will make certain judgements and assumptions about not only you but also our son. So you see, it's very much our business.'

The thumping in my head increased two-fold. I knew, if I wasn't careful, with everything else that was going on, I'd quickly wilt under her ongoing interrogation.

'We might need to agree to disagree on certain points,' I said, turning the car into our road at last. 'I'm trying not to become overwhelmed by Owen being questioned at the station and Michelle's worrying prognosis. Honestly, there's no room in my head for more trouble.'

'I'd say there's more than just trouble. My son is currently being treated like a common criminal. Owen simply isn't capable of a violent act like that.'

'Agreed,' I said. 'We both know that but the police are working methodically through their tick list. If Owen being questioned gets them closer to finding the monster that nearly killed my sister, then bring it on, I say.'

She turned in her seat to look at me but I kept my eyes on the road as I pulled into the driveway.

'And that's where our opinions differ, I'm afraid,' she said.

CHAPTER THIRTY-NINE

'Heavens. It must be very damp and drab around here by the looks of that roof.'

Brooke pursed her lips in disapproval, appraising the clumps of moss dotted on the tiles above us as we approached the house. Owen had enquired about a complete roof clean last year but the quote had been as much as a family holiday. With his reduced hours and my new business venture, we'd rightly decided against it.

If I opened my mouth to respond, I couldn't be sure what might come out.

I struggled behind Brooke's sweeping walk to the front door. I had too many bags and not enough hands. I put the shopping down and pushed the key into the lock.

Once in the hallway, I'd swear Brooke left her small, wheeled suitcase exactly in the middle of the walkway on purpose before heading for the kitchen. I held my breath and waited for it.

'I'll put the kettle on, shall I? Oh my!'

I knew she'd reached the chaotic space I turned my back on this morning. The one I'd imagined her seeing when I tried to put her off coming here in the first place. I hadn't emptied the dishwasher and reloaded it with our breakfast dishes. I'd opted instead to chuck all the dirty crockery in the sink to tackle when I got home later.

Empty cereal boxes and juice cartons littered the countertops and food scraps from making Zachary's packed lunch were still strewn here and there, betraying my sloppiness to Brooke's eagle eye. I realised, with a pinch of guilt, how much Michelle did around here that I didn't really even notice most of the time.

I shuffled into the kitchen and dumped the shopping on the worktop.

Brooke slipped off her coat and pushed up her sleeves. Then she pulled a pair of pink rubber washing-up gloves – complete with a feather trim on the cuffs – from her bag and put them on.

'Right, where to start... anti-bacterial spray?' She looked around, seeming doubtful I owned any cleaning products at all.

'In there.' I indicated the cupboard under the sink.

'I'd no idea you were struggling like this, Esme. I wish I'd travelled down earlier in the week now.'

'I really don't expect you to clean my kitchen, Brooke,' I said, taking food items out of the bags and slotting them into the cupboards, the fridge. 'I did warn you the house was in a bit of a state but I'm sure you can understand why things have slipped in the last few days.'

Who really gave a flying flip about the number of dirty dishes in the sink at a time like this? Not me.

A text message came though from Mo.

Have you seen this??

He'd included a link to the local newspaper, an online article I scanned about an attack in Wollaton Park on a woman in her thirties. I felt sick and dizzy and leaned back against the worktop for a moment.

'Like Eric says, we have to approach Owen's dilemma like a battle plan.' Brooke opened up the cupboard and frowned at the sparse array of cleaning equipment. 'And, as everyone knows, you don't win a battle by starting out disorganised.'

I slammed down a ready-made lasagne and she looked up, startled.

'It's not just Owen though, is it?' I said through gritted teeth. 'We know Owen is innocent, whatever the police might suspect, and I'm sure the truth will out. Meanwhile, Michelle is fighting for her life, so forgive me if I've been a bit lax with the scouring pad.'

Brooke closed the cupboard carefully and made a big thing of peeling off her flamboyant gloves and tugging down her sleeves again.

'I think I might leave you to it after all,' she said thoughtfully. 'The last thing I want to do is upset you, I'm so sorry if you misunderstood my intention.'

She padded out of the room and left me staring out of the window, feeling like I'd overreacted. Again, Simone's face drifted into my mind. In keeping with her descriptions of Grant Fischer's early covert control tricks, I'd do well to remember what a master manipulator Brooke was. She knew exactly how to play everyone to get exactly what she wanted, me included.

It was painfully clear she didn't give a fig about poor Michelle lying in hospital, unable to breathe on her own. Her only concern was for Owen. A natural reaction for a mother perhaps, but I felt sure most people would at least *try* to show a little compassion for what others might be going through.

Still, I decided I would be the bigger person here. It wouldn't be for long.

I finished putting away the shopping, then made two mugs of tea and took them through to the living room. Brooke looked witheringly at the mismatched crockery.

'A nice china tea cup prevents the natural tannins in the tea from sticking to the sides, did you know that, Esme?'

'I didn't,' I said. 'You learn something every day.'

She narrowed her eyes and took the drink. It seemed like she'd used the last five minutes to fully recuperate from her 'apology'. I sat on the sofa with her to show there were no hard feelings.

'I'd like to go with you when you pick Zachary up from school today,' she said firmly. 'As Eric and I were saying, we've been apart from our son and grandson for far too long and now's the perfect time to put that right.'

'I hope you've always felt welcome to visit,' I said testily. Something about her tone inferred it was our fault that they hadn't made more of an effort. 'I know you've both got lots of commitments and it's not always easy to get down to Nottingham but—'

'If I'm honest, Esme, I confess there has been an element of not wanting to intrude,' Brook said regretfully, pausing to sip her tea. 'You see, Owen was brought up to involve us in his life, to stay close to family, but I accept you've had different ideas with Zachary.'

'Now, wait a minute, I—'

She raised her hand in my face and I resisted the urge to slap it away. 'Now's not the time to argue about it. All I'm saying is that we want to put it right. We want to play a full part in Zachary's life from now on. That's not such a bad thing, is it?'

I was speechless. It felt like someone had flipped a switch and both Eric and Brooke had suddenly decided they would like to play happy families after all. From zero to full-on in what felt like sixty seconds.

'I'm very pleased to hear it, Brooke.' Although in reality I couldn't think of anything worse. 'I know Owen has explained to you the challenges we've had with Zachary since the accident. He doesn't do well with major changes to his routine, so we can sit down and plan how best to work towards you being part of his life to avoid too much of a disruption.'

'He's our *grandson*, Esme. Our flesh and blood. I don't think there'll be too many problems in us getting to know him better, do you?'

I took another sip of tea to avoid answering. It would be difficult, if not impossible, to make her fully comprehend how badly Zachary struggled at times. The best thing would be if she saw it for herself. She was clearly in no mood to take my word for anything at all.

I glanced at my watch and put down my mug. It was only half an hour before school was out.

'I'll show you up to your room,' I said, standing up and yawning. My night of broken sleep was catching up with me now. 'It's in a bit of a mess at the moment as we generally use it as the box room but I can tidy round later and put some fresh bedding on for you.'

She nodded and stood up, following me out of the room.

The pressure in my head continued to expand. There was so much extra to do now Brooke was on the scene. When Zachary got back from school, I planned to go upstairs and call the hospital for an update and also the police station to see if the situation with Owen had changed at all.

I walked upstairs, Brooke following just behind me lugging her case. I could feel the waves of ill-disguised fury rolling off her that I'd left her to do this, and to my shame I enjoyed a sharp thrill of satisfaction. On the stairs there were stacked toys, a pile of ironing and a couple of jackets. I imagined Brooke's face sagging in disbelief that anyone could live in this slovenly fashion. I felt like laughing but I just about managed to control myself.

Zachary's bedroom door was wide open as we passed, his bed unmade and dirty socks, underwear and other clothing strewn about the floor. I heard Brooke suck in air but I pretended I hadn't noticed.

'Is this room unused?' Brooke stopped outside Michelle's closed door.

'That's Michelle's room,' I said before thinking. Brooke frowned and I hastily backtracked. 'She uses it if she stays over.'

'I see.'

If she found out Michelle had been living here there'd be a tonne more questions and I'd probably have to tell her about our separation which would mean more antagonism.

I'd had no reason to go into the spare room for a few days and when I opened the door, even I felt shocked at the state of the place. 'Oh dear,' I said.

The first night Owen had stayed over, he'd obviously just scooped up everything that was on the single bed – all the winter clothes and other items without a home – and dumped them on to the floor. This bed was also unmade, the small windowsill lined with a crumbed plate and several used mugs and glasses.

I wanted to dive into a hole and stay there until Brooke went away again but there was no such luck.

'Sorry about the mess,' I said again, somehow managing not to say it was the making of her darling son. 'I'll sort it out when we get back from school.'

'It seems you'll be doing an awful lot when we get back from school,' she remarked drily.

I swore I could feel the ice crackle in the silence that sat between us.

CHAPTER FORTY

Trapped in the cool glare of Brooke's obvious disapproval of how I conducted my life, I felt relieved the school was only a ten-minute drive away.

A dark cloud hovered above me when I thought about how, when Owen didn't have our son, Michelle did most of Zachary's schools runs now. When would she be well enough to do so again? Soon, I prayed. I couldn't allow myself to think of the alternative.

I parked up a little way from the school gates and we walked down the road in silence. I scanned the road and school building for CCTV but the only cameras I could see were looking inward to the school grounds. There was nothing to cover the gates. When we got closer, one or two of the other mums recognised me and rushed over.

'Haven't seen you for ages, Esme! We heard about what happened to Michelle. It's so awful. Come here.' I couldn't help being a bit stand-offish at first, but then I found I actually felt better after their hugs and good wishes and I relaxed a little.

'Are the police any further forward in finding out who did it?' the mum of one of Zachary's school friends asked.

I shook my head. 'Not yet.' If the police didn't release Owen soon, it would only be a matter of time before word got out he'd been questioned. Especially now the attack had been reported in the media. 'But I wanted to ask… did any of you see Michelle talking to someone outside the school last Thursday morning? A man, perhaps?'

One of the women's face blanched paler. 'Was he *here*, at the school? The man who attacked her?'

'No, no. The police have just asked me to put the word out if anyone saw her on that last morning, that's all.' There was a grim finality to my words that made me want to weep.

'There were a couple of uniformed officers here yesterday,' someone else said. 'They showed around a photograph of Michelle, asking if anybody had seen anything unusual.'

I felt reassured. At least the police were looking into the prospect of the mystery man, even if they were still wasting time interrogating Owen.

Brooke shifted next to me and cleared her throat.

'This is Brooke, Owen's mum.' I introduced her. 'She's come down to help out with Zachary.'

The women made a fuss of Brooke and I watched, fascinated, as her snooty manner dissolved completely and she stood, head hanging, humbly accepting their compliments about how good she was to come down to help us.

'It's lovely to have the chance to spend time with our grandson,' she simpered, making it sound like something or someone had prevented them from doing so thus far. 'We miss him so much, living away as we do.'

When the women moved away again, Brooke swiftly returned to her usual spikey self.

'I'll meet Zachary's teacher while I'm down here, if I might,' she said when the end-of-school bell sounded.

'Oh, you have to make an appointment to see her if—'

'No, no, that's not necessary. I would like to just say hello, to introduce myself as Zachary's grandmother. I'm sure we don't need to book a half-hour chat to do that.'

The end-of-day procedure was usually for parents to wait by the gates until the children emerged from their classes, but I led Brooke across the playground to Zachary's classroom doors.

Brooke scanned the fabric of the building with a critical eye, taking particular interest in the windows.

'What was the last OFSTED rating at this school?' she sniffed.

'They got a "good" rating earlier this year,' I said, glad I was able to say so. 'They were in special measures a couple of years ago but the new head has really raised standards. And they've had new windows and built an extension at the back with extra funding he's secured for the school.'

'They're mostly private schools around us, but the one state school came out with an outstanding rating after their latest inspection,' she remarked. 'The thing I don't like about these places, these *state* schools, is the limited facilities. Eric always says it's a travesty for young boys if there are no fields on campus for rugby.'

'Girls play too sometimes, you know,' I mumbled under my breath, and she looked at me sharply. 'Zachary doesn't suffer in that regard since the accident. His leg prevents him participating in contact sports.'

The classroom doors opened and the children tumbled out, running across the playground. Zachary smiled when he saw me and walked over as fast as he could with the hindrance of his leg. When he spotted Brooke, he stalled.

'Darling!' Brooke rushed towards him. 'It's wonderful to see you. Have you got a kiss for Grandma?'

'It's best if you just let him…' My words were drowned out by the other children shouting and squealing. Brooke pulled Zachary towards her and he shot me a panicked look.

I walked over and took his hand, forcing a break in Brooke's pincer-like grip on him.

'Grandma surprised us. She's come to visit for a couple of days, that's nice, isn't it?'

Brooke smiled widely and Zachary swallowed and managed a single nod. I approached Miss Carling as she saw the children out of the classroom.

'Can I introduce you to Zachary's grandma, Owen's mother, Brooke?'

'Hello, very pleased to meet you!' Miss Carling said, giving Brooke a nice open smile.

'Very pleased to meet you, dear,' Brooke said grandly. 'I'm so pleased for the chance to chat. Myself and Zachary's grandfather hope to play a larger part in his life and I wondered if it would be possible to get a report on his current grades and teacher assessments?'

'I… well, yes, I could certainly put something together for you.' Miss Carling glanced at my stunned expression.

'I have all his school reports at home, Brooke,' I said archly, finally pulling myself together. 'There's no need to bother Miss Carling with this.'

'Perhaps my husband and I could arrange a mutually convenient time to pop in and meet with you, Miss Carling?' Brooke said, blanking me. 'School reports won't cut it, I'm afraid. If his grades aren't up to scratch then a remedial plan of action may need to be discussed.'

Miss Carling opened her mouth and closed it again.

'We can talk about this at home, Brooke.' I grasped her elbow firmly and looked at Zachary's teacher with an apologetic expression. 'We'll be in touch, Miss Carling. Thank you.'

I led Brooke away and she shook me off immediately. 'I didn't appreciate that, Esme. Frankly, I felt undermined.'

'Not as undermined as I felt!' I snapped back. 'You can't just barge into our lives and take over, Brooke.'

She shot me a hellish glare and swapped sides so she was next to Zachary.

'Now, let's see what we have in here, shall we?' She opened her cavernous Mulberry handbag and pulled out a large bag of sherbet-filled flying saucers. 'Here we go. A treat from Grandma!'

Zachary took them eagerly, then his face fell as he remembered our no-sweets-before-tea rule.

'Just have one,' I told him. 'As a special treat.'

'I always found depriving children and laying down rules about sweeties had the opposite effect,' Brooke remarked as we walk back to the car. 'Moderation was the way we raised Owen and look how he's turned out.'

Yes, he's currently in police custody, I'd have loved to snap back at her, but of course I didn't.

'Indeed,' I said instead.

CHAPTER FORTY-ONE

Back in the car, Zachary declined Brooke's invitation to sit in the back with her and climbed in his usual seat in the front next to me.

'Is Dad at home, Mum?' he asked, leafing through his new reading book as if he fully expected me to say that he was.

'He isn't yet,' I said lightly.

'Is he still at the flat?' Zach pressed.

'What flat?' I watched in the mirror as Brooke pursed her lips.

I continued as if she hadn't spoken as I pulled out into a gap in the traffic. 'We're hoping he'll be back home later and then—'

'Does he know his father's still at the police station?' Brooke said.

'Huh?' Zachary closed his book and shoved it back in his reading folder. 'Why is Dad still there?'

His voice sounded strained and he looked at me with dark, haunted eyes.

'That's Grandma's opinion entirely, Zachary,' she piped up again. 'It's ridiculous. They're questioning him about something he's had absolutely nothing to do with.'

'Brooke, can you please stop?' My face felt like it was on fire. I had to speak through my teeth because if I let rip I knew I'd never stop. 'I've explained to Zachary that Owen will be home soon. There's absolutely no need to burden him with any further details.'

'Well, I'm a big believer in telling children the truth,' she said tartly. 'People don't give young people the credit they deserve. Zachary is quite capable of understanding that his father is in trouble.'

'Is he, Mum? Is Dad in trouble with the police?' Zachary wailed, wringing his pale hands together. I pulled the car over into a lay-by, engaged the handbrake and turned fully in my seat until I was facing her.

'Brooke, it's about a ten-minute walk home from here or it's just two more minutes that you'll need to stay quiet if you want to continue the ride.'

Her mouth dropped open. 'Hang on a minute! I've done nothing wrong, all I said was—'

'It's not appropriate, Brooke. It's not the right place or time to be talking to Zachary about his dad. You can see how worried he is, as we all are. I won't have him needlessly distressed.' She hadn't a clue about the effect her ill-timed remarks could have on Zachary for days, maybe even weeks, to come.

'Message received and understood. You've certainly made yourself abundantly clear,' she said coldly, folding her arms and staring straight ahead, dismissing me.

I sat back in my seat and reached for Zachary's hand. 'Everything's going to be just fine, sweetie. You're not to worry, do you hear me?'

'But when will Dad be back?' he asked me in a small voice. 'The police said it was just a few questions and you said he went to bed in the flat last night. That he was out of the station.'

'What flat is this?' Brooke demanded.

'Your dad will be back soon,' I said, the words catching in my dry throat. I disengaged the handbrake and set off again. 'There's no doubt in my mind about that.'

In the back, Brooke sniffed and made a small noise in her throat. It was all I could do not to stop the car right there and then and order her out.

*

Back home, I sent Zachary upstairs to get changed out of his school uniform and in the kitchen, I called the hospital and asked how Michelle was.

'She's stable and that's all we're really looking for at this early stage,' the nurse said. 'The doctor is on his way around the ward now.'

I thanked her and ended the call. I couldn't take Zachary to the hospital to see his aunt while she was on the ventilator. It wasn't right, him seeing her so terribly ill. I rubbed at a small stain on the worktop with my thumb, trying to ignore the aching I felt inside.

'If you want to go to the hospital to visit Michelle, I'm happy to watch Zachary.' I jumped at Brooke's loud, clear voice. I didn't realise she was standing there in the doorway.

'It's fine,' I said, my voice sounding toneless. 'There's no change anyway.' The last thing I wanted was her filling Zachary's head with the 'truth' about Owen's precarious situation at the police station while I was gone.

'Esme, has Owen got a flat?'

I held my breath for a few moments. Do I outright lie? Do I refuse to answer?

'He... yes, he has. It's complicated. You can ask him about it when you see him, that would be best, I think.'

Her face darkened. 'If there's something happening I ought to know about then I'd appreciate you telling me now, Esme.'

With great effort, I pulled myself up to my full height and met her stare. 'Like I said, you can ask Owen when you see him.'

Brooke walked over to the breakfast bar and tapped her ruby nails on the countertop. 'Look. Perhaps I was a little hasty in the car and spoke out of turn in front of Zachary. If that's the case, then I'm sorry. It seems we have different ideas when it comes to what children can handle.' It sounded about as close to an apology as I was ever going to get from her. I picked up a dishcloth and rubbed at the persistent stain. 'I'll avoid mentioning Owen to him altogether if you'd prefer. I can make him some tea and he can do his homework, or whatever he does after school. I'm sure you'd like to get to see Michelle even if it's only for a short time.'

She was right. I would really like to go and see my sister with my own eyes. Whether she could hear me or not, I was aching to talk to her, tell her how much we were missing her. I hesitated.

'I give you my word,' Brooke said convincingly. 'Can we call a truce now, do you think?'

'If you're sure…'

'I'm positive. You get off now and I'll try and find out what's happening at the police station… well out of Zachary's earshot, of course.'

CHAPTER FORTY-TWO

It was an hour before I finally got to the hospital. The roads were busy with work traffic and the hospital car park was rammed. I had to drive round for a good five minutes until I was lucky enough to find someone reversing out of a space. But I got there and, although it stuck in my throat to say so, it was thanks to Brooke I was able to come.

We might have very different ideas of how to relate to children but I had to confess she'd pulled a masterstroke with Zachary before I left.

I told him I was going to the hospital and he started playing up.

'I want to see Aunt Miche! It's not fair. I want to tell her what I've done at school today, she always asks me. Every day.'

'Zachary, I've explained that she's feeling really unwell right now and—'

'I don't care!' He jumped up and tossed his game console aside. 'I want to see her.'

'And you will,' Brooke interjected gently when I closed my eyes, just so weary with it all. 'But today you need to stay here and let your mum give Auntie your love. Because I'm going to need some help with this.'

She handed him a big dinosaur activity pack and a bumper pack of coloured felt-tipped pens. The words emblazoned on the front of the pack read 'Everything Dinosaur', which was just about Zachary's dream apart from anything Nintendo.

His face brightened and he barely murmured goodbye when I left the house.

Just when I'd thought I had Brooke Painter pegged, she went and surprised me yet again.

*

They buzzed me in through the ward doors and I walked to the nurses' station, waiting to catch someone's eye. It was a different nurse on the desk today and I couldn't see the other one, but then I was visiting later in the day than yesterday.

'You're here to see…?' She was tall and thin and more officious than the previous nurse, but when I explained I was Michelle Fox's sister, she became a little friendlier. 'You're here again? I'm afraid there's little change from this morning. But you're welcome to sit with her, follow me.'

The bright lights and noise assailed my senses again. I glanced at the tangles of tubes and medical equipment clustered around each bedhead, reminding myself there was a patient just like Michelle under there, with a family as desperately worried as I was.

I didn't pay quite as much attention to my surroundings because something about the nurse's comment, and the way she said it, bothered me. *You're here again?* Surely it wasn't unusual for family members to visit people in ICU once a day.

'I haven't visited since yesterday,' I said slowly, the tendons in my neck tightening. 'This is the first time I'm seeing her today.'

'Oh?' She looked over her shoulder at me. 'I thought you'd visited earlier.'

'No… what makes you say that?' A crawling sensation started at the base of my spine.

'Someone mentioned it at the nurses' station this morning, I think. Said in passing that Michelle Fox's sister had just arrived.'

'Sorry, can we just stop walking for a second?'

She turned around, puzzled. 'What is it?'

'It wasn't me. If anyone came to visit Michelle this morning saying they were her sister, it was a lie. Can you check if she did have a visitor?'

She shook her head and set off walking again. 'I probably misunderstood, that's all. We're rushing around so much it's easy to get things like that wrong, hearing bits of conversations.'

I felt like something had a hold of my throat. There were no visitor logs or anything like that here, I'd not been asked to sign in yet. When I rang the ward for a progress report, they took my word for it that I was who I said I was. Maybe the nurse was mistaken this time, but the thought that people could just come and go here without being thoroughly checked out… it made my blood run cold.

What if the man who attacked Michelle came in here claiming to be her boyfriend or something? He could do anything if they left him with her like they did with me. The police were busy trying to pin the blame on Owen, wasting valuable time while the real perpetrator was still out there free to do as he wished. My head swam with it all and I had to force myself to focus on the here and now.

I wrinkled my nose against the smell of antiseptic as we reached Michelle's bed.

'Here we go.' The nurse picked up the clipboard at the end of the bed and studied the paperwork on there for a moment. 'The doctor's already seen her and there are no comments on here which means things are going as planned with the ventilator.'

'I'm worrying though,' I said falteringly. 'If someone's been here saying they're—'

'Honestly, you shouldn't worry. I'm sure I was mistaken. But tell you what, I'll ask at the nurses' station, OK?'

I nodded, grateful.

'Give me a shout if you need anything,' the nurse said before turning on her heel and walking away again. I bet she regretted mentioning the other visitor but now she had, I had questions.

I looked down at my sister... or what I could see of her through the rubber and metal and Perspex. If I came here every day for the next year I knew I'd never get used to seeing her in this state. Her skin was a mass of purple and blue bruising, her eyes even more swollen than yesterday, it seemed to me. It was like she'd been stripped of whatever it was that made her human.

The urge to fall to my knees and pray for her recovery was so strong I had to battle it. I pulled up a chair and sat down next to her instead, taking her cool hand in mine. I looked down and saw one of her nails had been torn off and the top of her hand was covered in deep scratches. I closed my eyes, bent my head and kissed her fingers.

'I miss you so, so much, Michelle,' I whispered. Even if she'd been conscious, with the noise of the ward and the rasping sound of the ventilator, she would have struggled to hear me. But I carried on just the same. 'I've taken you for granted, everything you do for me and Zachary. I've been too involved with the business, too obsessed with making it a success.' I swiped at my wet cheeks. 'I should've stopped to think about how you felt about being my general dogsbody. I'm sorry. I love you.'

I closed my eyes and tried to gather myself and then I looked around. The beds were set wider apart than in a normal ward. I couldn't tell whether the tube-cluttered patients either side of Michelle were male or female. There was just one other visitor across the other side, his back to me, hunched over his loved one in silent prayer. This was a wretched place that most people would never get to see. Lucky them. Hope didn't feel that strong here, but fear loomed large.

I inched my chair closer to her and spoke a little louder.

'I need to know you're safe here, Michelle. What happened? Did you know the person who hurt you? Who left you in the woods? Can you squeeze my fingers, just a tiny bit if you did know them?'

I held my breath and prayed for a tiny twitch from her hand but there was nothing at all.

'The police, they're questioning Owen. I know you two had issues but… I don't think Owen would hurt you. I don't think he would ever do that.' I could feel a strange throbbing sensation in my neck. What if I was in denial? I mean, why were the police so interested in Owen? The detectives both seemed competent and experienced… they must have had reason to be so preoccupied with him, to have a whole host of questions to ask, better done down at the station. But to keep him overnight? The thoughts scared me.

'Michelle, did Owen hurt you? I want to know. I *need* to know. Just a tiny, tiny squeeze… just a single twitch of your fingers to tell me. Did Owen have anything to do with what happened to you… I need to know for Zachary's sake. Please?'

I squeezed my eyes closed, half-terrified, half-hopeful for a sign. For anything at all to show she was there behind that awful rasping mask.

'Did Owen hurt you, Michelle?' I whispered hoarsely, closer to her ear. I waited for what felt like a long time, holding my breath, my senses on full alert. I was willing her to hear me so hard.

But there was no response at all.

CHAPTER FORTY-THREE

When I left the ward, the tall nurse caught me on my way out.

'I'm really sorry, looks like I was wrong. We've had a shift change but the healthcare assistants from this morning are still here and the ones I've spoken to don't recall Michelle having another visitor today.'

'That's good. Thanks for checking.' I still felt uneasy about it but they were super busy. I knew it was perfectly possible she'd made a mistake.

Back home, I pulled on to the drive and sat in the car for a few minutes.

I got a sinking feeling when I looked up at the house and saw a shadow pass in front of the small window at the top of the stairs. Brooke.

It was true I didn't know what I would have done with Zachary when I went to the hospital if Brooke hadn't turned up as she did, but the stress caused by having her around wasn't worth it. I found I didn't want to go back inside my own house.

I'd have liked to spend a little time with Zachary and then, when it was time for him to go up to bed, I'd pour myself a glass of wine and wrap myself up in a big soft fleecy blanket and sit with my misery a while. Obviously that wasn't going to happen with Brooke on patrol.

It occurred to me that I still had some sleeping tablets the doctor had prescribed for Zachary after his accident, to be used very sparingly. With Brooke in the house, it would surely be safe for me to have just one, just to take the edge off so I could get a good night's sleep…

Yet I had the long drive to HMP Bronzefield the next day to see Simone. I had to stay sharp for that.

The front door opened and Brooke stood there with her arms folded, peering out at the car. When I didn't move she went back inside but left the door wide open, signalling her expectation that I would follow her in. I questioned whether I had the energy to fight this woman. It was starting to make more sense to just go along with whatever she said.

Reluctantly, I grabbed my handbag and got out of the car, locking it and walking into the house. I felt a cool breeze on my face and shivered, pulling my jacket closer to me.

'I've been waiting for you to get back.' I jumped as Brooke stepped out of the shadows in the hallway, her voice low and raspy. 'Eric's been in touch. The lawyer has just arrived at the police station and is waiting to see Owen.'

'What? Have the police contacted you?'

'Eric contacted them. He's dealing with it now, to give you a bit of space to be with your sister. We thought it was for the best.'

The detectives knew we were separated but legally we were still married, and I had a responsibility to keep myself informed for Zachary's sake. 'They should have let me know, too.'

'You weren't here, Esme. You were at the hospital,' Brooke said crisply, revealing why she was so accommodating earlier, encouraging me to visit Michelle. She twisted her expression into something resembling pity. 'It's clear you're struggling and that's understandable. You can't do everything, you need to offload some of the responsibility. That's what I'm here for.'

'But… Eric can't just take over, he—'

'Someone has got to look out for Owen! You're barely functioning, your head's full of helping that murderer and your sister and little else. It's not fair for Zachary and Owen to suffer because your priorities are skewed.'

I couldn't have felt more winded if she'd punched me. I slumped against the wall in the hallway.

'I found these in the bathroom cupboard.' She shook a small brown bottle I recognised. Zachary's sleeping tablets. 'They were within Zachary's reach and I'm asking myself why a child of nine needs drugs to help him sleep. He's living in near squalor in that bedroom and he tells me you allow him to spend most of the evening playing computer games.'

Like most parents, I tried hard to monitor Zachary's screen time but it wasn't always easy. Still, what child, trying to pull the wool over his grandma's eyes, wouldn't try that line on them?

I pushed myself off the wall and stepped towards her. 'Why are you snooping around in my cupboards? You have no idea, not a clue, about how damaged Zachary was by the accident. Those tablets were prescribed by his GP who knows a damn sight more about my son than you do!'

I snatched the bottle out of her hands and she jumped back as if I might throttle her next. As much as I would have liked to do just that, I stepped back again. But I wasn't so far gone I was ready to roll over and let her get away with her insults just yet.

'And I don't know what your definition of squalor is, but I can assure you that for normal people who aren't living in a pink bubble, a sink full of pots and a few bits of dirty laundry on the floor don't count. If you must know, the spare room you're sleeping in was left in that state by *your* son.'

'So Owen was sleeping there, proving there *are* problems between the two of you.' She turned her back on me and walked into the kitchen. I could see Zachary through the living room door, engrossed with *Animal Crossing* which the little monkey had set up on the television downstairs while I was out.

The kitchen was spotless. All the surfaces glistened, not a soiled pot in sight. She'd moved the toaster and the kettle to the opposite worktop, repositioned the tea, coffee and sugar caddies. All the opened mail, school newsletters, old magazines that littered the worktops had disappeared.

I refused to give her any credit.

'What's happening with Owen?' I said. 'Why has the lawyer come down?'

She sprayed some anti-bacterial cleanser on the already flawless worktop and wiped it down smoothly and methodically with a cloth.

'Owen decided not to answer any further questions unless he has a lawyer present,' she said smoothly. 'Exactly the correct response, Eric says.'

'But won't that make him look as if he's got something to hide?' I cried out, and then bit my lip, hoping Zachary hadn't heard. 'He just needs to tell them the truth. I don't see what the problem is.'

'You're not a lawyer, Esme, so you won't understand. Bruce will soon avail himself of all the details and Eric will bring us an update when he has any news.'

'I'm the one who should be getting the updates,' I snapped, even though I logically knew Eric would be the solicitor's first point of call.

'But you're not his wife, are you? Not anymore. You threw him out, apparently?'

'How do you know th… we're still legally married. We aren't divorced and Owen moving out was a mutual decision.'

'You can't cope as it is, without getting involved in Owen's predicament, too. And for the record, I think my son will be much better off without you. Eric only gave it six months to last when you two wed, do you know that?'

I walked away before I started screaming at her. Upstairs I got changed in my bedroom. She hadn't even asked how Michelle was.

Tears streamed down my cheeks as I pulled on some old jeans and a top. It sounded silly but I felt too vulnerable in my pyjamas, in front of Brooke. Although she'd changed into an emerald-green, velvet lounge suit, she was still in full make-up and jewellery, looking like she was about to star in a QVC advert.

Didn't she ever just breathe out?

I stepped out into the garden for some fresh air and to try and calm myself down. I relished the cool breeze on my hot face and checked out the shrubs I'd planted last year and undertaken to keep trimmed and neat. I'd neglected them since then. After a few minutes of staring at the untidy borders, I opened up my emails on my phone.

I scrolled down the numerous messages and my breath caught in my throat when I spotted an email from Colin Wade, the local journalist who now worked on a national newspaper, congratulating me on the 'runaway success' of *The Fischer Files*. He wanted an exclusive interview about my interest in the Simone Fischer case and to ask how that was being affected by my sister's recovery from the, as yet unsolved, attack. I knew then it would only be a matter of time before the press floodgates opened and my personal life became a free for all.

Just about to click out of the emails, I saw there was one from Janice of the FSF group. She'd sent me Peter Harvey's telephone number. With so much on my mind I'd been distracted from my work on the podcast. I hesitated; glancing up at the house, I was all alone out here. I pressed the link, causing my phone to call him.

'Yes?' he answered curtly. He'd sound quite fearsome if you hadn't seen his diminutive appearance.

'Hello, Peter. This is Esme Fox of The Speaking Fox. Janice Poulter of the FSF group gave me your number.'

'Did she indeed!' He didn't sound pleased to hear from me. 'So, to what do I owe this honour, because last time we met you didn't seem that keen on speaking to me.'

'I think we got off on the wrong foot,' I said carefully. 'And I wondered if you'd be willing to meet up, either somewhere halfway or I'd be happy to drive to Ashford if that suited you better.'

He laughed. 'I don't live near the prison, it's just that my sister is incarcerated there. I'm in Melton Mowbray.'

Famous for its legendary pork pies and Stilton cheese, I'd been to the town a few times over the years. It was only about twenty miles from Nottingham. On a good drive I could do it in forty minutes.

'It's no problem for me to pop over to you there, Peter.'

He paused a moment and then said suspiciously, 'What's all this about? Why do you want to speak to me?'

'Just a general chat. You're the person who knows Simone best and it would be really useful to hear your opinion on what happened.'

'I want nothing to do with all that podcast nonsense,' he said airily. 'And I'm not being recorded.'

'That's absolutely fine,' I said, excited he might actually agree to see me. 'It's just an informal chat. Off the record.'

'Ha! I've never met a journalist yet who knows the meaning of that phrase. Things have a nasty habit of finding their way on to the news channels whether they were said *off the record* or not.'

'I give you my word, Peter,' I said, hoping I didn't sound too desperate. 'Would you be free tomorrow? I'm travelling down to speak to Simone anyway, so I could stop off for a coffee with you on the way? There's a Costa Coffee on the South Parade in the middle of town. I could meet you in there at say… ten o'clock tomorrow morning?'

'I suppose so,' he sniffed. 'Looks like you've finally realised who calls the shots when it comes to my sister.'

The person she banned from sitting in on our visits, you mean? I'd like to have added, but I got the feeling Peter's sense of humour wasn't his strongest point.

Nevertheless, I smelled a rat around Mr Harvey and I intended following my nose on this one.

CHAPTER FORTY-FOUR

I went back inside, already thinking through what I wanted to ask Peter. I pushed the worry about press interest in my own life to the back of my mind. They couldn't force me to speak to them.

In the kitchen I saw Brooke had laid the table with three place settings. That was something I rarely did anymore because we all tended to eat in different rooms. Something was bubbling away in the oven which ordinarily would've smelled delicious to me, but I had zero appetite and my stomach turned a little at the mere thought of eating.

Even before Owen moved into the flat, I'm ashamed to say we got into the habit of eating at the breakfast bar in the morning and then taking our evening meals on trays in front of the television. My fault, admittedly, but I knew Zachary was going to rail against Brooke's 'sitting at the table' expectation big time. He was used to eating while he watched his favourite television programmes.

Brooke glanced over at me as I hovered around the kitchen door, wondering how I was going to get out of this, too.

'Esme, look… we've got off on the wrong foot here. The things I just said… I'm stressed, too. We all are.'

Another pretty grovelling apology… by Brooke's standards.

'I've made a cottage pie,' she said before I could answer, in the kind of tone that implies no excuses will be acceptable. 'Zachary!' she called. 'Television off please and come and wash your hands.'

I heard the television fall silent and Zachary's murmurs of discontent but, to my amazement, he walked in the kitchen and washed his hands at the sink before taking a seat at the table.

When we were sitting down and Brooke was busy at the oven, Zachary turned to me.

'Did you see Aunt Miche, Mum? Did you tell her that I miss her?'

'I did, sweetie. She's very poorly.'

'Was she still sleeping?'

I nodded. 'They're still helping her to breathe but she has improved slightly, the nurse told me. Once she can breathe on her own, then she'll be awake and you can go and see her.'

I hoped and prayed Michelle's bruises and swelling would be much improved by the time Zachary went to visit. It was getting easier to talk about Michelle to my son, and that could only be a good thing.

Brooke carried an oblong earthenware dish over to the table, the contents still bubbling, and set it down on the heatproof mat in the middle of table. My stomach growled. The potato topping was perfectly browned and had been artfully scored with a fork, Mary Berry style.

'Yum!' Zachary's eyes widened and he licked his lips.

I had to admit it looked very good, even though I felt a sharp pinch of inadequacy when I thought of Zach's usual fare served after school. Fish fingers and chips or burger and potato wedges. Usually frozen. 'Looks amazing, Brooke.'

She looked pleased and went back to the oven for a second dish and our warmed plates. 'Here we are. Asparagus and buttered carrots to go with it.'

Zachary's nose wrinkled and Brooke saw it. 'No vegetables, no pie,' she said simply, and emptied a large spoonful of carrots on his plate. He didn't object.

'Can I have a glass of juice?' Zachary asked, watching his grandma as she placed a portion of cottage pie in front of him.

I pushed back my chair but Brooke shook her head and indicated for me to pass my own plate over. 'You shouldn't drink while you eat, Zachary, it dilutes the gastric juices. When you chew, the food starts to break down in your mouth, the first stage of digestion, before it even gets to your stomach. Did you know that?'

'Cool!' Zachary said, obviously impressed. No stropping, no backchat, no objections whatsoever. Where had I been going wrong?

Finally, when the food was all served, we ate.

'This is really delicious, Brooke,' I said, and I meant it. The mash was creamy, the rich meat and gravy seasoned to perfection and the vegetables were firm and fresh, not overcooked as I was prone to do.

I looked at Zachary and saw he was completely immersed in the experience of eating, no television or computer game to take his attention away. It was heartening to see my boy enjoying his food like this. If someone had tasked me to create this scenario I'd have said it would be nigh on impossible and not worth the trouble for the kickback I'd get from Zachary. And yet here we were. Brooke had somehow managed to work miracles.

She saw me watching Zachary and smiled knowingly. 'Children need the very routines and framework they like to kick against in my opinion,' she said rather smugly. 'All this respecting their views and giving them a voice is utter nonsense so far as I'm concerned. Children need gentle discipline. It's only when they're left to rule the roost there are problems.'

I put down my fork and dabbed at my mouth with a napkin. That told me then. There I was, believing the doctors when they said that Zachary's mood changes and difficult behaviour were as a result of the accident when it had been *my* fault all along.

I glared at her and she held my stare as if daring me to challenge her. But I didn't want Zachary witnessing more tension and harsh words at the table, so Brooke won again.

After tea, Brooke started clearing the table. I went to clear the plates and she put her hand up in a stop sign.

'Pop upstairs and change your T-shirt, darling,' Brooke told Zachary, indicating the gravy mark on his top. 'Bring that one down and I'll get it soaking so it doesn't stain.'

Nothing fazed this woman; nothing was left to chance. Zachary got up from the table and headed for the stairs to follow his grandma's instructions without any drama.

'I'm going upstairs to have a lie down, Brooke,' I told her. 'First, I want to call the police station to see if there's any news on Owen.'

'Don't bother with the police station – Eric has all that in hand,' she said dismissively.

I still felt annoyed the police were speaking to Eric at all, but there was nothing I could do about that. Despite our separation, I felt undermined. I opened my mouth to say as much when the doorbell rang.

'Expecting anyone?' Brooke said airily.

I shook my head, my heart thudding in anticipation of more bad news. Then, with a sinking heart, I remembered it could be journalists after a story. I walked out into the hallway and stopped when I saw the two familiar-looking male figures through the patterned glass.

With a fresh numbness gripping me, I began to move towards the door.

CHAPTER FORTY-FIVE

'Who is it, Mum?' Zachary stood at the top of the stairs and began hitting the bannister with a rolled-up comic. 'When is Dad coming home?'

'It's OK, Zachary. Just stay in your room a bit and I'll pop up shortly.' I felt so exhausted with it all. I held on to the bannister for a moment while I summoned the strength to deal with this next unwelcome instalment.

Zachary belted the comic harder on the wall. 'Is it those detectives again? Why are they here? Where's my dad?'

My bones felt so heavy with it all. 'Go to your room,' I shouted, too sharply.

'Patience, Esme. The boy's only asking,' Brooke called from the next room.

I opened the front door and looked steadily at the two detectives.

'I wonder if we might have a word?' DI Sharpe asked.

'Hello, Zachary,' DS Lewis called up the stairs, as they stepped inside. He raised a hand by way of a greeting.

The next moment, the rolled-up comic sailed downstairs and just missed the detective's head.

'Zachary!' I yelled, just as his bedroom door slammed shut.

'It's fine.' Lewis dismissed my concern with a hand gesture. 'I'm sure he's heartily sick of the sight of us.'

He wasn't the only one.

I led them both through to the living room. Before I could introduce Brooke, she stood up, heels back on.

'I'm Brooke Painter, Owen's mother,' she said imperiously. 'What's happening at the station with my son?'

'Well, that's what we're here to talk about,' Sharpe said in an affable manner.

Brooke's nostrils flared. 'You're here to talk about *what*, precisely?'

'Brooke, I think they're here to speak with me,' I intervened, rolling my eyes at the two detectives.

'It's fine for Mrs Painter to stay,' Lewis said, scuppering my attempt to get rid of her.

'That's if you're happy for her to stay,' his boss added pointedly, noticing my irritation.

'Perhaps you could make some tea for us, Brooke,' I suggested, gaining satisfaction from the flush of indignation that spread over her face.

Of course, she refused to be dismissed so easily. 'I could and will make tea for the officers… after I've heard what they've got to say.'

We both sat side by side on the sofa and waited. Sharpe's pleasant demeanour seemed to have dissipated and now the detectives seemed uneasy, glancing at each other. I held my breath. Were they here to tell me they'd arrested and charged Owen for the attack on Michelle? It couldn't be so. It just *couldn't*. My fingernails dug down hard into my palms.

I beat down the urge to ask searching questions about the information they were trying to get from Owen. I had to consider Zachary in this; I had to maintain my faith in Owen and not doubt him. The alternative terrified me.

'Have you found out something about Michelle's attacker?' I asked, desperate to hear if progress was being made in another area.

Sharpe hesitated. 'Investigations are still ongoing but I'm afraid we've nothing to report at this moment in time.'

'Nothing to report and yet here you are. How long are you intending to detain my son for?' Brooke demanded.

'We're entitled to hold Mr Painter for up to forty-eight hours.' Sharpe cleared his throat. 'We've asked him a number of key questions and I'm pleased to say he's answered most of them.'

'Well, he shouldn't have done so without his lawyer present,' Brooke snapped. 'At least that won't be happening now Bruce is on the scene.'

I glared at her and she pressed her lips together.

'He's still at the station?' I felt a bit lightheaded, wondering what was coming.

The detective nodded and took a breath, seeming to brace himself. 'As part of the investigation, we asked Owen, when he arrived at the station, if he'd be willing to give a voluntary DNA sample to assist us and he agreed. We are also checking a hair sample he gave but results will take a little longer for that to come back.'

'What?' Brooke stood up, outraged. 'I think that was way out of order, if I might say so, and—'

'It's standard practice where we deem it necessary, Mrs Painter. We were well within our rights to ask. Your son could have refused but he did not.'

Brooke sat down again, looking deflated. 'But then he'd look like he had something to hide, wouldn't he? He can't win.'

'Brooke, please. It might be a good time for you to make the tea because I want to hear what they're here to say without any further interruptions.'

She ignored me and looked down, her face crumpling. Mercifully, she fell silent.

'Because of the severity of the attack, we were able to get his DNA sample fast-tracked and when we compared it to samples found on Michelle…' I felt myself fading out, preparing for him to say it was a match. If Owen had to go to prison, Zachary would be utterly devastated, he'd never recover. 'There was no match with that sample.'

'Oh, thank God.' Brooke blew out air and my shoulders dropped.

Thank you, God. I whispered my own silent prayer. Now they could focus on finding Michelle's real attacker.

'However,' Lewis continued, looking straight at me. 'Your husband's DNA *did* match another historical sample on our system.'

'What?' I said faintly. It didn't make sense.

'The Forensic Information Database keeps all biometric information, such as DNA evidence, gathered at the scenes of crimes, including unidentified ones. Any new DNA sample is automatically checked against these and in this case, there is an unexpected match for Owen's DNA.'

Were they saying Owen had committed a crime in the past? Previous news stories I'd read whirred though my mind: people arrested for historical crimes like murder and rape that had happened when they were younger and that their families knew nothing about…

'Should you be divulging Owen's personal data to Esme like this when they've separated?' Brooke bristled and I couldn't help but marvel at her instant maternal defence mechanism before she even knew what Owen was accused of doing.

Creeping cold fingers worked their way up my spine. I didn't think I wanted to know. Whatever my feelings about Owen, he was Zachary's father, and my son would have to live with any fallout for the rest of his life. It took all my resolve not to run out of the room.

There was something about the detectives' expressions that chilled me. A tendril of fear wound its way around my throat and pulled tight. The odd look on their faces, the way they kept shifting in their seats… it all pointed to the fact that this was going to be big.

Even Brooke fell quiet and knotted her fingers together as if she was bracing herself.

Sharpe continued, looking at me. 'Eighteen months ago, your son was involved in a car accident, a hit and run.'

I nodded, unable to speak. Why would they bring that up now?

'Evidence-wise there was a handkerchief found close to the scene with Zachary's blood on it. There was also fresh blood from another source on the handkerchief, believed to be the driver's. The DNA from that piece of evidence was logged onto the database. The driver of the vehicle that hit your son was never found.'

They all stared at me, even Brooke.

'Ms Fox, I'm sorry to have to tell you today that Owen Painter's DNA is a match for that sample.'

'What on earth are you saying?' I heard Brooke demand.

Lewis answered. 'Mr Painter knocked his own son down and then he left the scene of the accident.'

I gripped the seat cushion. I felt like I was wading through thick fog, looking for clues to make sense of his words.

'Perhaps Zachary had his father's handkerchief on him when he was knocked over.' Brooke's voice sounded strained and high. She stood up, then sat down again. 'Perhaps it was—'

'Are you trying to say that… Owen was *there*, when Zach was knocked over by the car?' I said, still unable to put the pieces together. He'd been driving back from a course in Newcastle that day.

'Owen *was* the driver who knocked down your son,' Lewis said regretfully.

Old images hit me in a rush. Owen's injured hand the day of the accident. The fact that following the accident, he'd instantly stopped driving and insisted on getting rid of the family car, reducing his working hours so he could care for Zachary. His all-consuming guilt for supposedly not being there to protect his son… but no! It was still impossible – wasn't it?

Brooke was in full swing now, pacing around the room. 'This is outrageous. Completely ridiculous! There has to be some mistake…'

Sharpe cleared his throat. 'There's no mistake, Mrs Painter. Your son has made a full confession.'

A small noise escaped my throat. This... this was the stuff of nightmares. My mind was struggling to cope with it, trying desperately to find a logical reason why it couldn't possibly be true. It was a fruitless exercise because deep down, I know there was no mistake. It was real. Everything fitted and I'd chosen to ignore it. If I'd seen these clues play out in someone else's life, my journalist's nose for a story would have kicked in. I'd have started asking questions. But I'd been so blinded by my efforts to protect Zachary from any more trauma that I'd failed him in the worst way possible.

Owen was a liar. He'd nearly killed our boy. And the worst of it all was that he'd consistently covered it up. He'd accused me of being a bad mother. He'd let me think, all this time, that there was a person, a monster out there, walking around, living their life, getting away with what they did to our son. And all that time that person was *him*.

My beloved Zachary, constantly left in his father's sole care... *with my blessing.*

And then Michelle's injured face and broken body flashed into my mind and another thing occurred to me.

What else might Owen be capable of?

CHAPTER FORTY-SIX

When the detectives left, Zachary ran downstairs.

'What did they say?' he demanded, jumping on the sofa. 'When's Dad coming home?'

'They had some questions for me and Grandma,' I said weakly.

'Questions, questions, questions!' Zachary screeched, thumping the seat cushion in time with each word. 'I've got a question: where's my dad?'

'We'll have the answer for you very soon, Zachary,' Brooke said smoothly, and handed him the TV remote control. 'Put something on to watch and I'll bring you in a dish of fruit and ice cream, how's that?'

'Ice cream… yum! Fruit… yuk!' Zachary said cheekily, pointing the remote at the television.

In the kitchen, Brooke seemed unexpectedly concerned about me.

'Eric and Bruce will deal with Owen's case. I'll stop here at the house to support you and look after Zachary. You must rest, Esme, and gather your strength. It's a shock but we'll get through this terrible mess together, as a family. They can't pin such a terrible thing on Owen.'

'Owen has confessed,' I pointed out quietly. 'It's more than just a mess that can be neatly swept away.'

Brooke made a noise of disbelief. 'Owen is clearly under enormous pressure in that police station. He'll be tired and confused. I wouldn't put it past them to put the words into his mouth.' She laid a hand on my back as she passed me en route to the fridge freezer. 'Owen thinks the world of Zachary, you know that. He'd never do anything to hurt his own son. The very thought of it is laughable.'

The faintest glow of hope stirred within me. I wanted to believe her, I did. It was what I'd always told myself about Owen: he'd never do this, he'd never do that. *He'd never hurt Michelle.*

Was I deluding myself, always looking for the good in Owen… just like Simone had done for years with her husband? I shake my head, trying to break my thought pattern. Owen was not Grant Fischer. He was not abusive. He'd never hurt me or Zachary. He wouldn't.

And yet… there seemed to be rock-solid evidence that he *had*. He'd physically hurt Zachary very badly.

I couldn't stop my instincts now. I wanted to know the whole truth, no matter how awful. I could help and support my son through anything, but I had to satisfy myself it was the truth.

The day of the accident, the weather had been awful, most of the country lashed by torrential rain and howling storms. When the bad weather hit, Owen was in the middle of a pre-booked two-day fitness expo up in Newcastle. He'd stayed the night at his parents' house and, on the second day, was due to be back home about eight that evening.

The storm had continued and a short time after leaving Newcastle, a fallen tree had narrowly missed flattening the car, mercifully just grazing the bumper. Owen had cut his hand quite badly, helping another driver pull it out of the road. That's what he'd told me.

There had been a mix-up at school with a supply teacher and the children were inadvertently dismissed from their after-school club ten minutes earlier than usual. Most of them hung around and waited for their lift, but Zachary knew I'd be walking to pick him up and so, keen to get home and watch his favourite programme, even though he knew not to walk home alone, he slipped past the teacher, took a shortcut through the houses surrounding the school, and emerged on a quiet road he knew I'd be passing.

I breathed in and nothing happened... I couldn't get enough air in. My lungs started burning as a forgotten memory played out before me...

*

I'm three streets away from the school and, as I draw closer to the road, I hear sirens approaching. Not just one but two or three. Deafening. Then emergency vehicles whizz by me, one after the other, and I get this awful dark feeling that starts to rise up from my solar plexus.

I turn into the road as the vehicles all grind to a halt in front of me and before they have a chance to cordon off the area, I spot a small shape in the road. Despite the cold weather, I grow suddenly hot, as if a fever is rising up from the depths of my insides.

It's the lunchbox that catches my eye.

Several metres away from him. I see the logo on the front. Owen had ordered it on Amazon. It had taken a couple of weeks for it to get here because it came from China.

A police officer approaches me and says something about me moving back.

I sink to my knees in the road and start shaking...

*

'Esme? Can you hear me?' Brooke tugged my arm gently, looking alarmed. 'Are you alright? You've gone a funny colour.'

'I'm fine, I just... oh God, I can't stand it. I remember everything about that day, the accident...'

I went through it again, silently in my mind. How could Owen do that to his own son, to our boy? How could he be cold enough to act the devastated father so convincingly, for all this time?

'Come on. Let's get you upstairs for a lie down,' she said, slipping her arm around my shoulders. 'You're in shock. It's entirely understandable, the officers just blurting out a terrible accusation like that. We should consider making a complaint to the police commissioner!'

I allowed her to steer me to the bottom of the stairs. It wasn't an accusation. Owen had confessed to being the hit-and-run driver. He'd maimed his own son. Even Brooke and Eric couldn't smooth that over with their powerful contacts.

Brooke followed me up the stairs to my bedroom. I found myself wondering which scenario was worse: if Owen's DNA had matched Michelle's attacker or his admission of ploughing into our son and driving off like the most callous stranger imaginable.

After the accident, I became severely anxious, terrified of any of us stepping outside the house. Zachary wasn't even mobile at that point and the fear was completely irrational. I obsessed about all the things that could go wrong, things that could hurt him: intruders, cars driving into the house when we were watching television, a plane crashing into the house while we slept.

Owen sat with me for hours, holding my hand when one of my panic attacks struck yet again. He called the doctor out to the house and they spoke in hushed voices downstairs. The GP prescribed various medications to treat the anxiety disorder he diagnosed.

'It's just for a short time until you stabilise,' Owen told me afterwards. 'I know you're blaming yourself because you were late picking Zachary up but I want you to stop being scared. We can and will move on from this.'

I'd stayed on the medication for eight months, and became not exactly addicted, but certainly reliant. Again, Owen came to the rescue and got me to agree to slowly wean myself off them.

Then, when I started to feel a little more in control, Owen insisted on taking over Zachary's care almost exclusively. He took unpaid leave from work – being self-employed helped with this – and he gave me the time and space to get fully well again before drastically reducing his hours so he could be at home more.

He'd struggled terribly with his own feelings of guilt and regret. Or had seemed to. 'If I hadn't been at the fitness expo, I'd have been there to pick him up,' Owen had repeated continuously. 'All I can do is make sure he gets better and, if necessary, I'll give up everything so I can do that.'

When I felt fully recovered and I knew Zachary was safe in his father's care, my obsession with our son's safety seemed to switch to building the business. My twisted logic told me that if I could use my journalistic experience to build a successful podcast company, then Zachary need never want for anything again. I could afford the best treatment for his injuries, different therapies not available on the NHS.

Looking back, I could see I focused on the business to the exclusion of almost everything else. Owen, on the other hand, seemed perfectly happy to selflessly devote himself to Zachary. And now I knew why.

It was less a case of Owen putting all his efforts into caring for Zachary and more a case of keeping up appearances and possibly trying to quell the horror of his own guilt. All the time I thought he was being an exemplary dad, he was lying, pretending, hiding the truth and playing me like a violin. Now it was painfully clear that Owen wasn't being a model father at all, he was simply manipulating the both of us.

I'd felt so grateful to him at the time. I'd admired him putting our son's welfare and recuperation before anything else. That was before he started trying to dictate how I should be spending *my* time, too. Before his sole aim seemed to switch to making me feel guilty, an inadequate mother.

Now all I could ask myself was: *who exactly is this man I married?*

We all do it, don't we? We're all guilty of looking at others, questioning how they could have been so gullible… the British public openly wondered how someone like Simone Fischer could have just let her husband treat her like dirt for so long and stay in the marriage. Then the mirror flips and we recognise how we've somehow managed to do something quite similar in our own lives. We've managed to turn a blind eye because some part of us can't handle the truth.

I sat down on the edge of the bed.

'You're not to worry about a thing, do you hear me?' Brooke says briskly.

'But what about Simone?' I whispered. 'I have to keep my visit tomorrow. The whole podcast project depends on it.'

Brooke pressed her lips together. I could see her biting back her disapproval of my involvement with Simone.

'Do you think you'll be in a fit state to drive?' She frowned. 'You're obviously shocked. Perhaps you could rearrange?'

'That's impossible.' I croaked. 'But Zachary—'

She said, 'Zachary's not a problem. I'll take him to school and sort him out, whatever you decide to do.'

'I should be back by mid-afternoon at the latest.'

'I honestly think you're making a mistake, you know. That… that *woman*… is a cold-blooded killer. Is that really the sort of person you want to be spending time with?'

I sighed. 'I do know all that, Brooke.'

'Well then, you should think on. Do you really want more problems on your plate? I'd have thought you'd got plenty to deal with right now.'

'Simone's problems are hardly my own.'

'Have you heard of the term *guilty by association*? Evil rubs off. You'd do well to remember that.' She bustled out of the room, so confident of her own opinion, so dismissive of mine.

Owen had always said he was his mum's double in both looks and nature. Now that had new meaning.

At last, the mist had cleared and I could see everything so clearly. Without overthinking it I took one of my old prescribed sedatives before bed. I needed a good night's sleep and it was the only way to get it.

There was no more room for denial. I knew what I needed to do.

CHAPTER FORTY-SEVEN

The next morning I set off early. When I got out to the car, a short, plump man dressed in jeans and an anorak called out from the pavement.

'Esme! Did you get my email? I wondered if we could have a chat?'

He was a few years older and about twenty pounds heavier than before he moved out of the area but I instantly recognised Colin Wade.

'Not interested, Colin,' I said curtly, pushing my belongings into the boot and walking around to the driver's side.

'That may be so but there's a lot of interest in you at the moment. Is there any news on your sister's attacker?' I ignored him and opened the car door but he was undeterred. He raised his voice and leaned over the fence. 'Is it true your husband is in police custody?'

I felt a cold sweat at the bottom of my back. I slammed the door shut and jammed the car into reverse. Wade rapped on the window as I paused to check the road at the bottom of the driveway.

'Why are you trying to free Simone Fischer, a convicted murderer?' he shouted, louder than ever.

With a squeal of tyres and a pounding heart, I hit the accelerator and sped away.

It took me a good while to calm down but I managed it in the end. Wade couldn't force me to speak to him, and if he made a nuisance of himself I'd have a word with the detectives, see if they could help.

First stop was Melton Mowbray to meet with Peter Harvey.

I managed to find a spot on a side street with an hour's free parking. I was ten minutes early for our agreed appointment but when I walked into a nearly empty Costa Coffee, I immediately saw Peter sitting scrolling through his phone at a table near the rear of the café. He'd already got a coffee so I stopped off at the counter and got myself a small latte.

He looked up and scowled as I approached.

'Morning.' I placed my coffee down on the table before sitting down and slipping off my jacket. 'Thanks for meeting with me.'

'I hope this won't take long,' he said airily. 'I'm a busy man. Looking after Simone's affairs is a full-time job, especially as she's now asked me to work on various plans for the future.'

He watched me carefully, gauging my reaction, willing me to ask him to elaborate. But I'd resolved not to pander to his self-importance.

'It's just a quick chat, Peter.' I took a sip of my coffee. 'Particularly if we can be candid with each other.'

He laughed and put down his phone. 'Be as candid as you like. As the brother of Simone Fischer, I'm not sure anything *could* shock me anymore. That's why I'm the best person to write the book.'

'The book?' I played dumb.

He nodded, clearly delighted he'd finally brought the conversation round to what he wanted to discuss.

'I'm putting together a biography about Simone. About what really happened. A bit like your podcast, I suppose, but for people who'd rather read about it than listen. Simone has agreed, and between you and me, I think I'll probably have a bestseller on my hands. There are already publishers interested, although I've been sworn to secrecy.'

His eyes were bright and fixed to mine and I took great pains to keep my face impassive. I wouldn't get drawn in to this, despite Peter's best efforts to provoke a reaction.

I nodded. 'Sounds interesting. But I wonder if we can go back to what I wanted to see you about today.'

'Ha! How did I know it wasn't just the cosy, informal chat you tried to sell me?'

'I'll get to the point. Something doesn't quite sit right with me about the whole Simone-Grant situation.'

His smile faded. 'What do you mean by that?'

'Something just feels a bit *off* about everything I'm being told.'

'Go on.'

'It's vague and doesn't mean anything in itself, but I just get a strange feeling about the whole scenario.'

'Oh, spare me, please.' Peter dismissed me with a flip of his hand. 'What you mean is, the story isn't sensationalist enough for you. How disappointing and woefully predictable. I told Simone from the beginning that you'd just be the same as all the others, that you'd—'

'I don't mean that at all. But what I can't quite figure out is why you're always talking about how close you and Simone are, how awful it was for you knowing she was trapped in a loveless and abusive marriage, how you loved being an uncle to Andrew at the time and yet… Simone never mentions you as having been part of her life. And you're not in touch with Andrew any more, as far as I can gather.'

'That's not my doing. I took him in, you know. Saved him from going into care.'

I nodded. 'Have you tried to involve him with campaigning for his mother's release?'

Peter's mouth tightened. 'He wants nothing to do with it all. Totally useless. He still visits his mother occasionally but that's about it. He has no interest in getting involved in the FSF group even though it's Simone's best chance of getting out of that hell-hole.' He reached for his drink. 'Happy to wash his hands of the past and help strangers rather than his own mother.'

'Perhaps he just finds the memories too painful to bear,' I suggested. 'Grant was his father and—'

'That's just it, though. He claims to not have any memory of that afternoon. Nothing. So there can't be any pain involved,' Peter huffed. 'So much easier to go off and live your own life though, isn't it? Harder for me, to stick around and support my sister. Handle all the publicity, all the media interest on my own.'

His face shone.

'What does Andrew do?' I asked lightly, hoping he didn't close down the conversation. 'For a job, I mean.'

'Works with people with "complex needs" apparently,' Peter said scathingly. 'An all-round do-gooder. You know the type, aren't interested in their own family but they'll help any hopeless cause.'

I focused on my coffee for a few moments. I felt a desperate need to speak to Andrew, but that would be difficult if he'd made up his mind to try and live a life separated from the family's past.

'I sent him a message asking if he'd like to contribute to the book and he wouldn't even consider it. Selfish to the core, that's my nephew.'

I decided to go for the jugular.

'Do you think Simone is afraid of you, Peter?'

He laughed. 'That's not even worth a reply.'

'Part of me wonders if she's trying to protect you in some way.'

A shadow passed over his face and his brows knitted together as he leaned forwards. 'You're making up your own stories and that's not allowed, remember? I think you're trying to say I'm hiding something and I don't appreciate that. I don't appreciate it at all.'

His words didn't really amount to anything. His appearance though, was another matter. Within seconds his whole physicality had changed. He bristled, his mouth flattening into a sneer. His eyes seemed darker in colour and I could see the tendons pulling in his neck. Was he trying to hide something? I didn't really know yet, but one thing was certain; I'd hit a nerve.

'I told Simone she should have nothing to do with you,' he continued, his voice quietly menacing. 'You journalist types are all the same. If there's no story, you'll make one up. You're looking for something to make your meaningless little podcast sensationalist, that much is obvious. Be honest with me, I can take it.'

A flare of annoyance rose in my chest. I felt like he was playing games with me. Before I could bite my tongue, I said exactly what was on my mind.

'Maybe it's not Simone at all,' I said, keeping my voice level. 'Maybe it's *you* I don't trust, Peter. I'm going to keep going until I find out if my instincts are right. That there's something more that's not being said. Something important that's been carefully buried and concealed about this case.'

His expression didn't falter. If I was expecting him to explode and blab something telling out in temper, then I was to be sorely disappointed. But he did shock me with what he said next.

'I knew from the start you weren't the type to back off. Unless something really bad happened. And now I suppose it has. To your sister.'

He was trying his best to rile me and he'd succeeded. But it was worse than that. With those few words, something had clicked in my head and now I couldn't stop staring at him. I'd say Peter was about five foot nine. He had dark brown hair which was quite obviously dyed, and he was going thin on top. I ran through Zachary's description of the man he saw outside the school with Michelle.

He was tall with brown hair.

Peter couldn't really be described as tall for a man but to a nine-year old child… well, wouldn't any adult look tall?

'Are you actually listening to a word I'm saying?' Peter frowned. 'Do you realise the implications of getting Simone's hopes up? How unlikely it is she'll get an early release?'

'Have you ever met Michelle, my sister?' I said, fixing my eyes to his face so I didn't miss his reaction.

He looked nonplussed for a moment. Hesitated. 'Met her?'

'Yes. Have you ever spoken to her in real life?'

He frowned for a moment as if he were trying to recall something. Then he said, 'She's in hospital, isn't she?'

I felt dizzy, even though I was sitting down. 'I asked first. Have you ever met Michelle? It's a simple enough question.'

'No! I haven't met her. I'm sure of it.'

He looked away from me but I kept my eyes on him.

'You seem... uncomfortable, Peter.'

'It just seems a strange thing to ask me.' He swept a hand over the table to clear some scattered grains of sugar.

Every fibre in my body told me he was hiding something.

I recoiled at being in the company of this man any longer. I didn't like him. I prided myself in having the instinct to weigh people up within a minute or two; it had come in very handy in my career over the years. But I couldn't discern whether Peter Harvey was outright lying to me or not.

'Can I ask you how you found out about my sister being in hospital?' I said, reaching for my jacket and handbag.

'What?' He watched me collect my things together. 'Is that it then? I've disrupted my plans to meet with you and you're taking off now?'

'How did you find out Michelle was in hospital?'

'The Facebook page, of course!' he snapped. 'How the hell do you *think* I found out?'

*

Back in my car I sat staring at my phone – specifically, at the Facebook page I'd insisted Peter showed me before I left. He'd watched me, interested and amused as I took in an involuntary gasp of air, stood up and rushed out of the café.

I clamped my hand to my mouth when I looked at the page's main cover photograph again: a shot of the ICU unit at the QMC.

The pinned photo on the page was the same picture Michelle used on her own Facebook profile page. Just a head-and-shoulders shot I took of her at the coast, the same one I showed around the supermarket.

The page name was 'Pray for Michelle Fox'. The tagline: *A page created by Michelle's family and friends to share her progress. Your support is much appreciated.*

My heart felt like it might explode as I scrolled down to the one post, which was a link to the local newspaper report about an unnamed woman who was found badly beaten in Wollaton Park.

That was it. Nothing else. There was a total of twenty-two likes on the post but clicking on a few of the profiles, they looked like the kind of people who tended to like and support charity-type pages.

I could never have imagined the awful feeling wracking through my body right then. Someone had created this page and it felt a slap in the face, both for me and for Michelle.

I started shivering and couldn't stop. The nurse who mistakenly thought I'd visited Michelle twice in one day. Had the person who created this page been in, stood at her bedside, held her hand… it felt such a violation and made me sick to my stomach.

I clicked on 'Report this page' and then stopped. The police needed to know about this before I got it closed down.

I closed Facebook and opened my call list. When the automated voice at the police station answered, I entered the extension number of DI Sharpe. It went straight to his answerphone.

'It's Esme Fox here. I need to speak to you urgently. There's a Facebook page set up in my sister's name. Someone's done this and… I think I might know who.' I take a breath, aware my message will sound garbled when he listens to it. 'Look, I'm on my way down to Bronzefield prison to speak to Simone Fischer. I wish I could cancel my visit but I can't. I'll try you again when I'm on my way home.'

And then I texted Justine.

CHAPTER FORTY-EIGHT

THE FISCHER FILES

EPISODE FIVE: TOO MUCH TO BEAR

I'm speaking to you from outside HMP Bronzefield women's prison in Ashford, Middlesex. Today I'll be continuing my conversation with Simone about the day her husband, Grant Austin Fischer, died.

Simone is speaking exclusively to us and giving the most personal of insights. Only *The Fischer Files* has access to the truth of the case.

This is a Speaking Fox podcast and *I…* am Esme Fox.

*

Esme: Simone, before we go back to the day Grant died, I want to ask you a bit about your relationship with your brother, Peter, if that's OK.

Simone: Oh! That's… fine. Go ahead.

Esme: How much did you see of Peter, during your marriage?

Simone: How often, you mean?

Esme: Yes. I know Grant was keen to isolate you from your family, specifically your mother, initially. But I've spoken to Peter recently and he strikes me as a determined individual. Quite savvy. I wondered if you kept in touch, if he suspected all was not well in your relationship.

Simone: We didn't see much of him. The fact he was Andrew's only uncle meant nothing to Grant. He exerted full control over me and my son.

Esme: It's just that Peter is such a big part of your life now, I find it hard to believe that he so willingly backed off, didn't question why you were so insular.

Simone: That's because you have no comprehension what it was like.

Esme: I hope I haven't offended you, Simone. I'm just trying to understand and—

Simone: I'm trying to help you to understand. But I don't want Peter involved in this process. He doesn't agree with me doing it and I think it's best if you don't speak to him again. Likewise, I want my son to be afforded the privacy he has chosen. Peter is furious Andrew will have nothing to do with the circus around the case but I completely understand his choice.

Esme: I see. I apologise again if I've annoyed you.

Simone: I'm not annoyed. It's just… I think you should leave Peter out of this, OK?

Esme: OK.

*

Esme: Simone, last time we spoke, you told us about the humiliation and abusive treatment Grant Fischer meted out to you on November 13th, 2009. You described how he degraded you in a way no decent person would do. Was that the final straw... Did you just snap?

Simone: I did just snap, but it wasn't the degrading treatment that did it. He was in a particularly vicious mood that day. You'll recall I told you last time he came home early that day and was furious his dinner wasn't ready. Then he force-fed me raw pastry from the bin and sat laughing. Pathetic as it makes me sound, I was so low, at that point, felt so worthless, I'd have probably just cleaned myself up and got on with making his meal. But then he said something that made me go very quiet inside. Made me sit up and listen.

Esme: Can you share that with us?

Simone: He said, 'I bet you still get upset when you think about your mum's wedding and engagement rings, don't you? And your gran's ruby brooch, too.' See, we'd had a break-in at the house a couple of months after Mum died. They took a few things including her jewellery. Grant had dealt with the police but they weren't really that interested. At the time, he convinced me I must have left the back door open when I took Andrew to school, although I was almost certain I'd locked it. I spent months afterwards blaming myself, hopelessly wishing I could turn the clock back and ensure I'd secured it.

Esme: It must've been upsetting to lose your mum's jewellery.

Simone: I can't tell you how gutted I was. Especially after we'd drifted apart before she died. It was all I really had left of her. And my gran's ruby brooch had been in the family for a few generations. It was the way he said it, you know? Sort of mocking, as if he were amusing himself by talking about it.

Esme: How did you react?

Simone: As I said, I felt strange, as if he'd opened up something inside me just by mentioning the jewellery in that mocking tone he was so fond of. I said, 'Yes, I do still get upset, Grant. I'll always be upset and I'll always blame myself.'

He said, 'You really shouldn't blame yourself, you know. It wasn't your fault.' Like a fool, I actually thought for a moment he was consoling me.

But again, something about the way he said it made my throat turn dry. Then he said, 'You see, the jewellery wasn't taken in the break-in. That was just kids. They took a few electrical items and some cash I'd left on the mantelpiece. But it was just too good a chance to miss.'

I remember looking at him, tipping my head this way and that, trying to understand what he was saying and then he just told me. He said, 'I took the jewellery and sold it. Blamed it on the burglars. I got nearly a grand for it all, not a bad sum back then.'

He waited for my reaction and all I could do was whisper, 'You sold it?'

He laughed. 'I took a woman at work out, bought us a hotel room on it. Remember Liz Wood, that shapely little redhead? God, we had a good night on your mother's jewellery.'

Esme: That must've broken your heart.

Simone: It did break my heart, but it also opened my eyes. It was like someone had shone a spotlight on him, sitting there opposite me, and I could see him for everything he was. A cheat, a liar, an abuser. And all I could think was, *I can't raise Andrew here, with him. I can't do this anymore. I just can't.* I told him I was leaving him, that I'd go to the police and tell them how he treated me. All the time I talked, he laughed. He threw his head back and laughed so hard. He said nobody would believe a thing I said, that the whole neighbourhood knew I was unstable. He said he would kick me out instead and see to it I'd never see my son again.

Esme: And that's what did it… You just snapped?
   Simone?

Simone: Sorry, I was back there for a moment. Yes, I just snapped. He'd been so cruel that day, he'd outdone himself and the thought of Andrew being in his sole care…

Esme: What happened?

Simone: It felt like… like the eggshell surrounding me had cracked and I saw, for the first time, the extent of his cruelty, his abusive nature, his complete *vileness*. Before I knew it, I was across the other side of the kitchen and I saw his face drop. For a moment he stopped laughing. I saw his mouth move but I couldn't hear anything for the rushing sound in my head. I looked down at my hand and I was holding a knife from the block. A really sharp kitchen knife.

And then he was smiling again, his mouth stretched wide. He held out his hand for the knife and I just rushed forward and plunged it at his head. He turned as I went for him and it entered the soft bit behind his ear and the start of his neck.

Esme: There's no rush, Simone. In your own time, whatever you can remember.

Simone: I remember the blood. I still dream about it. Lots of blood spurting everywhere. My hand just kept going with the knife like it had a life of its own… in, out, in, out. I had to make sure, you see, make sure he couldn't get up, because he would have killed me. He'd have killed me.

When I looked down, he was slumped over the kitchen table, his eyes still open, a horrible gurgling noise in his throat.

Esme: When you realised you'd killed him, what did you do? Were you in shock? Did you panic?

Simone: I remember exactly what I did. I pulled some cloths out of the cupboard under the sink and I started cleaning up the mess.

END OF EXTRACT

CHAPTER FORTY-NINE

ESME

As always, on the journey home, I thought through my conversation with Simone. But it was the part before I started rolling the tape that was on my mind this time. The part about me.

When I'd entered the small room where we talked, I didn't know whether it was her smile, her welcome, her instant compassion when she saw I wasn't myself, but instantly, my eyes began to swim. Simone immediately gave me a clean tissue and reached for my hand.

'Sorry,' I'd said. 'This is unprofessional of me, I—'

'We all have bad days, Esme. I could see you looked a little low as soon as you walked in. How's your sister, is there any progress?'

'Michelle is just the same. Stable, at least but… it's not that. Last night… the police came over to the house and…'

I tried to fight the tears and keep my mouth shut but I'd been holding this stuff in, with nobody to talk to, for too long and I was really struggling.

Simone's voice was calming. She put me at ease. 'Take your time, Esme. Just let the tears come. That's it. I found out a long time ago it's better to let it all go. Scream and rant if you need to. It's OK. All those years with Grant, I did myself a disservice remaining quiet and compliant. It's what he wanted. I just played into his hands and it allowed him to continue.'

We sat quietly for a few moments, Simone stroking the top of my hand and me unable to cease snivelling.

Could I trust her? I felt I could. How open could I be with her? I was veering off the professional path...

Also, I was mindful I only had half an hour with her and I was wasting precious time. But once I opened up I couldn't seem to pull it back.

'You don't have to say a thing, if you don't want to,' she said, waiting.

'It's Owen,' I said quickly. 'I found out... I...' I dragged a big breath in and then just said it. 'He was the driver of the hit and run I told you about. Eighteen months ago, it was him who nearly killed Zachary.'

'What?' She was genuinely shocked, I could see it.

'He confessed to the police when they accidentally found an old DNA match with the hit-and-run driver's blood. All this time, I've blamed myself for being late to collect Zachary. And all this time Owen has looked me in the eye and accused me of falling short as a mother.'

'He's lied to you,' she said faintly. 'He's made *you* feel like the one with a problem.'

I nodded. 'He told me time and time again that any decent mother would be less worried about building the business and more interested in spending every minute with Zachary that day. But the reason I couldn't be there all the time is that I wanted to build a better life for my son.'

'Esme, you don't need to justify yourself to me. I, more than anyone, now understand that everybody has an agenda.'

'I never would have said Owen was a bully or tried to control me... he didn't "fit" my definition of a controlling man. I've always considered myself an independent woman, strong in my own way. Stronger before Zachary's accident, which knocked me sideways. Was it so wrong to have believed Owen was equally devastated when Zachary was injured?'

'There are a thousand ways to control or be controlled.' Simone gave a sad smile. 'We put our faith in our partner, our friend, a close relative. We want to believe they are good and true and so we do. We run with that. Then suddenly we can't see what's around us anymore; we can't spot the signs. We're blind to anything other than what they place right in front of our eyes and tell us is the truth.'

'I did just that! I believed him. I never had an inkling…'

'Afterwards, I used to think, "Why didn't I see what Grant was up to? Why did I let him treat me that way?" But then I realised that all the time I was taking the accountability that belonged to him and then carrying the weight of it on my own back. Mistrusting myself rather than him… every single time.'

It was exactly what I'd been doing since discovering the truth about the accident. Telling myself I *should* have seen through Owen's lies, I *should* have been sharper and smarter and realised what he'd done when, in fact, it was nothing to do with me at all.

All this time I'd shouldered the grief, the anger and the burden of easing a difficult future for my son. Effectively taking on the responsibility, and the blame of what happened, when it was Owen's doing all along.

CHAPTER FIFTY

JUSTINE

Justine came out of her meeting and read the text message from Esme asking for a meeting at the office.

Hi Justine,

Would you be free for half an hour this afternoon? I can come to the office if Mo's out? I need to speak to you alone.

Did Esme know? Was she planning to confront her?

With heat rising from her solar plexus, she tapped out a hasty reply that belied the squirming sensation in the pit of her stomach.

Sure. I'm in the office all afternoon.

This day was always going to come, she'd known that. But she'd never considered she wouldn't be the one to tell all in her own time, when she felt completely ready and had her story straight.

Now, it looked as if the unthinkable had happened. Esme had already realised exactly what was happening.

CHAPTER FIFTY-ONE

ESME

When I left the prison, I didn't mention to Simone what I planned to do. I didn't want her to feel anxious or to try and dissuade me.

The unauthorised Facebook page loomed large in my mind and I felt I had to do *something*. It was no good speaking to Simone about the matter because, if she was as nervous of Peter as I believed to be the case, I probably wouldn't get anywhere. Rather than sit around waiting for the police to call me back, I could make myself useful by acting on my gut feeling.

I'd telephoned The Spindles care home after leaving Melton Mowbray when I was on my way down to Bronzefield Prison. Andrew Fischer had already told me during our phone conversation that he lived on-site, so I knew there was a fair chance he might be in. When I explained I needed to speak to him as a matter of urgency, that Andrew knew me, the carer who answered the phone confirmed he was working.

From the A606, I followed signs for the village of Nether Broughton. I made a right turn on to Chapel Lane and turned again into a leafy driveway, parking the car outside The Spindles, which turned out to be a large detached Victorian house in its own substantial gardens.

I buzzed at the door and heard a click admitting me. In the large foyer with its parquet flooring and polished mahogany banister rail, a middle-aged lady with permed red hair and wearing a navy tabard walked towards me, wiping her hands on a cloth.

'I'm here to see Andrew Fischer if possible,' I said, silently praying she wouldn't present me with a reason I couldn't speak to him. 'I rang ahead.'

'He's in the main lounge, love. That door there.'

I walked into a large room filled with comfy seats and mismatched hardbacked chairs. The inside of the place was shabby but clean and ordered. The flatscreen television on the wall was on but the volume was low and I doubted whether any of the handful of young people in there who were staring at their phones could actually hear the daytime talk show.

I spotted Andrew right away. He was the only carer in the lounge. Tall with light-brown hair and slow, considered movements. He wore black trousers, trainers and a grey tabard top with short sleeves.

He was over in the corner helping a young woman out of a wheelchair and into a seat. His movements were careful, his touch light. He said something to her and she nodded, gave him a weak smile.

Andrew straightened up, turned and spotted me. He strode over, friendly and bright. 'Can I help you?'

'I'm sorry to just drop in on you, Andrew, but I'm Esme Fox. We spoke yesterday.'

He took a step back, surprised. 'Oh wow, and now you're here! Full marks for the detective work finding this place. We're somewhat tucked away.'

'You told me you worked at a place called The Spindles and… well, it wasn't too difficult…'

Andrew gave a small smile but I felt he was a little unnerved. I represented his mother's traumatic past. *His* past, too, and here I was, invading his 'normal' life. 'Now I know why you're a successful investigative journalist,' he said.

'I'm taking a chance, but there's something I need to ask you, something important. That's why I've come here. Is there somewhere quiet we could chat, just for five minutes?'

'Sure. We can sit in the staff room; everyone's had their break now so it should be quiet in there.'

He led me out of the lounge and down a short, carpeted hallway into a small, functional room that was two-thirds comfy seating and one third kitchenette. 'Coffee?' He asked, reaching into an overhead cupboard for mugs.

'Thanks. Milk, no sugar,' I said, the knot in my stomach growing by the second. Andrew seemed to think it was a nice thing I'd popped by, when in fact I was probably about to annoy him.

He brought the coffees over and sat across from me at the small, Formica-topped table. 'So. To what do I owe this pleasure? Not very often anyone visits me full stop, never mind here at work.'

I picked up my mug and sipped the strong, bitter drink.

'I want to apologise in advance, Andrew. There's something I'd like to ask you and it's rather awkward—'

'Don't worry about it. Just shoot. I'll help if I can.'

So I told him about the 'Pray for Michelle Fox' Facebook page. 'I've established the photographs on it are publicly available, so there's no question of anything being hacked into or stolen as such. It's just… well, frankly weird, and it feels really wrong. Invasive. That someone would be interested enough to go to the bother of doing this, you know?'

'God, yes, I do know. Even now when I see articles about my mother quoting an "anonymous source" which is so lazy, basically giving them a licence to more or less make lies up. And saying stuff about my dad who, whatever he did, isn't here to defend himself. It feels exactly that. *Invasive.*'

I nodded. He got it.

'The thing is… I didn't know anything about the page until your uncle told me about it.'

'Peter knew about it before you did?'

'Yes. He'd made reference to my sister being in hospital and it just struck me he seemed to know details that he must have gone to the trouble of finding. But it turns out he'd seen the Facebook page.'

'I didn't even know he had a Facebook account.' Andrew frowned.

'It got me thinking that… well, I wondered, if someone with an axe to grind was behind the page.'

Andrew seemed unfazed. He thought for a moment, scratched at his pale, freckled forearms and said, 'Why, though? Why would someone want to do that?'

'Well, here goes. This is the awkward bit,' I began.

Andrew put down his coffee and looked at me. He had his mother's eyes and I thought, from the photographs I'd seen of Grant Fischer, I could sense something of his father around his nose and mouth. 'Go ahead,' he said.

'Do you think… is there a chance that Peter might've created that page himself?'

I held my breath. Even if he didn't get on with Peter, he was his own flesh and blood.

I braced myself for a curt reply, but he didn't say anything. I'd caught him by surprise, I could tell.

I continued in the silence. 'Peter is annoyed with me, I think. He doesn't trust me, doesn't trust the podcast about your mum. You told me about his plans to write a book about Simone, maybe he wants to scare me off.'

Andrew raised an eyebrow. 'I wouldn't take that personally. It's true, I think, he wants her all to himself, has done since she got sent down. Peter's got this weird control thing going on with everything around Mum. Like the FSF group and stuff, he has to be the main contact. I've told Mum to remove his authority to speak on her behalf, but she says it's his way of dealing with what happened.'

'So… do you? Do you think Peter would stoop so low as to pull a stunt like this to unnerve me?'

Something wasn't right, and I had to vocalise it to Andrew, someone who knew Peter well. Simone appeared outwardly confident and acted as though she tolerated Peter. But my journalist's instinct kicked off every time I spoke to him. It was as if he wore a mask of respectability, a believable one. But every now and then it slipped, just a fraction, and the reality of what might lie behind it was terrifying.

Andrew paused for a moment before answering, as if he were thinking about what I'd just said, and I wondered if he'd ask me to leave. Then he said, 'As far as I know, he wouldn't have the skills to do it himself, but he has a vast array of contacts. So the answer is yes. I think it's exactly the kind of thing that Peter would be capable of.'

I breathed out. Someone else agreed with me that Peter was capable of doing something as awful. 'Thank you,' I said. 'I feel vindicated.'

'I didn't say he had done it, but I certainly believe it's possible. I'll do anything I can to help you find out if he is up to anything. You only have to give me the word.'

'Thank you,' I said and allowed myself to breathe out fully.

In a world where everyone seemed to be against me, it felt like I had an ally at last.

CHAPTER FIFTY-TWO

JUSTINE

An hour later, Justine had composed herself, and was all smiles when Esme arrived at the office.

'Let's go into the meeting room,' Esme said, her expression grim. 'This is... sensitive.'

Toby appeared from the back room. 'Esme, I wondered if... would it be possible to speak to you before you, before —'

'Later, Toby,' Justine said irritably. 'Esme isn't staying long.' Her heart felt like a battering ram on the inside of her chest. The last thing she needed was Toby prolonging the agony of what might well prove to be an unpleasant confrontation.

Distractedly, Esme turned to address Toby, but fortunately he'd already scuttled off again.

In the meeting room, the women sat opposite each other.

'I don't know where to start,' Esme said, stony-faced.

Justine curled her toes tightly inside her boots. 'I'm listening,' she said. She was ready.

'Before visiting Simone today I met with her brother, Peter, briefly. He seemed to know all about Michelle being in hospital and so I confronted him. Asked him how he'd found out my personal family business. He told me about a Facebook page that's been set up,' Esme said, her face darkening. 'It's called "Pray for Michelle Fox", and it's got her photo on there, a picture of the

Intensive Care Unit at QMC and also a link to an online news report about the attack.'

'Did Peter set up the page?' Justine said, her heart rate slowing marginally.

'He says not but I don't think I believe him. He said he thought I already knew about the page, that I'd created it. I don't trust him as far as I could throw him, frankly, and… I've spoken to Andrew Fischer, Simone's son, and he says his uncle is definitely capable of pulling a stunt like that.'

'You've managed to speak to Simone's son?' Justine gave a low whistle. 'That's impressive. I know he's a very private person.'

Justine's breathing settled a little. Esme's visit to the office wasn't about what she'd feared after all. She reached for her laptop and opened up Facebook. She typed in the name of the page and it came up immediately, Michelle's image filling the screen. Justine scrolled and tapped for a few moments. 'There's nothing on there that's not already in the public domain,' she said. 'But I can see why you're creeped out about it. That someone would do this anonymously…'

'Exactly. Somebody has gone to the trouble of effectively setting themselves up in some sort of alliance with Michelle,' Esme said. 'I wondered… with your research skills, if you could somehow trace who's behind it?'

'The world's full of crackpots and social media is their willing stage.' Justine closed the laptop. 'Tracing is notoriously difficult, nigh on impossible, on a platform like Facebook. But leave it with me, I have other ways and means of finding things out.'

'Thanks, Justine, I really appreciate it,' Esme said. 'It's just creepy as hell, and it feels invasive, even though, strictly speaking, it's not.'

'It is out of order though.' Justine frowned. 'This is the last thing anyone with a relative in hospital wants to see. I can't promise anything, but I'll have a good look at the page, interrogate its admin and stuff.'

Esme said, 'I just want the truth. I want to know who's doing this and why.'

Justine turned away and walked over to the window, pretending to look up at the sky to judge whether there might be rain.

She'd wait a little longer and then she'd tell her, but she felt certain of one thing.

Esme wasn't going to like the truth. She wasn't going to like it at all.

CHAPTER FIFTY-THREE

ESME

Five minutes after I'd left the office, my phone rang out on the car speaker and DI Sharpe's name flashed up.

'Hello, Esme,' he said pleasantly. 'I just picked up your voicemail.'

'There's a Facebook page,' I blurted out. 'It's called "Pray for Michelle Fox". Why would someone do that?'

'Whoa, let's rewind. What's this about a Facebook page?'

'I spoke to Peter Harvey, Simone Fischer's brother, as part of the podcast I'm doing about her case.'

'This is Simone Fischer, the convicted murderer, right?' It felt like he'd said that out loud to signal to a colleague the name and remind them who she was.

'Yes. I hadn't told him, but Peter knew Michelle had been attacked and was in hospital. To be honest, it creeped me out and I demanded to know how he knew this… I thought he'd been stalking me or something.'

'And what did he say?'

'He said he saw it on the Facebook page, as if it was something I already knew about. He showed me the page on his phone. It claims to have been set up by Michelle's friends and family to report on progress and gather support for her… but nobody knows her well enough to do that except me. And *I* certainly haven't created it.'

'One sec, let me pull this up on the screen.' A few moments elapsed. I heard muffled voices in the background. 'OK, we see it our end. There's not much on here.'

'No, but look at the cover photograph – it's the Intensive Care Unit at the QMC. That's exactly where Michelle is right now.'

'Hmm. It's a generic ICU picture though, easily available from a search engine. What I'm saying is that nobody has actually gone and photographed Michelle in hospital, thank God. Googling that location would bring up hundreds of examples.'

That was true. But still.

'They've used Michelle's actual Facebook profile picture,' I said. 'They have no right to do that.'

'It's annoying, I know, but sadly very easy to do. Anyone can take a picture from Facebook and appropriate it for their own use. Have you reported the page to Facebook as being unauthorised?'

My throat burned. 'No! I thought you'd want to investigate it first… find out exactly who's behind it. How do we know the person who attacked Michelle isn't responsible for this? It could be a massive clue as to what happened to her.'

'Sadly, our hands are pretty much tied when it comes to social media. It's notoriously difficult to prise any information from a company such as Facebook. Besides, this page is not threatening or abusive in any way.'

'So why does it feel so sinister?' I was aware my voice was rising higher and higher and I made a conscious effort to calm it. 'Surely there's something you can do!'

'I suggest, as a first step, you report the page, Esme. Hopefully they'll remove it if it's distressing you. But why would he draw your attention to the page if he'd gone to the trouble of secretly setting it up, pretending to be a member of Michelle's family?'

'I don't know. Because he's trying to unnerve me, maybe. Scare me off.'

'Tell me more.'

'Well, he's Simone Fischer's brother,' I said. 'He's bristly and unhelpful. He's made it clear he doesn't want me to do the podcast.'

'Really? What has he said about it?'

'Just that his sister is vulnerable and I should have approached him, not gone to Simone directly. But she's quite capable of making her own decisions. She's told him that, and I have, too.'

'And his reaction?'

'He's annoyed and doesn't try to hide it. He's planning to write a book about her case and I think he's angry I've encroached on that. If the podcast gives an interesting insight into what happened, the book won't be as exclusive as it might have been. In fact... I wondered if... oh, I don't know. It sounds silly when I say it out loud.'

'Go on.'

'Well, I wondered if Peter Harvey could be the man Zachary saw outside school with Michelle. He said the man had brown hair, which Peter has, but he also said he was tall. And Peter is only about five foot nine... which might seem tall to a kid.'

'Do you have a picture of him?'

'No but there are some online of him and one with Simone when she was outside the court.'

'Could you show Zachary his picture, ask him if this was the person he saw?'

'Yes! Yes, of course.' I bit the inside of my lip. My mind had been so full of Owen's treachery it hadn't occurred to me to do something as simple.

'One more thing. Do you have contact details for Peter Harvey? What do you know about him?'

'Not much. He lives in Melton Mowbray, he's Simone's brother. And yes, I have his number. Hang on.'

I pulled over at the next lay-by and pulled my call list up to read him Peter's number.

'I'll show Zachary his picture when he gets home from school and let you know what he says.'

Before I got home, I rang Peter Harvey's number myself half a dozen times to check he was around. There was no answer.

CHAPTER FIFTY-FOUR

When I got home it was mid-afternoon and I suddenly felt so tired I could barely keep my eyes open. Briefly, I said hello to Brooke and then went to my room for a lie down for half an hour before school pick-up.

I must have been exhausted, because I fell fast asleep for a while. Brooke woke me, entering the bedroom with a tray. Her make-up was immaculate as usual, but the formal jacket and jewellery were gone. She was wearing plain black slacks and a simple round-necked top.

'I came up earlier but you were asleep and I thought I'd let you rest. I got a cab and collected Zachary from school.' She placed the tray down on my bedside table. Tea, toast and a small dish of grapes.

'I'm so sorry,' I said, panicked that I'd missed school pick-up. 'You should have woken me. How long have I been asleep?'

'Only an hour or so,' she said. 'Don't worry about that. Everything is in hand. Zachary's downstairs and fine and Eric and Bruce are on Owen's case. If anyone can get Owen out of there, it's Bruce.'

Tough words, but I saw a shadow cross her face. In her quiet moments, even Brooke must have wondered what would happen to Owen if Bruce couldn't work his magic.

With Michelle still in ICU and Owen admitting to almost killing our son, I couldn't imagine our lives would ever be close to normal again. Brooke busied about around me, straightening the quilt, pulling back the curtains fully, and I thought about something Simone said earlier: *Everybody has an agenda.*

Here was Brooke, seemingly caring and considerate all of a sudden. But this was Owen's mother, the master manipulator.

'Can you ask Zachary to come upstairs please? I need to ask him something.'

'Hmm, I will but he's doing his homework now, and then—'

'No, Brooke, this is important. I need to speak to him.'

She sighed, walked to the top of the stairs and called down to Zachary. 'Come on up, poppet, your mum needs a word.'

My son walked into the bedroom and I held out my arms. We had a little cuddle.

'When can I go and see Aunt Miche?'

'Soon, Zachary. It won't be too long.'

'And when's Dad coming home?'

'I've explained everything to him,' Brooke interjected. 'Grandad's working very hard with Bruce to sort the mess out at the police station.'

'I've told you before, Brooke,' I said, injecting emphasis in my tone. 'He doesn't need to know *all* the details.'

She gave me a patronising smile that made me want to slap her. 'He's fine. Stop worrying.'

'How's school been today?' I turned back to my son.

'OK, I suppose,' he said unenthusiastically. 'Are you poorly, Mum?'

'I'm tired out, sweetie and I think I might be coming down with something.' I reached for my phone. 'Listen, I want you to take a look at this photo. Do you recognise this man?'

Brooke hovered in the doorway.

After my conversation with the detective I'd already saved a few different pictures on my phone of Peter Harvey from Google, some with Simone and others outside the courthouse. I chose the clearest image and pinched it open to enlarge Peter's face. I turned the screen to face Zachary.

He looked at the photograph and hesitated. I held my breath in anticipation, but then he handed me the phone back.

'I don't know him,' he said, and I sank back into my pillow. The little bit of hope I'd been harbouring was gone.

'You're certain this wasn't the man you saw with Aunt Miche outside school?' I said feebly.

'No,' he said. 'Mum, we've run out of malted milk biscuits.'

His favourite treat for after tea.

'I got you those nice rich tea biscuits from Waitrose,' Brooke said from the doorway.

'But they don't taste of anything!' Zachary wrinkled his nose. 'When are you getting up, Mum?'

'Come on now, let your mum rest. She's feeling under the weather. Back to your homework and then Grandad has sent over a fun gardening quiz for you to do.'

My eyes met his and Zachary seemed to silently plead with me.

'I'll try and get downstairs a bit later. This won't be for long,' I whispered, and gave him a squeeze to show I understood what he was having to put up with.

When Zachary had left the room, Brooke sidled over.

'I couldn't help hearing you say something to Zachary about a man… outside the school with Michelle.'

She fell silent and waited, like she fully expected me to fill her in.

'That's right,' I said, my tone curt.

'It's just… well, I wondered if your sister had a lot of boyfriends – acquaintances, if you'd prefer.'

Blood rushed into my face. 'What are you trying to say?'

'Nothing! Nothing offensive, it's just that, if she was seeing various *men*, things might be a little more complicated for the police and perhaps they ought to know about it. That's all.'

'As far as I know she wasn't *seeing* anyone, Brooke. I'm speaking to the police about all this and I don't want to rake it up again here, at home.'

'Of course. Yes.' She disappeared on to the landing and I breathed a sigh of relief to have a little bit of space from her exhausting behaviour.

I was halfway through drinking my cup of tea when I started shivering. I put down the drink and pulled the quilt up around my neck.

'What is it?' Brooke frowned, taking in my huddled appearance when she passed the open door with an armful of clean folded towels.

'I'm freezing. Cold to the bone,' I said, clutching the covers closer still.

'It's actually rather warm in here,' Brooke remarked with interest. 'The sun's shining outside and I've got the kitchen doors open downstairs.'

'Maybe I'm coming down with something.' My heart sank. The last thing I needed was some bug incapacitating me. I'd planned to visit Michelle in hospital after my rest, and with everything that had happened with Owen at the police station, it was crucial I was ready to respond at any minute.

'I'll go and get an extra blanket from the airing cupboard,' Brooke said, moving away.

I looked towards the drawn curtains and could see it was indeed still bright and probably warm outside. Hopefully, a couple of paracetamol and another little rest and I'd be good as new.

But when Brooke returned five minutes later and saw I'd kicked the quilt to the bottom of the bed, she raised an eyebrow.

'You're boiling hot now?'

I nodded, dabbing my damp forehead with the back of my hand and jutting out my bottom lip to blow air up into my face.

Brooke walked across the room and cracked open a window. A delicious wisp of cool breeze filtered in and fanned my blazing cheeks.

'Freezing cold and boiling hot within minutes… I don't need to tell you that's not a good sign,' she said sternly. 'You're going to have to stay in bed until you feel better, Esme.'

She spoke to me like a mother addressing her child. It was quite a novelty to be on the receiving end of Brooke's care and concern, and if it wasn't for my suspicion of her newfound empathy and the disastrous situation I'd found myself in, I'd be lapping it up. It was a shame I wouldn't be able to follow her advice.

'I can't afford to be ill, Brooke. There's Zachary to think of and—'

'Zachary is fine,' she interrupted. 'I can stay here as long as necessary, and while I'm around, you'll have absolutely nothing to worry about.'

A colossal understatement yet again.

'I'm very grateful,' I said weakly. 'But Michelle is in hospital and it's touch and go still. I have to see how she is, I can't just leave her in there all alone.'

'I thought you said she was unconscious?'

'She is, but the nurses say you can't be sure if someone can still hear or not. I want her to know I'm there.'

Brooke gave me a pitying smile. 'You're not thinking straight, Esme. Do you think, for a moment, they'd let you into ICU sweating and shivering like you are at the moment? You could seriously harm the patients in there if you have a fever or some kind of a virus.'

She was absolutely right. I wasn't thinking straight at all. A tear rolled down my cheek and plopped onto the quilt.

'Now come on. Don't get all down about it. Would you like me to call the hospital and get an update on Michelle?'

I nodded. 'Thanks.' I couldn't get used to this new, apparently helpful Brooke. I wasn't convinced by her at all.

She left the room again. On her return she brought a cool, damp flannel which she folded and lay across my forehead. 'See, everything can be sorted out, Esme. All you need to do is relax, get some rest and get better. You can leave everything else to me and Eric. Zachary is completely safe in our hands.'

I closed my eyes again, the end of her sentence seeming to fade into nothing. When I heard her leave the room, I opened them again and stared out of the window.

I'd gone from controlling all the parts of my life so easily to relying on my domineering mother-in-law for the simplest tasks.

Where would it all end?

CHAPTER FIFTY-FIVE

Later on, Brooke surprised me yet again.

'I brought you these. I found them in the bathroom cupboard.' She handed me a brown paper bag. 'I don't know if they'll be of any use to you.'

I felt relieved when I saw the familiar packets of tablets that nestled inside the bag. It contained the leftover medication the doctor had prescribed following Zachary's accident and I'd already rifled it for a sedative the night before… but Brooke didn't need to know that.

I longed for that blunted feeling again, a temporary respite from the cloying fear that nibbled at the edges of me.

Brooke watched as I pulled out a packet of tablets and inspected the small print. They were still a few months in date. I remembered these particular ones just took the edge off the panicky feelings. If I could just get on a level again, I'd be able to get back in the driving seat and feel more in control.

'We'll soon get you fighting fit, and in the meantime you can leave everything in my capable hands,' Brooke said.

It didn't sound like a choice.

*

For the next couple of days I drifted in and out of a kind of fog. I felt so ill, apart from saying two words repeatedly – 'Zachary' and 'Michelle' – I could barely manage to utter anything else.

I thought I heard voices on a couple of occasions but couldn't surface for long enough to see what, if anything, was happening around me.

I had no concept of time, just of drifting in and out of unpleasant hallucinations, anxiety dreams and the vague knowledge that I was sweating or shivering.

I wasn't aware of time passing, but I could feel a cool breeze and I heard a noise in the bedroom. Then a pleasant humming of a song. I had a sense of coming up, coming to the surface, and I opened my eyes and there was Brooke, smiling down at me.

'Welcome back to the land of the living,' she said.

'Wh – where's Zachary?' I stammered.

'Zachary is fine. In fact, he really seems to have brightened up in the last day or so. I think he's enjoyed the new routine. I'll ask him to pop up and see you in a few minutes; he's on the phone to his grandad and they're talking about dinosaurs.'

'Has Zachary been to school?'

'Of course he has! I've ordered him some new uniform too, his trousers were getting too short on him.'

I immediately thought about Michelle, my heart quickening at the thought of her alone in the hospital.

'Michelle…' I whispered.

'Michelle's readings have improved a little, apparently. I've kept in regular contact with the hospital on your behalf.'

Brooke had already told me the only person she cared anything about was Owen. So although I hoped it was true that Michelle had improved some, I knew I wouldn't rest until I heard it myself from the hospital. 'Thanks for speaking to them. Have the police been in touch with any news about the attack?'

'I'm afraid not. Do you feel up to sitting for a short time? I've made you some asparagus soup.'

My appetite was non-existent but I knew if I didn't build up my strength I'd never get back on my feet.

She helped me shuffle up into a semi-seated position and pummelled the pillows behind me to offer some additional back support. 'I expect you're worrying about Owen, too,' she said, fixing me with a cool look.

I wasn't so out of it that I'd thought about Owen's welfare.

'Yes. I'm worried about how Zachary is going to feel about the fact his dad nearly killed him and then lied about it.'

'Owen's predicament is not as straightforward,' Brooke said, as if I hadn't spoken. 'On Bruce's advice, he's retracted his admission about being involved in the accident. Turns out, as I suspected, he was put under certain pressures.'

Hope lurched in my chest. 'So, he didn't knock Zachary down?'

Brooke busied herself pulling the quilt straighter. 'There are circumstances to be taken into consideration, as I'm sure you'll understand.'

'I need to speak to the detectives myself,' I said. 'Could yo—'

'Asparagus soup coming up,' Brooke called as she headed hastily for the door.

What I really wanted to do was to jump out of bed and see Zachary and then get dressed and head for the hospital to see Michelle, but I felt far too weak. Perhaps Brooke's soup would fortify me.

I reached for the glass of water at my bedside and sipped it thoughtfully. It was hard to tell exactly what had happened with Owen at the police station, and Brooke, ever the defensive mother, wasn't the best person to level with me. I needed someone like Justine or Mo to find out exactly what was happening on my behalf.

I reached into the drawer of the bedside table to get my phone. Pressing the buttons, I soon realised it was out of charge and I tossed it back in, frustrated.

'Here we go, homemade soup. There's a full two bunches of asparagus in here so we'll soon have you full of beans again.'

My mouth watered at the delicious smell. Brooke placed the tray carefully on my legs. She'd even cut some bread to go with it.

'Could I trouble you to bring my phone charger up, Brooke? It should be in the kitchen.' I took a small mouthful of soup. 'This is delicious. I'd like Zachary to come up when I'm finished.'

'He's in his element, all the attention he's getting from me and regular telephone calls from his grandad. I'm not sure how much time you get to spend doing stuff with Zachary but Eric doesn't agree with children being left to their own devices, playing on computers all day long. I have to say the boy seems to have got into quite a bad habit of doing so.'

Hidden in her tone was a clear echo of disapproval, but I didn't rise to it. Brooke and Eric were of a different generation, an age at which some didn't really get that technology was now an integral part of kids' lives, and I did monitor Zachary's screen time. Nevertheless, it would be nice for him to see a bit more of his grandparents, and whatever I thought of them, they were Zach's family, too. I hoped this would be the start of a new relationship for them all.

'Eric is hoping to come down and stop over for a few days,' she said lightly. 'Owen needs all the support he can get.'

I never thought I'd say it, but I would have been in a far worse position if Brooke hadn't been around. But soon her domination of us all would have to stop. I seriously doubted I could survive Eric joining the Painter takeover of our home.

I needed to get my strength back and then get my mother-in-law out of my house and out of my life.

CHAPTER FIFTY-SIX

JUSTINE

Toby, the new assistant, was an absolute pain. He couldn't seem to use his initiative to do anything useful, and yet always seemed to be hanging around watching Justine at the most inconvenient times.

She'd taken a break from her clandestine activities, and had instead been looking at the unauthorised Facebook page Esme had shown her. She'd found some baffling and conflicting details she could do with speaking to her about. She'd called her a couple of times but her phone had been turned off. But the more she looked into it, the stranger it seemed, so she'd decided she'd focus on the details before involving Esme.

Justine had actually felt very sorry for Esme a couple of days ago when she'd asked for her help. She hadn't wanted things to turn out this way. If she could have avoided taking the necessary action before things had got so bad, she would have done. She wished she didn't have to disappoint her. But life often had a way of surprising you, and there was nothing left to do in these circumstances but deal with it.

And that's what Justine was doing. She was dealing with the circumstances the best she could and trying not to get caught.

She hadn't wanted to lie through her teeth to get into ICU to see Michelle, but she did. And she'd managed it, too. It was crazy how lax people and policies could be. She'd been shocked at just how easy it had been to get in there once she'd name-dropped

Esme and pretended to be Michelle's *other* sister. So much in life came down to whether people liked you. They'd willingly shelve a surprising amount of red tape if they did.

Justine had sat by Michelle's bedside for half an hour and talked to her solidly. The nurse had said it was unlikely Michelle would hear her, but you never knew. That had been all the encouragement she'd needed. From the moment she sat down she talked, explained why she'd had to do it, and, in a funny sort of way, it had made her feel better.

Whether or not Michelle understood in her comatose state, Justine didn't know. This was never meant to happen but now it had… well, maybe it was for the best.

Now, as part of her plan, Justine had to somehow speak to Esme without anyone else around. She'd heard from Mo that Owen's interfering mother, Brooke, had taken control of the family home, and that Esme had had some kind of meltdown.

Justine had only met Owen's parents once, when she'd been at the hospital at the same time as them, visiting Zachary after his accident. They were the kind of people who had this way of sort of dismissing you with a single look. Justine had sympathised with Esme, having to put up with them.

Mo had apparently visited the house yesterday and tried to insist on seeing Esme, but the old battle axe had kept him at arm's length, insisting Esme was ill in bed and didn't want visitors.

Justine's phone beeped now as an incoming text arrived. She opened it up and punched the air. She read Esme's message again and bathed in the warmth of a good plan falling into place. This was an unexpected bonus indeed.

Hi Justine, could you call in at the house? I really need your help and could do with someone to talk to.

Justine punched in her reply and pressed send.

I'll be there within the hour.

This was the chance she'd been waiting for, and she had no intention of wasting it. The time had finally come.

*

A heavily made-up Brooke Painter opened Esme's front door. She was wearing an emerald velvet lounge suit paired with pale gold flat pumps and, judging by Justine's impromptu sneezing fit, had recently drenched herself in YSL's *Opium*.

'Who are *you*?' she said without welcome.

'We've met before. I work with Esme. I'm—'

'Are you another one at that office who approves of fraternising with convicted murderers?' Brooke said, not giving Justine chance to reply. 'What can I do for you?'

'I'm here to see Esme.'

'I'm afraid you've made a wasted journey. I told your colleague yesterday that Esme's not well right now,' Brooke said, blocking Justine's access. 'She's not taking any visitors.'

Justine stood her ground. 'Esme herself texted me. Asked me to drop by for a chat.'

Brooke's face darkened. 'She's taking prescribed medication so is quite confused most of the time. She's sleeping now.'

Justine craned her neck to look over Brooke's shoulder. The house did seem very quiet. Then Zachary appeared at the end of the hall.

'Hi, Zach!' she called, raising her hand. 'Are you OK?'

'Of course he's OK, he's with his family. What do you expect?'

Zachary took a few tentative steps down the hall. Brooke spun around.

'Get back in the kitchen and don't move until you've finished your reading,' she snapped. Zachary's face blanched and he slunk back, out of view. Brooke turned back to Justine. 'As you can see, we're up to our eyes in it here.'

Justine tried again. 'It's just… well, Esme did text me a short time ago, so could you just check if she—'

'I have a thousand and one jobs to do.' Brooke folded her arms. 'She's sleeping. Understand? You'll have to call back another day.'

'Justine?' a faint voice called from within the house.

Surprised, Brooke took a few steps back and Justine took the chance to slip inside.

'Esme? Get back into bed!' Brooke thundered, rushing to the stairs. 'You're supposed to be resting.'

Justine was shocked to see Esme appear at the top of the stairs, holding on to the bannister for support. She looked so frail, dressed in pale grey sweatpants and a thin white cotton top.

Brooke began to climb the stairs. 'Esme, you must get back into bed at once. You haven't the strength to—'

'I want to see Justine!' Esme wailed in a thin voice.

The look on Esme's face was one of pure panic, and so Justine moved forward.

Brooke reeled around. 'What do you think you're doing? You can't just barge in this house. You need to leave, now!'

'I want her to stay,' Esme said, her voice so weak now, Justine expected her to collapse at any moment.

Justine continued to advance upstairs. 'You heard her, she wants me to stay,' she said, more confidently than she felt. 'This is Esme's house and a quick chat isn't going to do her any harm. I won't stay long.'

Brooke's face reddened. Justine could see she was fighting a full-blown temper tantrum. This was a woman used to getting her own way, completely unaccustomed to being challenged. Esme slumped against the wall.

Justine rushed forward to assist her and helped her back into the bedroom.

She plumped the pillows behind Esme and helped her take a few sips of water.

Esme seemed too exhausted to speak. While she gathered herself a little, Justine took a look around the bedroom. The first thing she did was open the curtains a touch. Instantly, the room looked less gloomy and Justine spotted a pile of medication on top of the chest of drawers.

She picked up several empty foil packets and inspected them, frowning before returning to sit at Esme's bedside.

'Did the doctor come out to see you?' Justine asked.

Esme shook her head. 'I think it's been the shock of everything that's happened. I just became exhausted, it knocked me off my feet.'

'There's quite a bit of medication there. Looks like you've been popping pills for England.'

'Brooke rescued my old medication. They're the same drugs I took after Zachary's accident, they just take the edge off. I figured if I could relax properly and get some rest…'

'Are they sedatives?'

Esme shrugged and swallowed more water. 'They're supposed to have a calming effect, that's all. But I've felt really out of it. Brooke doesn't know but I haven't been swallowing the tablets today but I was able to gather the strength to shout downstairs to you.'

'Well, thank God you texted me.'

'Zachary secretly brought my charger up and that's how I could finally contact you. I'd asked Brooke for the charger a few times but she conveniently kept forgetting. I realised I'm no match for her in this state; she's basically taken over.'

'She's formidable. I'd tried everything to reason with her but I was on the verge of walking away when you shouted downstairs.'

Esme nodded. 'I've not seen Zachary today and I can't visit Michelle in hospital. I'm feeling better without the drugs until I stand up and then I feel so weak again. I really need your help, Justine.'

'Brooke was quite sharp with Zachary downstairs just now. He looked pretty miserable.'

'The saving grace is that I know Brooke does care about him, she's just old school. A big fan of discipline and routine,' Esme said. 'Poor Zachary. It's not ideal but thank goodness he's been safe at least while I've felt so ill.'

Justine reached for her hand. 'What do you need me to do?'

'Can you check on Zachary? And I need you to speak to the hospital to find out Michelle's progress, and also the police. I've heard nothing about any progress finding her attacker.'

'What about Owen... is he still in custody?'

'I don't care about Owen at the moment,' she said in such a vehement way Justine didn't feel she could ask why.

She'd hoped to speak to Esme about what she'd found so far on the unauthorised Facebook page, but there was something more important that had to be said.

Esme said, 'Would you drive me to the hospital later, when I feel a bit stronger? I haven't been to see Michelle for days now. Brooke says she's kept in contact with the hospital and nothing has changed but... I need to see her for my own peace of mind.' She sighed. 'I'm missing her so much, I just want her home.'

Justine said, 'I think it's best you don't go there at the moment, Esme.'

'I wouldn't ask, it's just that...'

Justine took a breath. 'Look, I have something to tell you. I don't know how to begin.'

'Just say it.' Esme was trying to smile. 'Nothing can hurt me now.'

It took Justine a long time to speak. 'This is not easy, Esme. What I've got to say is... upsetting. In fact, that's an understatement. It's going to knock you for six, and you're going to be hurt and angry but—'

'You're making me nervous! I'll let you know if I'm annoyed. Just tell me.'

Justine said, 'I've been doing some research work… on the side. It's taken a while because I've had to make absolutely certain I was correct before speaking to you.'

Esme gave a sad, wry smile. 'You've found yourself another job.'

'That's not it.' Justine reached down to her bag and pulled out a thick sheaf of paperwork. 'These are my findings. This is the evidence behind it all, if you like,' she said.

Esme frowned. 'Evidence for what, exactly?'

Justine tapped the pile of paperwork. 'I've set it out just like one of our projects. So you can see at a glance how I've come to the conclusion that I have.'

'Goodness, you're scaring me now. Spit it out!'

'Esme, I'm so sorry it's fallen to me to tell you something that's going to break your heart. For the past six months, your sister has been betraying you in the worst way possible.'

CHAPTER FIFTY-SEVEN

Esme's face seemed to melt like wax in front of Justine's eyes.

'Tell me everything,' she whispered.

Justine spread the papers out on the bed: printouts of emails, scrawled notes and telephone records showing highlighted key numbers.

'From what I can gather, Michelle and Mo have been romantically involved for about a year now,' Justine said. 'But six months ago they changed gear, set up a podcast company called MiMo Productions with the two of them as joint directors.'

Esme lay a flat hand on her chest and took some deep breaths.

'Are you OK?' Justine said. 'Do you want me to give you a few minutes?'

'No. I want you to tell me everything,' she whispered.

'It started when I overheard a conversation between Michelle and Mo in the office about a month ago. They thought they were the last two members of staff around, but I'd popped to the loo before leaving the building,' Justine said. 'As I came down the corridor, I heard Michelle's voice. She said, "It won't be long now and we'll be the ones making the decisions." I peered around the corner and saw she was talking to Mo.'

'Did you say anything to them?' Esme asked.

'No! While they were talking about you ruining everything the company did by insisting on being so honest, I crept back up the corridor. I waited a few moments and then made a noise walking down so they knew I was there. I couldn't be sure who they were talking about but I guessed it was you. Still, it made no sense. I mean, I know how close you and Michelle are.'

'What did they mean… too honest?'

Justine shrugged. 'That you were planning on being so transparent with Simone, that she would get to approve every word of the final aired podcast, I guess.'

She added the 'I guess' bit to make her colleague and friend feel a bit better, but in reality, Esme's commitment to such pure honesty irritated Justine, too. They were supposed to be journalists, not saints, and it was hard to put out a good story without upsetting someone. It had been that way since the beginning of time.

Justine braced herself for Esme to become emotional when she showed her the email she'd salvaged from the deleted emails folder on Mo's laptop. She turned the screen so Esme could read it.

'This was sent to TrueLife on the afternoon of your meeting with them,' Justine said quietly.

'Oh no…' Esme whispered.

Mo had emailed the confirmation of a meeting with his new company, MiMo Productions, with Damon Yorke, the CEO of TrueLife Media. The message reassured him that 'myself and Michelle Fox are the two major contributors to *The Fischer Files* podcast production and responsible for its success. Esme Fox has had minimal involvement, which explains why she couldn't effectively present to you at your planned meeting when Michelle Fox was delayed and unable to attend.'

Esme seemed to visibly shrink, growing weaker in front of Justine.

'I'd noticed you'd changed in your manner at work,' Esme said, her voice thick and still seeming a little out of it. 'I thought you were getting sick of the company. In fact, I thought that you were going to tell me you'd got another job.'

'I wish that's all it was,' Justine said. 'I have felt frustrated at times but I haven't felt I could approach you until now.'

'But – are you sure? Are you positive about all this?'

'Yes. I've followed them, eavesdropped on them, tracked back how long they've been seeing each other. I've even sat waiting in the nature reserve, watching as they snuck out of work to meet in Mo's Audi. Sorry.'

'I know it can't have been easy to come here today and say what you had to say, Justine. You've had my back on something I hadn't a clue about and I thank you for that. But this still doesn't make sense. If they're so close then why isn't he crying by my sister's bedside?'

'Because that would have blown everything wide open. Michelle may recover and so he needs to keep their plans to himself. But it has affected him badly. When you came into the office he put on a brave face but I've noticed he's been distracted and down. He's cancelled some meetings and avoided all but minimum contact with me. This definitely wasn't part of their plans.'

'Do you think he knows what happened to Michelle? Or has an idea who might have done this?'

Justine shook her head. 'I don't think he has a clue. He's walking around with this baffled, worried look on his face.'

Esme was acting surprisingly calm, as if she'd taken everything in her stride, but Justine wasn't fooled. Her fingers twisted together and her foot tapped incessantly on the floor.

Justine paused before continuing. 'In view of what you now know, do you still want to go to the hospital to see Michelle?'

Esme stared at the wall for a few moments.

'I do. I have to,' she said at last. 'I don't know why she'd do this to me, but I intend to find out as soon as I'm able. Michelle's out of action in hospital, so that just leaves Mo here to do his worst. I need to stop him going any further with this, stop him ruining the business completely. Not easy to do when he's the IT manager. If I just fire him he could simply take all the documentation and all our clients with him at the click of a button.'

Esme untangled her fingers and Justine saw that her hands were shaking.

'Leave it with me,' Justine said. 'I'll see what I can do. In the meantime, I've restored all the information on Michelle's laptop. Mo had run an overnight programme to remove the security on the machine, but I got in the office the next day before he did and wiped it clean so he never saw all the files on there. It looks like Michelle was stockpiling information for MiMo Productions. They've been stealing data – your contacts and the supplier contracts – for some time, so they could hit the ground running with their new company.'

'I don't know how to thank you,' Esme said, opening the laptop. She looked sickly, so pale.

'I'm going back into the office now. Hopefully, if I can find Mo's laptop – not an easy task, as he usually takes it home every night – I can use the flash drive to take data from his, too.'

'Bring Zachary up here to me,' she said. 'I don't want Brooke anywhere near him now.'

Justine turned to leave when Esme's phone began to ring. She waited while Esme answered it and watched as the colour drained from her face in an instant.

'Thank you,' Esme said faintly. 'I'll get there soon as I can.'

She dropped the phone onto the bed and stared open-mouthed at Justine.

'That was the hospital. It's Michelle… she's awake.'

CHAPTER FIFTY-EIGHT

ESME

While Justine used the bathroom, I swung my legs over the side of the bed and sat there for a few moments before standing up. My legs still felt a bit shaky but I took my time. My head cleared slightly and I took a few steps forward.

I could barely concentrate on moving for racking my brains about what Justine had just told me. I found myself thinking back, combing over the last year, since starting The Speaking Fox. I couldn't come up with one hint or incident that should have rang an alarm bell and told me that Mo and Michelle were an item.

Mo and Justine I could have handled. But Mo and my *sister*? It was crazy. Michelle and I had been through so much stuff together. We'd stuck together as kids, supported each other after Mum's death. We dreamed up the business together, she moved in after Owen left… had I imagined all this stuff? No! We were as close as sisters could be, sharing our home life, work and even leisure time. There had been *no room* for Mo; her life had been full of me and Zachary.

And another question loomed large, too. Zachary knew Mo well. He would have said if Mo was the man he'd seen Michelle with outside the school gates; there would have been no mystery about it. So it must've been someone else. But who?

Slowly, I padded out of the bedroom and down the landing. I could hear voices downstairs. As much as I hated to do it, I had one more favour to ask of Brooke.

I heard feet pounding up the stairs and I froze. I was acting like a kid caught in the act in my own home! I just don't know how it got to this so quickly.

'You should be sleeping.' Brooke stood, hands on her hips. 'Back to bed, I think.'

My legs still felt a touch wobbly but I hid it as best I could and turned to face her. 'Michelle is awake,' I said. 'Justine is going to drive me to the hospital and I wondered if you'd mind watching Zachary for me? I'm not sure what to expect and the hospital is no place for him.'

Her frown disappeared. 'Of course. He's quite safe here with Grandma.'

'Mum? Where are you going?' Zachary appeared at the bedroom door. I looked up and saw the unhappiness etched on his face.

'Come over here, sweetie. I've just heard that Aunt Miche is awake.' I held out my hand to him and forced a brighter tone. 'I'm going to see her now and hopefully, it won't be too long before I can take you with me.'

'I want to come with you,' he said, glancing nervously at Brooke. I felt his desperation to be with me and I took him in my arms, held him to me.

'Soon,' I murmured, into the top of his head. 'Soon, I promise.'

Brooke patted his arm. 'Come on, we can work on that welcome home card for Daddy.'

With a last lingering look, Zachary reluctantly broke away from me. His spirit, his fire, seemed so dampened.

I felt a thread of steel winding through my insides. I would pick my time to face Brooke. I wanted both her and her lying son out of my house and out of my life for good.

But first things first.

*

Justine and I barely spoke on the way to the hospital. I couldn't. I just needed to be quiet and think. Try and get my head around everything that had happened.

Halfway there, I thought about asking her to turn the car around and take me back home. I thought about sending Justine to speak to Michelle instead. But ultimately, I said nothing. I knew I had to face her. It was constantly running away from facing reality that had got me to this place.

Justine waited outside in the car and, slowly, I made my way up to the ward. I still felt weak and had no energy. They buzzed me into ICU, and before the nurse took me up to Michelle's bed, the doctor came over to speak to me.

'Her body has incurred a lot of damage from the attack. It's still touch-and-go but, if she's lucky, she'll make a slow, steady recovery,' the doctor said.

'Will she eventually get back to being her normal self?'

'Visually, she will be left with scars on her face, forearms and torso. Mentally, in some ways, she may never be the person you remember, but only time will tell. That's a long way ahead, and there are many obstacles still to get through. For now, our priority is getting her stabilised.'

Little did he know she was already someone different from the person I remembered.

The nurse escorted me on to the ward and every step I took felt like a mile. I still felt so sick and weak and the thought of facing my treacherous sister made me want to turn around and leave. But I forced myself to carry on walking.

'She has some memory loss, which is to be expected,' the nurse told me. 'Her memory may well return, but for now she can't recall anything about the actual attack, though she may remember other, earlier, events. The brain works in peculiar ways.'

My heart sank as I realised the torture would continue. I'd hoped for answers about Peter Harvey but now… Michelle probably wasn't going to be able to tell me anything at all about the attack.

When we reached her bedside, I saw her eyes, wide and dark, staring at me. There was a lighter, more transparent oxygen mask over her face, but the bruising and swelling seemed just as bad.

The nurse gently removed the oxygen mask from Michelle's face. 'If she seems to be struggling, just pop it on again for a short time, OK?'

'Thank you.'

'I'll give you some privacy,' the nurse said, leaving us.

'Esme,' Michelle whispered, and her fingers moved on the blanket. I touched her hand and she grasped mine. In a rush, I forgot everything she'd done and we were just sisters again. Our eyes met and I could tell she felt it too… our indelible genetic link that ran under everything. That which surely could not be erased. Was it possible we could somehow get over the lies and betrayal?

'Can you remember anything about the attack?' The words were out there. I couldn't help myself. 'Anything at all?'

She gave a tiny shake of her head and let go of my fingers. 'Nothing.'

Her voice was almost inaudible, the word emerging like a scrape in her throat.

'Zachary asks about you every day,' I said. 'He misses you so much.'

She closed her eyes briefly before opening them again and staring at me. I couldn't go on like this. I had to say something. 'Michelle… I know,' I said. 'I know about you and Mo. I know about MiMo Productions.'

I watched as a tear blossomed and traced its way across her purple swollen cheek, trickling down into her ear.

'I'm sorry. I never meant to hurt you,' she whispered hoarsely. There was no sense of denial, just regret.

'You can remember?'

She gave a single nod. 'We… we got carried away. Mo was angry, I – I betrayed you.'

She could obviously remember the months before but not the actual attack.

'But why?' I bent closer to her. 'I just want to know why. When we've always been there for each other as sisters, our whole lives? How could this come between us?'

She turned her head slowly and looked at the glass of water on the side. I reached for it, held the back of her hot, damp head while she took a couple of sips.

'You remember… differently to me.' She spoke slowly, taking in breaths between every short burst of words. 'You never… see what's in front of… your own eyes.' She paused before continuing. 'In the end I just… I resented you. I'm sorry.'

'What? I thought we were close, thought…'

'Sometimes you've been like… Big Brother watching over me… telling me what I should do, how I should live,' she whispered. 'When Mum died… you just took control… expecting me to want what you yourself wanted.'

'But I was just looking after you! And we've had such good times, too. I can't accept that—'

'Listen to yourself. "I can't accept."' She paused to rest, taking a few breaths under the mask again before continuing. '*You* can't accept that people have their own lives… *you* can't accept your way is not always the best way.' The words bled out of her. 'You try to control every last detail in your life, including the people around you, because if not… well, you'd have to stand back and look at yourself, wouldn't you? See you're far from perfect, see that you don't always know best. Could you cope with that? I don't think so.'

I felt stone cold to my bones. The things she was saying, what she'd secretly thought of me all this time. Was there truth in any of this? Some of what she said reminded me of Simone, talking about Grant. But I wasn't a controlling person... was I?

Was wanting to make money to secure the future of my son more noble than wanting to make money for pure profit, like Michelle and Mo did? I'd say so.

She was sorry for what she'd said, but not sorry for what she'd *done* with Mo. That much was clear. Whatever bond I thought we'd shared, it now lay in tatters around us. I didn't know what the future held for us as sisters, and that thought left me hollow inside.

'Best to let her rest now,' the nurse said softly at my shoulder, and I put up my hand.

'Just a few more seconds,' I said, a flood of heat rising through my chest into my neck and face. 'Michelle, have you heard of a man called Peter Harvey? He's Simone Fischer's brother.'

Michelle's eyes widened a touch and then she nodded, her face crumbling.

'How? What was your contact with him?' If she recalled Peter, then her memories were coming from before the attack. Could he be the man Zachary saw her with outside school? 'Did you get into his car? That morning, did you—'

The nurse sighed loudly. 'Please. The doctor insists she has to rest now.'

'I just need to ask her a few more questions. Michelle?'

I looked at my sister, waiting for her to ask the nurse to give me a little more time, but she simply glanced at me one more time and then she closed her eyes.

CHAPTER FIFTY-NINE

Justine dropped me off back at the house before she left again for the office.

'I'm hoping I might have some information about the origins of the unauthorised Facebook page soon. It's confusing. At first glance it looks like one person's work, but then it could easily be the work of another.'

'Sounds… well, confusing, as you say!' I frowned.

I sat with Zachary in the living room and scanned the files that Justine had recovered from Michelle's laptop.

There were a lot of them, and I felt sure that hidden in one or more of them would be protected documents giving details of Mo and Michelle's treacherous plans to undermine The Speaking Fox.

But instead of searching for those now, I double-clicked on the folder labelled *Meetings*.

Several documents were filed within, and I worked through them. The first document detailed the schedule for my meetings with Simone at HMP Bronzefield. The second contained the meeting notes with the TrueLife executives… very detailed ones that explained everything clearly and would have helped me immeasurably. As it was, she'd just left the short cryptic notes on her desk that meant little to me.

This all now made perfect sense. Michelle must have planned to desert me for the meeting. She'd wanted me to fall flat on my face, had never intended turning up. But fate must have intervened and she was attacked by someone. The two incidents – her not turning up and the attack – were separate things, which I hadn't realised until now.

When I opened the third document, my fingers froze above the keyboard. This document was more interesting. This document wasn't meant for my eyes at all.

It was a list of various meetings she'd set up for MiMo Productions to discuss spin-offs from *The Fischer Files* podcast – meetings I obviously knew nothing about. But I couldn't focus on the short list in front of me, because one meeting in particular drew my eye immediately, and I couldn't look away.

The last entry in her meeting list read:

11 a.m. Meeting with Peter Harvey at The Ruddington Arms

According to this entry, made two weeks ago, my sister met with Simone Fischer's brother. The man who told me he'd never met Michelle.

CHAPTER SIXTY

I called DI Sharpe and left a hurried message. My throat felt so tight I could barely get the words out, but he needed to know about the meeting Michelle had with Peter Harvey. I was getting so frustrated with the police response to Michelle's attack. I felt I could probably do a far better job myself in following up the leads.

Why would Peter lie about never having met Michelle? It could only mean he was hiding something.

A sickly swirling started in the pit of my stomach, a bitter taste rising up into my mouth. Peter was rude and obstructive, but he didn't seem unhinged. But then Michelle was a determined woman, and if she'd put forward proposals to him about Simone he didn't like – plans that could scupper his book, the project he hoped would make him a lot of money – and she refused to back off, then maybe he'd snapped. I'd seen glimmers of his belligerent nature myself.

Yet my feelings of dread about the attack now mingled with disbelief at what Michelle and Mo had done to me. A band of coldness wrapped itself around my heart and squeezed hard. The reality had been there all along in front of my face, I'd just chosen not to see it.

Zachary seemed a bit listless, but he was OK. 'Is Aunt Miche better, Mum?' he asked half-heartedly. I'd knocked back his requests to visit so many times, he'd all but given up.

'She's still very poorly, sweetie. But she was awake for a few minutes and that's a great sign.'

'I made you a cuppa.' Brooke came in with a drink and a foil strip of tablets. 'Good news: Eric has travelled down from Newcastle. Owen is to be released pending further investigations! He and Bruce are calling at the house, they're just a few minutes away now.'

'Dad's coming home?' Zachary said with an element of disbelief.

'Yes, darling, isn't it wonderful?' Brooke simpered, full of unbridled joy.

I kept my expression blank, thanked her for the tea and waved away the tablets. I felt much stronger thanks to the absence of medication. Learning of Owen's terrible deed that nearly killed our boy had devastated me, and he was the last person I wanted to set eyes on. I wasn't in the least surprised I'd fallen ill. Brooke might have been trying to help, or she might've had darker motivations in keeping me out of the picture. Who knew?

One thing I was certain of: Owen would not be coming here. And there was no way I could stomach Eric staying at the house, too. It was time for me to tell them to go home.

My stomach tilted when I looked over at my son, his eyes trained blankly on the television. He looked so quiet, like someone had knocked the Zachary-shaped stuffing out of him.

'Are you OK, sweetie? Come here.'

He walked over to me like a little robot and I cuddled him, closing my eyes and resting my chin on the top of his head. He was stiff and unyielding in my arms, and I felt a pang of guilt that he'd had to suffer like this. But I was feeling better now. I could take care of my son again.

'Can I stay at Dad's flat if you're still feeling poorly, Mum?'

I opened my eyes and Brooke was staring at us with a strange look on her face.

'Leave us a while,' I told her. It wasn't a request.

Without comment, she turned and walked out, closing the living room door. I spoke to Zachary, keeping my voice low in case she was still lurking outside the door.

'Things are different now, Zachary. I know it's been tough, sweetie. I've felt so ill but now I'm OK again so I can look after you. Has Grandma been nice to you?'

He looked into my eyes and my heart started hammering. He looked, I don't know, *strange*, for want of a better word. I knew Brooke wouldn't have mistreated him, but…

'What have you been doing downstairs while I've been sleeping so much?' I asked.

There was no reply. He pressed his lips together, as if he'd been told to say nothing and was afraid the words would just pop out on their own. I shook his shoulders, gently, and pressed my face close to his. 'Zachary, speak to me, sweetie, so I know you're OK.'

'Grandma wouldn't let me come upstairs and see you even when she brought your food up and you were awake,' he whispered. 'But I'm not supposed to tell you that.'

His words sounded very slightly slurred at the ends. Was it possible…

'Zachary, you can tell me anything you like. Do you hear me?' He gave a tiny nod. 'I feel better now and I'm your mum. I have something to ask you and I want you to tell me the truth. Don't be frightened.'

He looked at me, his eyes dark and wide.

'Has Grandma given you any tablets?'

He shifted uncomfortably. I waited.

'She… gives me a tablet to make me sleep at night, that's all.'

'Out of the bathroom cupboard?'

He nodded.

I already knew Brooke had found Zachary's sedatives in there when she confronted me with them, saying it was an unsafe place to store them. Yet *she* was the danger to Zachary, not the medicine.

I braced myself as a black Jag pulled up outside the house. Eric. A tall man in a navy suit I hadn't seen got out of the passenger door – Bruce, I presumed.

'I don't want to go,' Zach suddenly whined when he saw the car. 'Please, Mum, don't make me.'

I shook my head, not understanding. 'Go where?'

'To live with them.'

Eric and Bruce walked up the path, and I heard Brooke open the front door.

'What? You're not going to live with them, you silly sausage!'

'Grandma said me and Dad had to go and live with them when he gets out of the police station.'

I pulled him close again and his tense little body softened a touch. 'I'll never let anyone take you away.'

As I finished the sentence, the lounge door opened.

'It'll just be for a while.' Brooke walked in, followed by Eric and Bruce. 'It's for the best.'

'He's going nowhere. I want you to all leave now.' I suddenly felt exhausted again, but I made a big effort to keep my voice sounding strong and determined.

'That won't be possible, Esme.' Eric stepped out from behind his wife, a wiry little man with weathered skin full of deep creases. 'We're going to be taking Zachary up to Newcastle for a few months until you get the treatment you need.'

'He's going nowhere,' I repeated. Zachary stood in front of me and I pulled his back against me and wrapped my arms around his shoulders. 'Leave now or I'll call the police.'

'You're clearly suffering from anxiety and depression. Don't make us go to court or we'll make sure it's all over the newspapers,' Brooke said. 'Colin Wade has made it clear he'd love an exclusive interview with us.'

I didn't doubt them for a minute. Wade would love to hear Brooke's side of things after my involvement with Simone Fischer.

I couldn't even hit back at Brooke and say the press would be more interested in vilifying Owen than me. The man who nearly killed his own son. I couldn't say a word with Zachary here to hear it all; the shock would send him spiralling back down into that dark place he inhabited for so long.

No, I'd have to be altogether cleverer about it.

'Leave me and my son a while. I want to talk to him. Explain everything.'

'I don't want to go! You said I wouldn't have to!' Zachary yelled, burying his face in his hands. I squeezed his shoulders and hoped he got the message of calm I was silently trying to convey to him.

Brooke's face brightened. 'Thank goodness you've decided to see sense, Esme,' she said, all heart now. 'It will only be for a short time, until you're feeling your old self again.'

She turned to Eric. 'Come on. Let's give them a little time, dear.'

When they'd gone, I whispered in Zachary's ear. 'Be smart and play the game. You're going nowhere. I promise I won't let them take you. But we have to pretend for a short time. Do you understand?'

He nodded and I felt him relax against me.

My phone rang, causing us both to jump. DI Sharpe's name lit up the screen and I felt like crying with relief.

'Thank goodness you called,' I say in a low voice. 'I need your help. Can you come to the house?'

'Are you in danger, yes or no?' he said, his voice suddenly more alert.

'Not yet… but that might change soon,' I said.

CHAPTER SIXTY-ONE

Five minutes later, Brooke tapped on the door and opened it without waiting for an invitation to come in. The more time I spent with her the more I saw the origin of Owen's worst traits.

'I'm going to get some of Zachary's things together, Esme. I've already packed some of his things while you were at the hospital. We won't be taking a great deal; I think he's in dire need of a wardrobe refresh anyway.' She looked so incredibly smug I had the urge to throw something at her. 'I'll send a courier for the rest of his things and just so you know, Bruce has gone back up to Newcastle and Eric will be staying here tonight. We can all celebrate Owen's release and then we'll all travel up together tomorrow morning.'

'I don't want to go!' Zachary wailed, and I secretly squeezed his hand.

'Shall I bring you something to eat?' Brooke said graciously, as if she wasn't planning to steal my son away at all.

'No thanks, Brooke,' I said, equally pleasantly. 'Soon, I'm going to be far too busy to eat anything.'

She hesitated, then frowned. 'Too busy? Doing what, exactly?'

Before I could answer, an urgent, heavy knock came at the front door.

Brooke clutched her throat. 'Heavens, who's this?'

I peeled back the quilt and sat on the edge of the bed.

'It's the police!' Zachary said, bounding out of the room past an astonished Brooke.

*

Laughably, puny Eric squared up to the detectives. 'He's our grandson! There's no crime in taking him back to Newcastle with us. His mother clearly can't cope with him; she spends half her life in bed and the other half chatting to a convicted murderer.'

Lewis held up his hands. 'If Ms Fox says you're not to take Zachary then you're not able to do so, sir.'

'It's thanks to her my son is in custody.' Brooke spun around to face me, teeth bared.

Again, I was unable to retaliate with Zachary by my side. I couldn't bring up the hit and run with him here, so I plumped for a dignified silence. But Brooke hadn't finished.

'Taken in for questioning because your cheap sister had been putting it about. Getting into strange men's cars outside the school.'

'She got in someone's car and therefore you're saying she *deserved* to be beaten to within an inch of her life? No wonder your son has a skewed idea of what's acceptable!' I stepped towards her and a little distressed voice stopped me in my tracks.

'Someone beat Aunt Miche up?'

My heart squeezed, and I turned to hug Zachary. 'I'm sorry, sweetie. Mum's just upset. Ignore me.'

I turned to Sharpe and Lewis. 'I've asked Brooke and Eric to leave my house and they're refusing,' I said simply, refusing to be sidelined by Brooke's senseless accusations.

'You heard her,' Sharpe said curtly. 'You need to get your things together, please, and go.'

'Now look here, this is all getting a bit out of hand,' Eric said in a jolly manner. 'Why don't we sit down like adults and talk through—'

'I want you both to leave,' I repeated stoically.

I could have kissed Zachary when he stamped his foot – as well as he was able, anyhow – and yelled, 'Get out of our house!'

'We're family! This is ridiculous,' Brooke blustered, looking wildly between Eric and the detectives.

'It's ridiculous I've allowed it to carry on so long, yes,' I said levelly. 'But you need to go now. And take your bloody furry pink washing-up gloves with you.'

*

Thirty minutes later, Brooke and Eric were finally gone. Zachary and I sat in the living room with Sharpe and Lewis.

'We'll need to be careful what we say.' I swivelled my eyes meaningfully towards Zachary, who sat next to me playing on his Nintendo Switch. 'Little ears.'

'Understand completely,' Sharpe nodded. 'I wanted to let you know that we've been trying to locate Simone Fischer's brother, Peter Harvey, but to no avail. We've called at the house and left messages. Did he mention going away for a few days, perhaps?'

I shook my head. 'No, he didn't. But then he never mentioned the fact he'd met with my sister, either.'

Lewis took out his rough book and a pencil. 'So, let's start at the beginning. What's been happening here then, with your in-laws?'

Zachary looked up from his Nintendo, just for a second, and I knew he'd tuned into the conversation. I shook my head discreetly at Sharpe.

'I think we can cover all that when things have settled down a bit,' he said meaningfully to Lewis, who looked confused. 'In the meantime, we are going to carry on trying to find Mr Harvey. If you hear from him can you let us know?'

'Course,' I said, standing up as they both walked to the door.

'Any *further problems* family-wise, just let me know,' Sharpe said meaningfully, glancing at Zachary. I received his coded message loud and clear, and was grateful for it. With Brooke and Eric gone, I felt a sort of draining away of at least part of the dread that had been trickling into every pore.

'What's happening with Owen?' I ventured in the hallway behind them, keeping my voice little more than a whisper.

'I realise it must have been a terrible shock, Esme,' Sharpe said with a sigh. 'He'll be released, pending further investigations, but just between you and me, he's likely to be charged with the hit and run very soon.'

My skin crawled when I imagined having to explain this to my son at some point.

'When he is charged it's likely he'll be released until his court hearing, as he's not deemed to be a danger to the public.'

'Well, he won't be coming back here,' I said firmly. 'That I can assure you.'

When the detectives had left the house, I made Zachary a snack and a glass of juice. 'OK, sweetie?'

He nodded. 'When's Dad coming home, Mum? And when can I see Aunt Miche?'

'Not sure for both of those things yet, Zachary,' I said, watching his face drop. 'You've got to trust me here… I'll do what I think is right for you every time, do you understand?'

'Not really.' He frowned.

'What I mean is that sometimes there are things happening behind the scenes that you don't know about. Yes?'

'You mean like a plot twist?' he said. 'We did those in creative writing.'

I smiled. 'Yes, Zach, that's a great way of looking at it. And you never really know what the twists are until the end of the story, right?'

He nodded again. 'I think I understand now,' he said.

'You're a clever lad.' I smiled and kissed the top of his head.

In the meantime, I'd have to think of how and when I could break the news to him that his own father nearly killed him and then proceeded to lie to us both for almost two years.

CHAPTER SIXTY-TWO

We'd had a good night. Zachary had stayed in his own bed, and I luxuriated for a moment in the knowledge that the house was our own again.

When I opened my eyes, my phone was flashing. I reached across and picked up my phone from the bedside table. A call coming through from… Owen.

I sat up in bed and rubbed my eyes. The call ended and a list of eight notifications was revealed on screen. Texts, missed calls and a voicemail message. I felt gratified I'd thought to double lock the front door last night so he couldn't use his key.

Owen clearly had his phone again and was desperately trying to make contact. That meant he was a free man.

I listened to the voicemail. 'Esme, it's me. I'm out. Listen, I didn't want to just turn up at the house but I need to speak to you about… well, about everything. I know what happened with Mum and Dad, that you put them out of the house and… I'm shocked. Whatever you think about me, you shouldn't take it out on them. I can come round this morning. I want to see Zachary. Could you keep him off school? Call me when you get this message please.'

He was shocked I asked his parents to leave after they tried to take my son away? Spare me.

I glanced at the other messages, assuming they would all be from him. But there was one from Justine.

*Hi Esme, I know life must be crazy atm. If you want me to
look after Zachary for a few hours after school, maybe take
him to the new dinosaur art exhibition at the Contemporary
gallery... just let me know.*

Justine's offer couldn't have come at a better time. I didn't want
to see Owen yet, didn't feel ready to hear his pathetic excuses or
admonishments. My stomach turned when I thought of him
anywhere near Zachary. I knew I was going to have to get over
that somehow, but that didn't have to be right now.

Janice from the FSF group had sent me a message yesterday to
say Simone had asked if I could visit her this morning. I'd read it
quickly and hadn't replied because I thought I wouldn't be able
to make it with everything that was happening.

But now I found myself thinking about visiting Simone after
all, it sounded like she wanted to talk to me. Yes, it was a long
drive, but I relished the thought of the thinking time it would
give me and the added benefit that it was a perfect excuse to stop
Owen coming round to the house.

Zachary knew Justine well enough, and anything dinosaur-
themed would be sure to be a hit. It was just the thing to take his
mind off all the crap that was happening around him. And it also
meant we'd be out of Owen's reach for most of the day.

I tapped out a hasty reply to Justine.

That would be amazing. Call you when I've had coffee!

An hour later, Zachary had happily gone to school, excited
for his trip to the gallery later, and I was on my way down to
Bronzefield Prison.

If Owen came to the house looking for tea and sympathy, he
would be sorely disappointed.

CHAPTER SIXTY-THREE

ESME

Simone's face lit up when Officer Kat opened the door to the visitor room and I walked in. It felt a novelty that today was purely a visit, not a recorded episode.

Her cheeks were flushed and her eyes bright. She was sparkling. She rushed forward and flung her arms around me. I saw Kat open her mouth to issue an admonishment and then she closed it again, giving me a small smile.

'Janice says she's had lots of positive messages after episode two, and that public opinion seems to be on the turn. She thinks we'll have a fighting chance of getting a retrial.' Simone tucked her long brown bob behind her ears.

It was very early days to assume such things, but I knew the positive reaction to episode two and growing popularity of the podcast had contributed to this raging optimism. But a successful podcast and the Supreme Court deciding to reopen a case were very, very different things, and weren't dependent on each other. It was true that there was at least a glimmer of possibility her case might get reviewed in the coming weeks, but it wasn't a foregone conclusion by any means. It was hard to dim someone's shining hope though, particularly with so much misery around me already.

'Let's hope we hear soon,' I said, hugging her back with affection.

Simone stepped back and looked at me, her hands still on my shoulders.

'It's going to be alright, isn't it, Esme?' she said earnestly.

'There's a lot of public support for you now, so that will help bring the case to the court's attention. If coercive control was at play, which it clearly was, then there's a good chance the wheels could start turning. But obviously I'm not a lawyer, so you'll need to get professional advice. I'm sure Janice will already be on the case.'

Simone covered her face with her hands and let out a muffled scream. 'A whole tub of Ben & Jerry's cookie dough ice cream… that's the only thing I want when I get out.'

I smiled. I wouldn't talk about Michelle today; I didn't want to sink down into the pits of her betrayal. It might take some time, but there was a real possibility that Simone's life could change for the better, that justice might be served in the future. Despite my own life falling to pieces, I was delighted to see her so happy. This result had come from a podcast my company made, and despite everything else that was happening, that made me feel really good. Like we were making a difference to real lives.

'Your truth shines through in the podcasts,' I told her. 'The public couldn't fail to like you once they got to know you.'

Simone stared at me for a moment or two and then looked at Officer Kat. 'Can we just have five minutes' privacy? Just five minutes?'

The officer looked like she was going to refuse, and then she sighed. 'Five minutes, that's all. I'll be standing just outside, so no funny business. If this thing does work out for you, you want to make sure you don't mess it up, Simone.' She walked out of the room and closed the door behind her.

'You and I, we've been honest with each other, and it's worked well,' Simone said, clutching my arm.

'I think of you as a friend now, Simone,' I said carefully, suddenly sensing an opportunity. 'And friends are completely honest with each other, right?'

'Of course,' she said, a little guarded.

I tipped my head to one side and braced myself. 'This is a difficult question to ask you but I feel like I have no choice. I need to know the truth.'

The smile dropped from her face and she turned pale. What on earth did she think I was about to say?

'Go on,' she whispered, her eyes flitting to the door.

'Do you know anything about Peter meeting up with my sister? I have evidence that he did. I found an entry in her online diary. She met him two weeks before she got attacked.'

'I swear I don't know,' she said, her expression strange. 'Peter… he's not so bad.'

'Are you sure about that? Sometimes, you seem almost afraid of him.'

'I want to tell you the truth,' she said simply.

'Simone…' My insides were cramping. I was half dreading her response, half desperate to hear what she had to say. 'If you know something please don't protect Peter. Please don't lie to me.'

'I haven't *lied* to you exactly, Esme. But you seem such an honest person, I've lost sleep over the fact I haven't told you the full story.'

'Which is?' My heart hammered on my chest wall. If she confessed that Peter had attacked Michelle, I'd have no option but to go straight to the police.

'I didn't plan it. I want you to know that.'

I frowned. 'Plan what?'

'Grant had been so cruel that day, he'd outdone himself. In the end I just lowered my head to the table and closed my eyes against it all. And that's when it happened.'

'What happened?' I swallowed hard, the sound of my own blood rushing in my ears.

'Grant was sitting across from me at the table. He had his back to the kitchen door and… I opened my eyes and Andrew was behind him clutching the biggest knife out of the block. Grant had this thing about keeping them super-sharp all the time. I cried out at the same moment as Andrew plunged the knife into the soft bit of flesh behind Grant's ear and the top of his neck.

'It was horrific. Blood spurting everywhere, Grant with his eyes still open, a horrible gurgling noise in his throat… I jumped up and ran to my son. He was frozen like a statue, the knife still in his hand. I snatched it off him and pushed him out of the door.

'Grant's head was on the table but his eyes were still open and he was staring at me, blinking at me, blood running out of his mouth, and he sneered. Even in that state, he sneered at me, and I just lost it.

'I took the knife and I stabbed him again and again and again. Then I cleaned Andrew up and stuck his clothes in the washer. He put on his pyjamas and sat in front of the television and he didn't say a word. I made a cup of tea when I'd tumble-dried Andrew's clothes. And then I rang the police.'

I glanced at the door. I could see the officer through the glass, shuffling her feet, ready to come back in.

'Andrew attacked Grant? Killed his own father?'

Simone shook her head. 'He wasn't dead. Andrew didn't kill him. Grant would have recovered and I knew for certain that Andrew would have been taken into care. That sneer… it meant Grant had still won, you see. I couldn't stand the thought of a life being without my son but still being under Grant's control.'

Thoughts were whizzing around in my head at a hundred miles an hour, but I couldn't stop Simone from talking now.

'I'd do it again. I'm not sorry. Andrew had heard what was happening in the kitchen, how Grant was treating me. I opened my eyes at the moment my son walked in, calm as anything. I could see he was staring into space as if he was in some kind of a trance.'

The officer opened the door and walked back in. Looked at our faces.

'Is everything OK in here?' she said.

*

Back outside, I took some deep, cleansing breaths and stood at the end of the footpath on the edge of the parking lot. Cars crawled past looking for vacant bays. Vehicles came in and out of this place all the time, a vital visitor support network for the prisoners within. I felt like I was looking at everything with new eyes, as if Simone's truth had shone a light on the whole world outside.

I pulled my thin cardigan closer against the cool breeze I hadn't noticed when I arrived. More than anyone, I understood the love of a mother and the need to protect her son, but Simone's confession also proved she'd made the decision to kill her husband solely to disguise the fact Andrew had stabbed him.

In anyone's book, that made Simone Fischer a murderer.

Didn't it?

CHAPTER SIXTY-FOUR

My phone started ringing when I was just a few yards away from my car in the prison car park.

I pulled it out of my bag and glanced at the screen. Unknown number. I almost rejected the call, but then, worrying who it might be, I answered.

'Is this… Esme Fox?' a woman said, unsure.

'Speaking,' I said.

'This is ICU at Queen's Med. Your sister has suffered a sudden setback. The doctors have said you should get here as soon as you can if—'

'I've got a two-and-a-half-hour drive in front of me but I'm on my way.'

I pushed the phone, call still connected, in my bag and rushed for the door, cursing my decision to come here in the first place.

*

I drove like a maniac, earning myself beeps of annoyance and frustration from at least half a dozen other drivers on the way.

My mind lurched between Simone's confession and what I'm morally obligated to do about it and the need to make peace with my sister, possibly before she dies.

Mercifully, there were no delays on the roads, and two-and-a-half hours later I pushed my way out of the lift and ran towards the double doors of ICU.

A nurse took me directly to Michelle's bed, explaining what had happened on the way. I tried hard to take it all in, but only her key words got through.

'Setback... Breathing... Relapse...'

In the main ward I spotted immediately that there was a small group of medics standing around her bed. I broke away from the nurse and started to run, calling out Michelle's name. They turned to look at the disturbance and the senior doctor stepped forward and held up his hands for me to stop.

'Is she... is she going to be OK?' My words emerged broken and incomplete.

Slowly, he shook his head. 'I'm very sorry,' he said quietly, respectfully. 'Your sister passed away just a few minutes ago.'

CHAPTER SIXTY-FIVE

I sat on the small kitchen sofa with a cup of coffee, staring out of the window at the garden. I felt so quiet inside, and inconsequential, as though I was partially invisible.

Having Brooke installed here and spending so much time feeling unwell in my bedroom had given me a new appreciation of my home. Despite Michelle's newly discovered betrayal, I felt completely hollowed out with news of her death. In that moment, I felt empty and utterly alone, and yet I could not cry.

My phone buzzed with an incoming text. I looked over to the worktop but didn't rush to get up. The world wasn't going to fall in if I took a little longer to drink my coffee.

The phone started to ring.

I stood up and ran across the kitchen.

The lit screen revealed Peter Harvey was calling. I hesitated and then answered.

'Esme? What the hell is happening? I got a voicemail from you and then another three from the police! Is this something to do with your sister because I told you, I've never—'

'My sister is dead,' I said quietly. 'I got to the hospital too late.'

The tone of his voice changed completely. 'Oh God, I'm so sorry to hear that, Esme. Is there anything I—'

'Save your breath,' I said. 'I know, Peter.'

'You know *what*?' He was a good actor. He sounded completely confused.

'I know you had a meeting with Michelle. Just a couple of weeks ago. To talk about *The Fischer Files* podcast. I know all about her and Mo deceiving me now, setting up their own company.'

'Are you completely *mad*? I haven't a clue what you're talking about. I have never met your sister, never mind attended a meeting with her.'

So many lies. Everyone I knew was telling lies.

'I've got access to Michelle's meeting dates. There's a diary entry for a meeting with you two weeks ago. She confirmed it with you by email.'

'She didn't. And that's a fact. Hang on, I can check now.' I heard him tapping a keyboard. 'There is no email on here at all from your sister. Nothing from anyone regarding a bloody meeting in a pub two weeks ago!'

'Peter. I need to ask you something straight. It's going to come out because the police are looking for a murder suspect now. They'll be doubling their efforts. Level with me. Did you create the Facebook page about Michelle? I warn you that the police know about it and I spoke to Andrew and he—'

My voice faded out as I tripped myself up.

'And he what?' Peter snapped.

'Well, he said it was possible, just possible, that you might have—'

'Be careful who you trust, Esme, is my advice,' he said in a sinister voice.

I thought about Simone's confession. Was it possible Michelle had suspected something about Andrew's involvement in the death of his father and had asked to meet with Peter to discuss it? She'd never mentioned it to me, but then she wouldn't… a shocking revelation like that would set her new business off to a flying start.

'It's time for this to stop,' he said cryptically. 'I'll be in touch.'

Before I could reply, Peter had put down the phone.

I stared at the wall feeling disturbed but not knowing exactly what to do about it. I felt like I was fighting in a swamp of grief and pain. Unresolved questions from the death of my sister, mixed with disbelief over what she had done to me.

Then, in the midst of that dark place, I had a glimmer of an idea. I pulled up one of the photographs featuring Peter Harvey that I'd downloaded from Google to show Zachary and I texted it to Justine.

When you pick Zachary up from school, could you show him this photo? Ask him if he recognises anyone on it.

Then I headed back out to the car yet again.

CHAPTER SIXTY-SIX

Before I started the engine, I entered the address for The Spindles care home in Nether Broughton into Google maps on my phone, and then I set off on the twenty-five-minute journey.

I left the radio off, preferring to recall memories of when Michelle and I were just kids. In the summer months we'd spend entire days in the garden, hunting for evidence that fairies and goblins were real. During wintertime, we'd build dens under the dining room table and hole up stores of biscuits, pop and crisps, pretending we were in the Arctic with snowdrifts as big as the house outside.

It was the two of us against the world back then, and we were so close nobody could have ever come between us. No hidden agendas, no duplicity. Betrayal was a world away from touching us. However rocky the road ahead would be, this was the way I'd try to remember my sister.

A call rang shrilly from the hands-free, bringing me back to reality with a jump. I answered and Justine's voice filled the car, low and concerned.

'Esme? I just showed Zachary the photograph you sent. I'm putting him on now.'

There were a couple of moments silence, then my son's bright, innocent voice. 'Mum?'

'Did you have a good day at school, sweetie?'

My heartbeat felt as though it had relocated to my throat, but I tried to sound normal. I didn't want to make a big deal about the photograph, and I didn't want him to ask about Michelle. I didn't want to lie to him, but he'd be broken when he found out his auntie had died.

'School was OK. Justine showed me a photo and the man who Aunt Miche was talking to outside school is on there.'

The picture I'd sent over was taken outside the court when the Free Simone Fischer group had tried to force a retrial last year by a demonstration. I hadn't shown Zachary this one the first time, as it had more people than just Peter Harvey in it, and I'd wanted to keep it simple.

'So which man is it?' I managed to say, even though I could barely breathe.

'It's the man stood on the steps away from the group of people,' Zachary said. 'That's the man I saw Aunt Miche with outside school.'

I knew the press tagline underneath the photograph read: *A rare sighting of Simone Fischer's son, Andrew Fischer.*

*

Heart racing, I made a phone call.

'DI Sharpe.'

'It's Esme Fox. Zachary has recognised the man Michelle drove off with at school as Andrew Fischer, Simone Fischer's son.'

'Not her brother, Peter Harvey? That's who you were concerned about.'

'He's picked Andrew Fischer out, and I'm heading over to him now. I've had contact with him already through the podcast. He lives and works at a care home called The Spindles, in Nether Broughton.'

'Listen to me, Esme… hold fire, you mustn't go there. I'll speak to my colleagues, we'll need to check out what you say.'

I end the call without committing to anything. I didn't turn the car around; I continued with the journey.

I didn't know why I was going there, didn't know what I thought I might do when I got there. Part of me knew I should leave it to the police, but I needed to hear what Andrew had to say after all the lies he must have told me. I needed to hear the truth with my own ears.

Simone's confession burned brighter in my mind. I'd tried to push it away; it was information I didn't want to have. I didn't want the burden of it on my mind, constantly swaying between the right thing to do.

But if I'd known about Andrew attacking his father, I'd have instantly been cautious. As it was, he was so personable and friendly, so different to Peter, and I'd trusted him. Simone's lies might have inadvertently caused Michelle's death, because she'd allowed Andrew to live his life unhindered.

When I arrived at The Spindles, there were only a couple of cars out front, but the entrance door of the house was wide open.

My skin prickled as I began to wonder what Andrew might be capable of. What was his state of mind under the respectable exterior he'd perfected over all these years? Had he really no memory of what happened that day, or was it just buried deep, festering and waiting for its moment?

As soon as I stepped inside the building, I heard raised voices. I rushed over to the main room and saw a couple of carers encouraging the young people in the lounge to go back to their rooms. Then I saw Peter had Andrew by the scruff of his neck up against the wall.

'Peter, wait!' I ran over, my heart racing.

'He's admitted it.' Peter clenched his teeth. 'Looking through my emails. Deleting my messages. It was him who made that Facebook page!'

I thought about Justine's observation that the origins of the page looked like one person had created it but that it could actually be another. That hadn't made sense at the time, but now it did.

'You're crazy… get off me!' Andrew yelled, his face puce. He pushed Peter hard and his uncle staggered back.

'What about the emails?' I asked Peter, trying to find out what was happening.

The older man's face was flushed and sweat peppered his upper lip. 'When you said your sister had sent me a message about meeting up, just something about it made me think. On a few occasions I've tried to find an email containing important information only to find it had disappeared into thin air. Before I'd always blamed myself for my lack of technology skills. But after I spoke to you today, I asked Janice Poulter who oversees the FSF website to take a look.' He turned to glare again at Andrew. 'She found a whole bunch of deleted messages in the virtual bin of my email account. Including one from Michelle Fox asking to meet up. In the message, she'd said she had a lucrative proposal she wanted to discuss with me.'

Andrew smirked at Peter. '*You're* the one who met with her. You're the reason she ended up in hospital.'

'You've always been a coward,' Peter said, quieter now. 'Even as a child, you stood by and let that pathetic excuse of a father of yours terrorize your mother.'

'That's not fair. I was just a kid.' Andrew's face darkened.

'I don't know. I think most teenagers would have tried to protect their mum. But you just stood by, let him abuse her. You've always been such an inadequate, weak individual.' Peter assumed a mocking tone. 'He can't even remember what happened, do you know that, Esme? How convenient, forgetting how his mummy had to fend for herself against that monster of a—'

'That's where you're wrong… I remember everything!' he spat the words out. 'Every last detail. Him stuffing food into her mouth as if she were just a vessel for him to abuse, the filthy things he called her, the way he'd try and drag me into it all. I'd seen him with one of his women in a coffee shop when I walked by a week before. He'd rushed out, explained it was just someone he worked with. But I'd seen the way she'd looked at him, traced over his hand with her long red nail. I was a naïve kid, but it all felt wrong.'

'So you remember it all?' I repeated.

'Yes! When I heard Mum cry out and I saw his hand take a handful of her hair I just went for him. I saw the knife, the biggest one in the block. Mum must've used it because the blade seemed almost illuminated, so bright, as if it were beckoning me to pick it up.' He turned to Peter. 'So don't you dare say I just stood by. I was brave. Do you hear me? I was brave!'

Peter sneered but I stepped forward. This was my chance.

'Why hurt Michelle though, Andrew? You met with her and then attacked her… why? She'd done nothing to you.'

'She wanted to hurt Mum, hurt me, to make money. She had no intention of helping Mum's cause like you did. And when I told her I wasn't interested in working with them, she turned nasty, said she'd do it without me.' He hesitated, his face turning pale. 'Then she said she'd done some digging and maybe I wasn't telling her everything. She said she was going to write an article assassinating my character, raising the question of my involvement in Dad's death.'

I shook my head. 'She couldn't have known that. She would be bluffing and you fell for it.'

'I just flipped. She was just a bitch and she deserved everything she got… just like my dad did.'

Voices began shouting from out in the foyer.

When I turned to look, DI Sharpe stood in the doorway and uniformed officers charged towards us.

CHAPTER SIXTY-SEVEN

ONE MONTH LATER

Mo had been arrested on a number of charges – fraud and stealing intellectual property – but DI Sharpe informed me he refused to speak about anything to do with Michelle. Without Mo speaking out, I would probably never find out the truth.

I wasn't interested in the business side of their deception; what I really wanted to know was why? Why did my sister, to whom I felt so close, betray me? Mo was the only key to me finding out now. Michelle was gone, and every day I mourned the sister I used to have, the one I knew and loved.

'I'm sorry to have to say this, Esme,' Sharpe said regretfully, 'but it's highly possible Mo Khaleed just intends for their secrets to stay buried.'

Andrew Fischer had been sectioned under the Mental Health Act, as he was deemed to be a danger to both himself and other people.

'Although we didn't get a full and detailed statement from him about the death of his father and also Michelle, we did get some answers,' Sharpe said grimly. 'He made arrangements to meet with Michelle, but became aggressive and that got Michelle's curiosity up. She approached him a second time, suggesting – and most probably bluffing – that maybe *he'd* been the one to kill his father, not Simone.'

I said, 'It tipped him over the edge, forced him to face the past he'd tried to hide from, and he became violent. Michelle didn't stand a chance.'

'Exactly.'

'But why did he meet her at school?'

'Apparently, Michelle was keen to keep you from suspecting her involvement – no surprise there,' Sharpe said. 'Fischer insists she'd told him to meet her after the school run as it was one of the rare times she wasn't in the office with you. They drove out a couple of times to parkland to talk, and it was on the second meeting he lost control and attacked her. He swears he never meant to hurt her, just that things got out of hand.'

'But Michelle had called me from the supermarket to ask what to get for tea that day,' I said, frowning. 'That was *after* she'd seen Fischer the second time.'

Sharpe shook his head. 'That was a ruse just to ensure you were safely at work and going through with the TrueLife meeting. Fischer said she'd told him she had no intention of turning up for the meeting and it was all part of the masterplan that you'd mess it up so Michelle and Mo could approach the television company directly after the event.'

He'd beaten my sister to death because she'd stumbled on the possibility there might be more to Grant Fischer's death than first met the eye.

There was a further piece of devastating information DI Sharpe came to impart.

'Owen's parents knew all along that he was the driver in Zachary's hit and run. Both Owen and they maintain it was a complete accident, an awful coincidence, and that he has been wracked with guilt ever since.'

I shouldn't have been surprised, given everything else they'd done, but… it was shocking. I felt an electric bolt shoot through me, and I knew, in that moment, I probably wouldn't be able to fully trust another human being again. I had refused to meet up with Owen and refused to let him see Zachary so far. But I knew that couldn't continue. I had to face him at some point.

Sharpe said, 'Owen told us his parents helped him plan how to get over the accident, and also form a contingency plan in case it did come out that he was the culprit. This involved him agreeing to his parents taking temporary custody of Zachary so you wouldn't have the power to keep his son away from him. They'll probably be charged with perverting the course of justice.'

Apparently, Owen kept all sorts of evidence to show I was an unfit mother – even video footage of me drowsy on prescribed medication after Zachary's accident. Just in case I found out what he'd done and he needed it to blackmail me, keep me quiet. It made me feel physically sick to think about his duplicity.

But if Brooke and Eric Painter got their comeuppance at last, then there was hope of some justice being done, at least.

CHAPTER SIXTY-EIGHT

Justine had taken Zachary to the local park while the detectives were over under the ruse of getting him away from his screens for a while. When the police left, I finally called Owen to say it was a good time for him to come over to talk.

His car pulled up outside the house and I opened the front door to him. He looked as if he'd aged ten years from the last time I saw him, the day he went to the police station.

His skin looked dry and grey, his clothes hung shapelessly on a leaner, less flattering frame. He wouldn't meet my eyes.

'Go through to the living room,' I said. 'I'll make us some tea.'

I followed him up the hallway, and when he turned into the living room, I carried on into the kitchen. When the police told me about the DNA match from the accident that day, I swear, if Owen had walked in, there and then, I'd have gone for him. Clawed, punched, kicked… I was so angry. So hurt, betrayed and bent on revenge.

But now those feelings had settled and I felt very little towards him. The revelation of what he'd done had killed off any emotion I felt towards Owen at all, and now, when I looked at him, I just felt flat and empty.

I took the tea through and sat as far away from him as I could.

'I don't blame you for hating me,' he said, his voice thick. 'For what it's worth, I'm sorry. I'm very sorry for what I did to you. To Zachary.'

'What exactly happened, that day?'

He sighed as if he didn't want to talk about it. 'I was so tired, driving down from Newcastle. I hadn't slept well the night before and I'd had a bit more wine than I should with colleagues at lunchtime. Instead of stopping for a coffee and resting on the way back home, I drove through the bad weather to get back earlier. I had this idea I might be able to pick Zach up from school, surprise you both. An important call came through, about some work at a plush new gym in the city. They asked me for some information that was on paperwork just to my left, on the passenger seat. I took my eyes off the road for one second – I swear that was all – and… I hit something. That dull, heavy thud is in my nightmares.'

I closed my eyes against the horror of the vision in my head. Owen hitting our boy.

'I slammed on the brakes and got out to look. I thought it was a dog, an animal, but I felt sick to my core. It was as if, deep down, some part of me knew it was a person. The road was so quiet, nobody was around. The last person I expected to find was a child. I was on a quiet side street, not outside the school gates. I got out of the car and walked around it into the road and saw the legs, the shoes… his head and torso were hidden under the car. I thought, it's Zachary. It's Zachary! And then I told myself I was an idiot, that it couldn't be because I knew you were picking him up from school after his club. I heard some shouting, people on the next street, and I knew they'd be coming around the corner any minute and I…' he squeezed his eyes closed, 'I bent down, dabbing at his bloody leg with my hanky, and I thought, they'll get help. The people will help him. I sort of watched myself get back in the car and backed up, drove off in the same direction I came in. It was like I was a witness to myself, but the person who'd done that… it wasn't the real me.'

'But it *was* the real you.' My voice sounded cold and level. 'And you'd dropped your handkerchief.'

'Yes. I'd dabbed my own cut hand with it, too. I wasn't in my right mind. I swear I thought a thousand times about telling you, about giving myself up, but I couldn't. I couldn't, because I knew I'd lose you both.'

I took a sip of my tea and looked steadily at him. 'You're the person who has to live with what you did for the rest of your life, Owen,' I said. 'In five, ten, twenty years, when Zachary is frustrated because his leg injury prevents him from doing something he wants to do, stops him playing football with his own children. Every single time he'll think about your lie. Despite you trying to blame me and pile guilt on my shoulders, you can never escape what you did, and the blame will always lie squarely at your door.'

I felt a cold indifference to him. I couldn't look at him.

He looked down at his hands. Nodded. 'I know. The thing that gives me nightmares is telling him… telling him what I did. And what I've come here to say, apart from apologising to you, is to beg for you to let me see my son. I understand you must hate me; I take ownership of the terrible thing I did to Zachary. But I can't live without him. I just can't.'

His voice broke and, pathetically, he covered his face with his hands and began to sob.

I sat silently and said nothing. When he removed his hands and roughly wiped his cheeks, I spoke up.

'I'm not going to make any snap decisions. Zachary loves you so much; he worships the ground you walk on. It would break his heart not to see you.' A sob caught in Owen's throat. 'But we can't keep this a secret. He has to know the truth, and we'll need professional help to do it properly, to do it in a way that will hurt Zachary the least, and that he can understand.'

'Anything,' he said, sitting up a little straighter. 'Whatever you want, I'll do. I just need to be part of my boy's life. He can come to Mum and Dad's with—'

'You'll need to come here to spend time with him. I don't want him anywhere near your parents for the foreseeable.'

'But—'

'It's not negotiable, Owen. It's the only way I'll agree to you seeing him.'

'Fine. If that's what it takes, that's what I'll do. But I hope in time you and I can rebuild our relationship. Be a family again.'

My days of pleasing Owen were long gone. Zachary was my only priority now.

'And there's one more thing I need to tell you,' I said. He looked up hopefully. 'I want a divorce.'

CHAPTER SIXTY-NINE

TWO MONTHS LATER

Little by little, I'd begun to pick up the threads of the business I'd built with my own sweat and tears. It was just me and Justine now, but we were managing. Everything was very low-key, but The Speaking Fox still existed, and that was a miracle in itself.

Mo seemed to have disappeared off the face of the earth, taking with him lots of valuable documentation. We discovered several remittances had been billed under the company name but using his own bank account details.

The police were investigating, and had frozen his financial assets.

I let the office lease go and Justine and I started using the two spare bedrooms upstairs in the house. Toby had stayed with us, and was like a different young man now that he no longer worked with Mo. The meekness had gone and he was blossoming.

'I strongly suspected something was happening between Mo and Michelle and a few times, I came close to telling you, Esme. But I kept running scared, and my mum told me not to get involved or I might lose my job.'

'There's no fear of that, Toby,' I told him. 'We're lucky to have you.'

When Mo disappeared, Justine worked miracles. Single-handedly she kept the remaining episodes of the podcast on track. With her production experience she was able to release each subsequent episode on time so the listeners hadn't a clue of the chaos that was happening behind the scenes.

The Fischer Files had been a resounding success. Streaming and download records had been smashed, and we were now considering options for our next project. There had been a big surprise in a recent phone call; TrueLife Media were back on the scene. Thanks to the local journalist, Colin Wade – who'd turned out to be an enormous support and had produced a detailed article about my ordeal – Damon Yorke, the CEO of TrueLife, had heard the truth of what had happened, and wanted to restart talks. Early days but exciting times.

I wasn't yet ready to think about taking on new staff yet to replace Mo or Michelle. But it was wonderful to feel a growing interest in potential new projects, and there were a couple of cases I had my eye on. Cases that sparked that interest in me, that I felt I could believe in. Just like how I felt about Simone Fischer's case back at the beginning.

Simone. I'd had to make a call as to what to do. Did I tell the detectives she'd already confessed to me that Andrew had attacked his father first, but that she'd finished the job? I decided, as Andrew had been charged with manslaughter for Michelle's death and the detectives were investigating the death of Grant Fischer again, justice would prevail one way or another.

I knew plenty of people would disagree with the path I'd chosen, the one of least resistance, but I settled on what I believed to be the right decision for myself and my son. So I said nothing.

And then I got a call from DI Sharpe.

'I wanted to let you know everything is tied up with the case now, but we had a bit of a last-minute surprise,' he said. 'You're not going to believe it.'

'I can try,' I said.

'OK, well, Andrew Fischer has confessed that actually, it was him who murdered his father. Simone didn't kill Grant at all.'

He paused, waited for my stunned reaction.

'Wow!' I managed. 'What will happen now?'

'Simone has confirmed she didn't kill her husband and the wheels are in motion for her release. That would probably have happened anyway, with the change of law on coercive control, but now… well, turns out she was always innocent. Nothing like the love of a mother, I guess.'

'And Andrew? Will this add to his sentence?'

'He was a child when he killed his father, so probably not. But I thought you'd want to know.'

'Thank you,' I said, just before the end of the call. 'It's the final piece of the puzzle.'

Simone wasn't a killer. She'd been forced, under extreme circumstances, to protect herself and her son. I couldn't condemn her for that. Would I get in touch when she was free? I wasn't sure. The only thing I felt certain of was that when Grant Fischer died, the world contained one less abusive, misogynistic bully, and I wasn't going to waste a moment feeling bad about that.

Peter Harvey had been in touch, just a short note to say he was looking after Simone's affairs together with Janice Poulter from FSF, and that he was sincerely sorry about what had happened to Michelle. I sent a note back thanking him and apologising for accusing him instead of the real culprit, his nephew.

I sat next to Zachary on the sofa. He was playing a computer game, and I slid my arm around his shoulders.

I'd been surrounded by people who'd consistently buried their emotions, buried the truth, and now I'd added myself to that list. I was far from over Michelle's betrayal and her subsequent death. I was still confused about whether I'd done the right thing trying to keep quiet about Simone's confession to me, and probably always would be.

I was more concerned in doing the right thing by my son, and I couldn't shake the feeling I was making a mess of that, too. He was still under the impression that Michelle was in hospital.

There was a steep uphill climb ahead of us, and the time had to be right to sit my son down to face a truly awful reality. Next week, with the help of a family liaison worker from Zachary's school, we'd start to address the very difficult issues he needed to know about.

Justine had accompanied him a couple of times on a visit to the park with his father, and soon I'd be telling him a whole host of truths that a nine-year-old boy should never have to hear. The death of his auntie and exactly what had happened. The terrible truth about the hit-and-run accident that would probably break his heart.

But the shining star amid all the horror and gloom was that I had come to appreciate the present moment. Instead of worrying about Zachary's future and working all the hours God sent to combat what might go wrong in years to come, I was counting my blessings right now. Yes, Zachary would have issues with his health as he grew older, but he was here now, he was happy and we had each other. We had *today*.

I glanced at the clock. 'Come on, sweetie, time for our swimming session.'

'Yesss!' He immediately cast aside his gaming controls and jumped up to gather his things. Swimming was just one of the activities we took part in together now. We'd enrolled on a baking class together, and Zachary was teaching me how to appreciate football, even though, to his increasing frustration, I continued to struggle with grasping the offside rule.

Before he could take off upstairs to get his things, I grabbed his arm.

'I love you,' I said softly.

'Mu-um!' He wailed, trying to free his arm. 'I love you too, but we're going to be late for swimming class if we don't get a move on!'

I smiled and hugged him tighter. DI Sharpe was right. There was nothing like the love of a mother. And in a world where nothing was simple, nothing was certain, I now knew one thing that was surely cast in stone.

Nothing would ever come between me and my son again.

A LETTER FROM K.L. SLATER

Thank you so much for reading *The Evidence*; I really hope you enjoyed the book. If you did enjoy it and would like to keep upto date with all my latest releases, just sign up at the following link. Your email address will never be shared and you can unsubscribe at any time.

www.bookouture.com/kl-slater

Readers are always interested in how ideas for stories come to be, and *The Evidence* started to develop when I had the idea of incorporating podcast extracts within a story. I've been a fan of podcasts since listening to the gripping *Serial* by Sarah Koenig in 2014 and, as *The Evidence* was initially released exclusively in audio format, this spurred me on to create the character of Simone Fischer, a British woman serving a long sentence for the murder of her abusive husband. At the same time, the character of Esme Fox, an investigative podcast journalist, began to take shape.

As the character of Simone Fischer developed, I began to research women who kill and became interested in exploring how society and the justice system often view and treat women accused of violent crime in contrast to men. During this research period, I looked at real-life cases involving Sally Challen, Emma-Jayne Magson, Farieissia Martin and Emma Humphreys. I read about cases where there was strong evidence of chronic psychological abuse and/or violence, and yet the victims were charged and convicted of murder as opposed to manslaughter. On the website justiceforwomen.org.uk, I was shocked to discover a long list of similar cases documented there.

The thing about control, particularly coercive control, is that the traumatised victim (usually female) doesn't necessarily recognise what's happening to her and can't always articulate why she killed her partner.

In *The Evidence*, Simone Fischer talks about her own experiences at the hands of her abusive husband, Grant. I wanted to underline the concept of this 'invisible' control and have the main character, Esme, slowly becoming aware that she may also have been subject to manipulation and control in her own marriage.

There are excellent resources available, for anyone who wants more information or needs help and support, by searching generally online. Also, the Resources section of the Justice for Women website provides a good place to start.

This book is set in Nottinghamshire, the place I was born and have lived all my life. Local readers should be aware I sometimes take the liberty of changing street names or geographical details to suit the story.

I do hope you enjoyed reading *The Evidence* and getting to know the characters. If you did, I would be very grateful if you could take a few minutes to write a review. I'd love to hear what you think, and it makes such a difference helping new readers to discover one of my books for the first time.

I love hearing from my readers – you can get in touch on my Facebook page, through Twitter, Goodreads or my website.

Until next time…
Kim x

 KimLSlaterAuthor

 @KimLSlater

KLSlaterAuthor

 www.KLSlaterAuthor.com

ACKNOWLEDGEMENTS

Thank you to my editor at Bookouture, Lydia Vassar-Smith, for publishing *The Evidence* and for her enthusiasm for the book.

Thanks also to Camilla Bolton, my literary agent at the Darley Anderson Literary, TV and Film Agency, and to her assistant, Jade Kavanagh, who was my first reader and gave feedback for the earliest draft.

The Evidence started life as an audio recording and I'd like to record my thanks to the various editors, copyeditors and proofreaders for their valued input and suggestions along the way, including Karen Ball, Sam Bryce, Dushi Horti, Neil Burkey and Maddy Newquist. Special thanks to Bookouture's editorial manager, Alexandra Holmes.

Thank you to the bloggers and reviewers who do so much to support authors, and thank you to everyone who has taken the time to post a positive review online or has taken part in my blog tour. It is always noticed and much appreciated.

Last but not least, thank you SO much to my wonderful readers. I love receiving all your comments and messages and I am truly grateful for the support of each and every one of you.

Made in the USA
Monee, IL
27 July 2022

10386661R00184